"I didn't know."

He kept his eyes on the road. "You didn't know what?"

She felt her face flush an even darker red. "I mean, I didn't know that you—thought of me that way. I thought you saw me as a . . . little sister, or something."

He turned to her, surprised. "Antonia," he said. His voice was husky with longing, his mouth slowly curled into a smile, and his caramel-colored eyes gleamed. He gently unhooked her hand from his thigh and lifted it to his lips and kissed it. Then he ran his lips over the palm of her hand and up to the tip of her index finger and sucked, bringing it into his warm, soft mouth and biting down gently before pulling away and carefully placing her hand back down on his thigh.

"I have never," he said, his voice lit with amusement, "thought of you as any kind of sister."

Nacho Figueras Presents:
Ride Free

NACHO FIGUERAS
PRESENTS:

Ride
Free

Jessica Whitman

Book Three in The Polo Season Series

FOREVER

New York Boston

Copyright © 2016 by Ignacio Figueras
Excerpts from *High Season* and *Wild One* copyright © 2016 by Ignacio Figueras
Cover design by Elizabeth Turner
Cover illustration by Alan Ayers
Author photograph by Claudio Marinesco
Horse images © Steve Greer/Getty Images
Cover copyright © 2016 by Hachette Book Group, Inc.

Forever
Hachette Book Group
1290 Avenue of the Americas
New York, NY 10104
hachettebookgroup.com
twitter.com/foreverromance

Printed in the United States of America

OPM

First Edition: July 2016
10 9 8 7 6 5 4 3 2 1

Forever is an imprint of Grand Central Publishing.
The Forever name and logo are trademarks of Hachette Book Group, Inc.

The publisher is not responsible for websites (or their content) that are not owned by the publisher.

The Hachette Speakers Bureau provides a wide range of authors for speaking events. To find out more, go to www.hachettespeakersbureau.com or call (866) 376-6591.

ISBN 978-1-4555-6372-2 (trade paperback edition)
ISBN 978-1-4555-6371-5 (mass market edition)
ISBN 978-1-4555-6370-8 (ebook edition)

I want to dedicate this book to horses.

Horses help bring out the best parts of you and have been my partners throughout my polo career. I love horses as much as I love polo.

Dear Reader,

I first learned to ride a horse when I was four years old and started playing the sport of polo by the time I was nine. Tango was the horse on which I learned to play, and Tango was my first love. I fell in love with the beauty of horses and idolized the strength and bravery of the best players. In my native Argentina, everyone has a chance to go to polo matches and see how thrilling they are. It has been my dream to share the game that I love, the game that has given me so much—as a person and athlete—with the rest of the world.

I think polo is very appealing. After all, there's a reason Ralph Lauren chose it. There is something undeniably sexy about a man and a horse and the speed and the adrenaline.

It was at a polo match that I met my wife. I was in the stands and she was coming up the stairs, and I looked at her and she looked at me, and we looked at each other. I had to know more, so I asked her cousin Sofia to introduce us and she told me, "That's funny; she just asked me the same thing." So the cousin introduced us, and we talked for a little bit. It was the beginning of the summer, and we didn't see each other for two or three months. After the holiday, we started dating, and we have been together ever since...

I am very excited to present the Polo Season series, which blends my favorite sport with a little bit of romance. Whether you're already a polo fan or completely new to the game, I hope you will enjoy these characters and their stories.

Nacho Figueras Presents:
Ride Free

Chapter One

When Sunny started crow-hopping, Enzo Rivas didn't worry. The big mare had always been hot, and it wasn't out of character for her to occasionally get a little bored and try to test her rider.

But when Sunny started to buck, Enzo knew something was seriously wrong.

The pony threw her head down, kicked out her legs, and whinnied fearfully, almost sending Enzo out of the saddle. He pressed his knees against the saddle, grabbed the reins, and battled to pull her head back up. She fought him, flinging her head down again and heaving her back legs into the air.

For a moment, he thought he was going to be thrown, and his body automatically tensed, preparing to hit the ground, hard.

It wouldn't have been the first time Enzo lost his seat to an unruly horse. It was part of his job, after all. Nobody trained horses and didn't occasionally get thrown. But that didn't mean he wouldn't fight it.

Sunny came back down onto all four legs again, and Enzo, sensing a split second of opportunity, yanked the reins sharply to the right, forcing the pony's head so far over that her nose touched his knee. She screamed in outrage and spun in a circle, but she was powerless to kick her hind legs from this position.

Enzo kept her in that stance, letting her spin as many times as she wanted, speaking to her softly in Spanish, until he could feel her temper start to ebb and her muscles soften, one by one, under him.

He relaxed the reins and let the pony's head back up. As they cantered forward, he noticed a large, bald-faced hornet floating away from them.

"Ah. Poor girl," he said, "you got stung."

Sunny snorted complacently as if in agreement, then reared up, threw Enzo backward into the grass, and bolted, riderless, down the pitch.

Enzo lay there for a moment, the breath knocked out of him, staring at the cloudless Florida sky. It had not been a bad fall, as falls went, and he knew that once he could breathe again, he'd be fine. But he was also pissed, and he knew it would be better to get his temper under control before he chased down the errant horse. It never helped to be mad when dealing with ponies.

"Rivas?" came a distant voice that made him close his eyes and smile ruefully. *Of course* she would find him like this.

"Enzo, are you okay?"

She was closer.

He struggled to a sitting position, still a little winded but determined not to be on his back when she reached him.

"I'm fine," he said, and then almost fell over again, he was so dizzy. Damn that horse. He bent his head to his knees and closed his eyes.

"You don't look fine. You look like you got knocked on your ass."

He slowly turned his gaze up toward Antonia Black and felt his heart speed up in a way that had nothing to do with his fall.

It was getting worse. He could hardly look at her anymore without being filled with an almost paralyzing ache of attraction.

She reached out her hand, her dark eyes twinkling with amusement, and after a beat of hesitation, he took it and let her help him to his feet.

For a moment after he stood, he let his hand linger in hers, allowing himself the luxury of feeling the tingling heat that seemed to generate from her skin into his. But then he dropped it, remembering the runaway horse.

"Did you see where Sunny went?" he asked.

She laughed. "She pranced right into the barn. I'm sure one of the grooms has her by now."

He nodded and winced, already sore from the fall. "She got stung," he said.

"Oh," said Noni, "I know. I saw the whole thing."

He smiled and rubbed his neck. "Hot horse," he said ruefully.

She smiled back. He felt his chest squeeze in response. "Hot horse," she agreed. She looked him over. "You sure you're all right?"

He nodded. "I'll probably be sore, but nothing is broken."

"Good," she said.

They gazed at each other for a moment.

"Are you going to Hendy's party tonight?" he finally said, needing to break the tension.

Her mood suddenly changed. She frowned, and a red flush touched the creamy skin of her cheeks and chest. "Yeah, I guess," she said in an abrupt tone. "Anyway, if you're really okay, I'm going to head on home." She quickly turned to go. "I'll see you at the party."

He watched Antonia walk away, heading for her truck. He had the impulse to call out, stop her, ask her what was wrong. But before he could act, Noni swung up into her truck, her platinum blond hair streaming behind her, slammed the door with a bang, and was gone in a cloud of dust.

He clenched and unclenched his fist, reminding himself that every time she slipped away, it was better for both of them. Less complicated, safer.

Nothing good, he reminded himself sternly for the ten millionth time as he started back toward the barn, *could come from anything happening between us.*

She is my boss's sister. She is a Del Campo. I would only end up hurting her.

The words were his litany, but lately they were starting to lose their power.

He shook his head. Being stern with himself wasn't working anymore. He could feel that he was starting to weaken. Being around her at work, being her friend and confidant, without ever hinting at his real feelings, had begun to exhaust him.

It was a part he knew he could not play much longer. All his good reasons for keeping his distance, all the rules of the barn and vows to himself that he had clung to over the years had started to feel weightless compared to his growing feelings for this woman. The many times he had repeated to himself that it was unprofessional, that he wasn't fit to be in a relationship, that he didn't deserve her, that she was too fragile... it was all beginning to feel as insubstantial as a fairy story. A cautionary tale he'd heard as a child, meant to keep him away from gingerbread houses and wolves in the woods.

Because she was different these days. She was stronger and happier and more stable. And her happiness made her all the more irresistible.

And maybe, he thought, *I'm different, too...*

He turned back around at the barn door, watching the lingering trail of dust that her old blue truck had left behind. He thought of a moment in the barn earlier that day, when he had held the head of a pony for her while she bent over its hind leg, hammering in a new shoe. For just the quickest second, she had looked up and met his eyes, and a devilish smile had danced over her mouth. It had been the kind of carefree grin he would never have imagined on her face when he had first come to know her. It seemed to prove that she was finally mended. Certainly, she was a changed woman from the one he'd met all those years ago.

* * *

Eight years earlier

The barn had been fizzing with gossip for days. Enzo's boss, Alejandro Del Campo, had flown to Berlin to find his newly discovered half sister. She was a scandal no one in the Del Campo family had even known existed before reading Carlos Del Campo's posthumous will.

There were rumors circulating all over the farm about the mystery woman. The grooms were whispering that Alejandro had bailed her out of jail, a student rider swore she heard that the sister was an opium addict, and the Argentine vet said she had been living on the streets, doing what she must to survive.

Of course, not one of those things had turned out to be

true, but on the day that Alejandro had first brought Antonia to the barn, anything seemed possible and none of it was good.

Enzo had been leading out a little black mare named Hex for training—she'd recently started to get spooky on the field and he'd wanted to pinpoint what, exactly, was setting her off—when Alejandro slid open the doors and entered with a small blond woman trailing behind him. The usual buzz and chatter of the barn suddenly stilled.

The woman immediately stopped to look at a pony and turned away from Enzo, so that his first impression was just a swath of pale, creamy neck and long, silky white-blond hair, the kind of hair so fine and smooth that it looked like it couldn't be bound, as if it would just slide right out of a clip or hair band. At first glance she seemed a child, sylphlike and vulnerable, in an oversized black button-down flannel, baggy faded jeans, and worn work boots. But when she turned her head and glanced at Enzo, he'd felt himself go still.

This was no child.

She was stunning. With high Slavic cheekbones, a wide and generous mouth, a heart-shaped face tapering to a stubborn little chin, and, most startling, Carlos's eyes. Large, slanted, and raven dark, hauntingly shadowed in her pale face, with long, sooty lashes and dramatic black slashes for brows. Except that, unlike her father, whose gaze had always looked a bit dulled by overindulgence and self-satisfaction, this woman had eyes that glowed like live coal—filled with raw intelligence, hurt, anger, and challenge. She looked like a desperate, wild thing who had just been trapped into captivity.

Her beauty was undeniable, but it wasn't just her physical presence that moved Enzo. He recognized something in her—a fierce and anguished aura—that made him want to reach out and touch her, to gentle her, to comfort her, to find out exactly what had happened to make her this feral and fix it in any way he could.

The pony beside him had nipped him then, impatient to get outside. Enzo swore in pain, and Antonia laughed—a silvery sound that sent electric chills down his spine. For a moment, her whole face lit up. She was transformed. She lost that hunted look, and she was, if it was at all possible, even more beautiful than she had been seconds before.

Then her smile slipped away and her eyes clouded back over, and Enzo realized that he would gladly spend the rest of his life doing just about anything to try to make her laugh again.

She walked over and scratched Hex's ears. "She wants out," she said. Her voice was soft and husky and thoroughly American—not a trace of the Argentine accent that the rest of her family, and Enzo himself, sported.

Hex closed her eyes and nibbled at Antonia's hair. Enzo smiled. "She likes you," he said.

Antonia arched a dubious brow. "She likes to be scratched."

The sleeve of her shirt fell back as she continued to rub Hex's neck, and Enzo had been shocked to see all the scars—some shiny white and healed, but others still pink and raw—that dotted her hand and wrist.

Without thinking, he reached out and touched her hand, tracing the marks under his fingertips, feeling the tight, raised flesh and then an incredible heat that seemed to emanate from her skin. She felt like she was burning with fever.

She went absolutely still, met his eyes defiantly, and then shook him off.

"Not that it's any of your business"—she flipped her hand over and showed him a small tattoo of an anvil on her inner arm—"but I'm a metalworker. Burns are just a hazard of the job."

He felt hugely relieved and then annoyed with the force of emotions that were raging through him. What business was this of his? Why should he care how she got her burns?

"A farrier?" he asked, trying to hide behind polite conversation.

She shook her head. "No, mostly casting lately." But she looked around the barn, a hint of speculation in her wide dark eyes.

Then Alejandro had joined them and Enzo had suddenly been shocked back to reality.

His boss's little sister. A member of the Del Campo family.

If ever a woman had been off-limits...

Alejandro led his sister away, wanting to show her the rest of the farm, and Enzo had been left with Hex, who was starting to paw the ground in her eagerness to get out of the barn.

In the field, Enzo rode the pony, trying to figure out what she was shying away from, but his thoughts kept returning to Antonia. The silken curtain of her hair, her obsidian eyes, the way her skin seemed to burn from within, her scent— something sweet and hot like black pepper and cinnamon...

Under him, Hex suddenly tensed and Enzo broke from his reverie to take note of their surroundings. There it was—an old black garden hose on the field that someone had left out. It looked too much like a snake to the sensitive little mare. He'd tell a groom to take care of it right away.

He rode the pony back in, wondering whether he'd see Antonia again, wondering where she was staying...

He shook his head.

He had not felt this way in years. Perhaps he had not felt this way ever. And it shook him to the core.

* * *

The dust had cleared now, the truck was long gone, and Enzo finally went to find Sunny and make sure she'd been taken care of. He knew he would see Noni later that night, at Lord Henderson's end-of-the-season party, and thought that he might ask her then what had made her so angry.

Ducking back into the cool, fragrant barn, he flashed on her face again—that slightly wicked smile—and he felt his whole body tighten in response.

He closed his eyes for a moment, took a deep breath, and tried to banish her from his thoughts, push her away, in the same way he'd been doing for years.

But something stuck and held.

It was getting harder and harder to let her go.

Chapter Two

Antonia burned herself as she pulled the red-hot piece of steel from her forge. The coal spit fire when she grabbed the metal rod with her tongs, and a tiny piece of ember landed on her arm, but she didn't even wince. She merely flicked the glowing spark off her wrist with the careless air of someone who had been burned many, many times before, slammed the burning rod onto the horn of her anvil, and set to work hammering it out.

Antonia was making horseshoes. They were pointless, really. She knew that her homemade shoes would probably just end up reforged as something else later. When shoeing the costly ponies in her care, she only used "polo plates," machine-made, lightweight, specially designed shoes whose carefully dulled edges and rims were beyond her abilities as a smithy. She would never dare put her relatively crude work on a Del Campo pony. But when Antonia was upset, when she had something she needed to get off her mind, when she needed to check out, she went back to the first thing she had learned to smith. Which happened to have been horseshoes.

She hit the steel with more power and less precision than she normally would. But, at the moment, all Antonia wanted was the satisfying feel of metal against metal, the shower of sparks she created every time she landed a blow, the smell of burning coal and hot steel, and the resonant clank of her hammer shaping the work.

She'd had a bad day. Not because anything had gone wrong professionally. Everything had been fine as far as her farrier work went. She'd successfully shod three ponies, managed to fix a problem in the gait of one of her favorite horses just by opening up the back left heel a little and recalibrating the balance, and she had noticed a narrow but deep sand crack in the hoof of another pony and trimmed it down before it became something much worse.

But all that accomplishment came to nothing after Pilar Del Campo had shown up at the barn.

Antonia moved the metal to the center of the anvil and hit it still harder. Her hammer made an explosion of sparks bloom and fly, bouncing in a small hail of embers off her heavy leather apron.

Usually, Antonia didn't let Pilar's attitude get under her skin. In fact, she often had sympathy for the woman. After all, when Carlos Del Campo had died, Antonia's existence had come as a surprise, not just to Pilar but to the whole Del Campo family as well. Suddenly Sebastian and Alejandro had a twenty-two-year-old half sister they'd never even met, and their mother had a flesh-and-blood reminder of her husband's infidelity.

Antonia continued to hit, trying to draw the metal out into a curve, but the steel was losing heat and pliability now, no longer a bright orange-yellow but fading into a darker red.

She threw the shoe back into the forge for another heating.

At the end of the day, Noni and her older brother Alejandro had been in the barn office discussing the pony with the sand crack in her hoof. Alejandro had been effusive in his praise, telling her that he had picked that pony's feet that very morning and completely missed the injury.

"I am in your debt, Noni," he'd said. "That crack would have been a disaster if you had not caught it in time. What can I do to thank you?"

Antonia had shrugged him off. It was her job, after all, but her brother laid a hand on her shoulder and met her eyes with a warm smile. "Come, *hermana*, there must be something you would like."

Antonia's heart had beat a little faster than usual, and she'd thought, *Now's the time.* She took a deep breath and tried to seem as casual as possible when she'd said, "Maybe we can just, you know, play a little stick and ball together sometime? Even get Sebastian out on the field, too?"

Alejandro had looked surprised for a second, and then his smile had grown even wider, and he'd opened his mouth to answer her, and Antonia had been filled with a breathless hope, when the door to the office had banged open and Pilar had come charging in. Ignoring Antonia completely (as she always did), Pilar had started in on Alejandro in rapid-fire Spanish about what he was going to wear to Lord Henderson's party that night since the dry cleaner had failed to return Jandro's good tuxedo on time.

And just like that, the moment was gone. Jandro had rolled his eyes and shrugged at Antonia before plunging into a good-natured argument with his mother. Antonia, after catching an impatient sideways glare from Pilar, had stood there for just one more agonizing moment before she gave up and left the office.

For a brief time later, talking to Enzo after she'd helped

him off the ground, she'd felt a little better. But then he'd gone and reminded her of Hendy's party, too, and all her disappointment and anger had flooded back.

She'd driven straight home to her shop, lit up her forge, and started making horseshoes.

She opened the door to the forge and caught up the partially made shoe in her tongs. Holding it in the air, she stared at it for a moment, chewing her lip. It was pulsing and alive—exactly the right temperature, she could tell by the yellow-orange color—as pliable as clay, ready to be thrown onto her anvil and hammered into something useful.

Instead, Antonia reached over and plunged the half-done work into her water bucket, extinguishing its heat and glow with a steamy hiss. Then she threw the thing, dripping, cold, and worthless, into her scrap pail, took off her safety glasses and apron, and shut down her forge.

"Luna, Mojo," she called.

A black and white mass of fur curled up in the corner of the shop untangled itself into two separate huskies, one fluffy white, one glossy black, but both with the same slanted ice-blue eyes.

"Come on," said Antonia, giving her thigh a little pat as she left the shop.

The sisters, tongues lolling, obediently trotted after their mistress. Next time, Noni thought as she strode into the soft Florida dusk, she wouldn't let Pilar Del Campo stop her. Next time, she wouldn't hesitate. She would make her move.

Chapter Three

Enzo was at the foot of the stairs at the back of the barn, heading up to his apartment, when a figure riding a black Ducati motorcycle pulled up next to him.

Enzo smiled as the rider took off his helmet, revealing a young blond man with a friendly grin. "Mark Stone," said Enzo. "It has been a while. Nice bike."

Mark dismounted awkwardly. "It's new. Still getting the hang of it." The motorcycle began to lean, and he caught it just before it fell. "Obviously."

Enzo laughed. He had always liked this young Internet genius. Enzo had given him polo lessons when Mark had substituted for Sebastian on the Del Campo team a few years back. Since then, the amiable billionaire had been a regular at Del Campo events.

"Where is Camelia?" Enzo asked, referring to Mark's new wife, an ex-groom from the Del Campo farm.

"Training," said Mark proudly. "It looks like she and Skye have a really good shot of making the Olympic dressage team this year." He frowned. "Oh, but hey, if you see her, do me a favor and don't mention the bike, okay? She'd pitch a fit if she knew I was riding it."

Enzo snorted. "I am sure she just wants to keep you alive."

Mark smiled roguishly. "One hopes."

"You just missed Alejandro," said Enzo as he started back up the stairs. "He left about thirty minutes ago, but I think you can probably catch him at the farm."

"Actually," said Mark, "it's you I want to talk to."

Enzo paused, surprised. "Oh?"

"I'm putting together a team, Enzo."

Enzo raised his eyebrows. "A polo team?"

Mark nodded. "Yes. High goal. I'm going to be the patron and play number four, and I've got two other players—a guy from Mumbai and another guy from Australia—lined up. They're both incredible. But I need a fourth player, a team captain, to play the number three position."

"Ah," said Enzo, "that is very exciting. Congratulations. Actually, there is a young groom in the stables—he's from Philadelphia. I don't know if he's ready to captain, but he's an incredibly promising player—"

"No, no," said Mark. "You misunderstand. I want you to come play number three. And be the *piloto* of my team."

"*Pilotos* don't play," said Enzo automatically, "and I have a job here with the Del Campos."

"I'll pay you twice what they pay you," said Mark, "and who says that a *piloto* can't play?"

"I should have said that good *pilotos* don't play," said Enzo. "It splits their attention."

"I think you're capable of doing both."

Enzo laughed. "Well, thanks for the offer, but—"

"I'll pay you three times as much," interrupted Mark.

Enzo was silent for a moment. It wasn't the money. It was the timing. He knew that he was starting to weaken when it came to Antonia. Perhaps putting some distance between them wouldn't be the worst idea...

Mark seemed to sense his hesitation. "Or listen, if you don't want to play, just come and be my *piloto*, then. You can help me find my fourth player."

Enzo chewed on his lip. "Can I think about it?"

Mark smiled happily. "Absolutely! Take all the time you need! No hurry. I want to get this right."

Enzo nodded. "Okay. In the meantime, check out the kid I told you about—his name is David Jefferson. He's got a lot of potential."

Mark shook his hand enthusiastically. "Okay, I will. Ah, man, I'm so excited! This is going to be an amazing team!"

Enzo laughed. "Don't get too excited. I just said I'd think about it."

Mark grinned. "Better answer than I expected. I never figured anyone could poach you away from the Del Campos."

Enzo shrugged. "It just might be time for a change is all."

Chapter Four

Noni stood in front of her closet and considered her choices. Dressing for these Wellington parties was always a chore. She dearly wished she could just show up in her worn jeans and T-shirt, but she knew that wasn't an option.

She pushed aside a pile of half-hung sweaters, ignoring the ones that slipped to the floor. Like the rest of her house, the closet was a mess. Though she kept her smith shop immaculate, her cottage was something of a disaster zone. Noni was halfhearted about housecleaning at best, and even though she knew she could afford a housekeeper, she couldn't get over the idea of a stranger cleaning up after her.

She sighed, fantasizing about ditching the whole night, staying home with Chinese takeout and bingeing on her backed-up DVR. She was in no mood for a party, and getting dressed felt like such an effort.

Not that Antonia didn't have the clothes. In fact, for the first time in her life, she had plenty of clothes. She had wanted for nothing since that winter eight years ago when Alejandro had found her in that nearly empty studio in Berlin.

* * *

The heat had been turned off, so she'd taken to staying in bed as much as possible, fully dressed and huddled under five layers of blankets. When someone had knocked on the door, she considered not answering, afraid it was the landlord demanding the last two months' rent. But then she had thought, what if it was Jacob? What if he wanted her back? And just the faint hope of that possibility had propelled her out of bed and to the door.

But it hadn't been Jacob. It had been Alejandro Del Campo, her eldest brother, whom she had never before met. She'd recognized him immediately, though. Tall, dark, and broad shouldered, with Carlos's strikingly handsome and imperious face. Except that her brother had ocean-blue eyes, not black, and a much kinder, though sadder, smile.

He was there, he said, to let her know that she would inherit quite a large sum of money from their father and would need to return to America to claim it. He would take her back home with him, if she was willing.

She stared up at her brother as the breath left her body. She hadn't known their father had died.

It had been like a twisted fairy tale. Suddenly, after years of neglect, Carlos had finally claimed her, just as she had always dreamed he would. But instead of her strong, handsome father swooping in to take her away, there were just words on paper, signatures, and lawyers, and red tape, and no father at all. Only this stranger of an older brother here to deliver the news, who looked as grim and reluctant as Noni felt.

Alejandro had noticed her shivering then and frowned. She'd watched him realize that her flat was no warmer than the ice-cold hall he was standing in.

"Let's get a cup of coffee," he'd said. Then, peering closer at her frail form and pale cheeks, his face softened. "Or perhaps lunch?"

She had hastily agreed, and after two bowls of soup, three cups of hot tea, and a slice of Linzer torte, she had also agreed to go back to Florida with him, where, he assured her, it was very warm, and she would be welcome to stay as long as she liked.

"I'm sorry I did not know of you sooner, Antonia," he said, taking her hand. "It's a crime and a shame what our father has done to you. And to me and Sebastian. *Somos familia*. This should not have been the first time we met."

And she had blinked, trying to keep back the tears. "Call me Noni," she'd offered weakly in return, already starting to love this big brother she had always imagined she hated.

Since then, she'd had everything. A monthly stipend from her inheritance, her little cottage and blacksmith shop on the beach, the farrier job, the ponies, the clothes, world travel with the Del Campos, the parties, the connections, the glamour.

Once the initial rumors had cleared and everyone accepted that she was neither a junkie nor a prostitute, she'd been treated like a mysterious long-lost princess by the Wellington horsey crowd. She'd been invited everywhere, cultivated, and accepted like a true Del Campo.

Except that she was not.

Her brothers Jandro and Sebastian and, later, their wives Georgia and Kat had offered her nothing but kindness and friendship. They had welcomed her into their home—and what a home it was. The Del Campo farm was even more impressive than she had fantasized it would be. And once she had completed her blacksmithing classes, they had hired her on as their team farrier. She'd now been with them for almost eight years, and yet, she still felt like the little girl she had been—the one whose mother had constantly told her that her rich, handsome, and powerful father wanted nothing to do with her. She still felt she was watching her family from the outside, with her nose pressed up to the window. And they were all gathered around the table, laughing and teasing each other and having the loveliest time. Noni longed to be invited in, could almost touch them, they were that close... but somehow she could never make it past the door.

Part of the problem was Pilar. Hell, most of the problem was Pilar. Even as Alejandro and Sebastian had rallied around their little sister, inviting her into their lives, Pilar had made it very clear that she preferred Antonia to stay well outside the family. She would, for her sons' sake, tolerate Noni's presence, and of course, she'd never be so gauche as to actively confront Noni with her displeasure, but to her, Antonia was simply Carlos's bastard. Just the greatest disappointment in a lifetime of disappointments visited upon her by her charming, wretched, late husband. And despite all her brothers' good intentions, this attitude kept Noni firmly out of the inner circle.

Antonia could have left, of course. Certainly she had never planned on staying for long. But she'd been so weak in the beginning, still reeling over what had happened to her in Berlin. She had just wanted to rest. Rest somewhere sunny, and easy, and beautiful, somewhere she didn't have to struggle. She'd fallen into life with the Del Campos like a sleep-deprived child tucked into a warm, soft bed.

Just a little break, she had promised herself. Just a little time, and once she was stronger, then she'd be on her way.

She'd inherited a generous monthly allowance from Carlos, and when she turned thirty, she was due to receive a full fourth of the Del Campo estate, making her worth hundreds of millions of dollars. She didn't need her job. She didn't need anyone to support her. She could start her life over somewhere remote and quiet and pretty, where no one knew her name or wondered about her history. She could do or be anything.

It was the only gift that her father had ever given her, and she had fully intended on taking advantage of it.

But as Antonia had grown stronger, as her pain had dulled, she had started to notice things about her brothers. She had spent her whole life thinking of them as spoiled, untouchable aristocrats. She'd only seen them as distant strangers who kept her father out of her life. However, now that she had finally gotten the chance to know them, she realized that, even though Alejandro and Sebastian had grown up with wealth and privilege, their lives were not necessarily so easy either.

When Noni first arrived, before Alejandro had met Georgia, he'd been entangled in his own kind of grief. He'd recently lost his wife in a fatal riding accident, and he was raising a difficult teenage daughter, Valentina, on his own. The whole Del Campo legacy was on his shoulders, and Noni could see that he was struggling, barely keeping his head above water, and that he desperately needed help.

Handsome, green-eyed Sebastian had, at first, seemed the opposite of Alejandro—full of joy and mischief, always ready to have a little fun. But Noni soon became aware that he had his own demons. All his partying was simply a front for a man who didn't think he would ever measure up, who was so afraid of failure that he never allowed himself to try.

As Noni got stronger and started to heal, she'd found herself falling in love with her brothers and her niece—with her *family*—and she longed to help them as much as they had helped her.

She did whatever she could to help them through their hard times. *My rock*, Alejandro had once called Noni, and just hearing those words had sent a thrill of joy zinging through her, had made her feel important and necessary and included in a way she'd never felt before.

And then her brothers had both married women who were strong, and smart, and funny, and interesting, and Noni had fallen for them as well. Valentina had moved away for college and then started her career dancing with the San Francisco Ballet, but Alejandro and Georgia had baby Tomás, a beautiful, laughing child with Alejandro's black curls and Georgia's wide, hazel eyes.

When Noni held her nephew for the first time, she wept. After a lifetime of having no one she could truly depend upon, Antonia's circle only seemed to be growing bigger.

That was an almost impossible thing for her to walk away from. All of a sudden, she no longer wanted out; instead, she desperately wanted in. She wanted to belong to these people, heart and soul; she wanted the family she'd never had. She wanted to truly be a Del Campo.

* * *

Antonia attacked her closet with renewed force, just hoping to find something clean. She wanted to be a Del Campo? Well, then, she had better suck it up, get dressed, and get to the end-of-the-season party for the Del Campo team. She was already late.

Her hand snagged on a dark brown leather gaucho belt. A gift from Enzo. She smiled, remembering the way he had surprised her with it. He had brought it back from Argentina after he had gone back home to visit his family. He claimed it was no big deal, that he had just seen it and thought she would like it. Noni had been so touched, tears had sprung into her eyes, and she'd had to turn away to hide them. No one had ever given her a gift "just because" before.

Her fingers lingered on the belt, tracing the brightly colored embroidery, as she experienced the familiar butterflies swooping in her stomach that she always felt when she thought of Enzo. Enzo sitting on the pitch that day, looking up at her as he took her hand. She blushed, wondering if he'd noticed the way she'd held on to his hand just a bit longer than she should have, but she hadn't been able to bring herself to let go.

Enzo, her best friend, which meant all the more to Noni since she had never had many friends, and certainly never a best one. Enzo, who had, from the beginning, helped her and advised her and kept her spirits up even when she felt her darkest. Enzo, who, aside from her brothers, was the kindest, truest man she'd ever met. Enzo, who always made her laugh. Enzo, who was smart and strong and so incredibly good-looking and pretty much the sexiest man on the face of the planet as far as Noni was concerned. Enzo, who would only have to crook his finger and beckon and Noni would be out of her clothes and into his bed before he could count to three...

Except, she reminded herself, that Enzo had never shown any interest in her beyond brotherly affection. He'd never even made the smallest move on her. As far as Noni could tell, she was so thoroughly friend-zoned that it seemed pointless to even think about trying to turn what was between them into anything more.

She frowned, shaking her head, and dropped her hand from the belt. Now was not the time to be thinking of Enzo.

She finally found a white Calvin Klein suit, brushed off the dog hair (living with two huskies, there was no avoiding it), and examined it. It was blessedly clean. She decided that, rather than dig out a proper blouse, she would wear the jacket buttoned up with nothing underneath. It had a plunging neckline, but Noni was small-breasted and slight and she knew that, even with a lot of skin exposed, her boyish figure would keep her from looking like she was showing too much.

The suit was immaculately cut but bordering on severe, so to dress it up a bit more, Noni untangled a thick gold lariat necklace from her dressing table and gold cuffs she had made herself for each wrist. She topped the outfit off with flat, metallic gold sandals.

She pushed her hair behind her ears and despaired at getting it to do anything but what it always did, which was basically hang there looking lank. She applied a little tinted moisturizer, a lick of mascara, clear balm to her lips, and called herself done.

She didn't like to look in the mirror for too long, as it was too easy to start focusing on all she was not, but she gave herself a quick last glance, making sure everything was basically in place and that there were no errant stains or holes she had somehow overlooked before impatiently turning away. She fed her dogs, gathered up her bag and keys, and hurried out to her old Chevy truck, determined not to be any later than she already was.

She would talk to her brothers tonight, she decided as she turned the ignition. Do or die.

Chapter Five

Enzo looked over the crowd in the nightclub and was grateful he had a good suit.

It was a relic of his past life. Custom made on Savile Row. Hand-crafted, bespoke. It was tailored to fit him perfectly, and though he'd worn it for almost two decades, it looked as good on him now as it had when he'd first bought it.

There weren't many things that Enzo had taken with him when he'd left his old life behind, but he'd never been sorry that this suit was one of them.

As always, his eyes skimmed the glittering mass of partygoers, unimpressed by the wealth and celebrity, searching the room for the only one who mattered.

There she was. Standing alone at the end of the bar, wearing a white suit that plunged in the front in a way that made his breath catch, nursing her usual Jameson and water, easily the most beautiful woman in the room. She looked bored, oblivious, as always, to the stares and attention she was drawing from every corner.

Enzo frowned as he watched a handsome pop star, recently made notorious for an enormously revealing wardrobe malfunction at one of his concerts, approach Antonia. The singer smiled at her, leaning in much too close, and whispered in her ear.

Noni's face stayed coolly neutral. She took a sip of her drink, then answered him without even meeting his eyes. Whatever she said made the man's face wash over in an angry pink before he turned and walked stiffly away.

Enzo grinned. God, she could be as cool as ice, his Antonia.

She looked up, spotted him, and her face lit up. She wrinkled her nose impatiently, gesturing for him to stop hanging around in the doorway and to come join her. By the time he crossed the floor, she had procured his usual Grey Goose and soda, which she handed to him with a double kiss of greeting.

"Feeling better?" she asked him.

He took a sip of his drink. "I will be in a moment."

"I love it when you wear this suit," she said, casually adjusting his tie and then running her fingertips down his lapel. "Gives me a Javier Bardem vibe."

Enzo swallowed and took a step back. He should be used to her careless touches by now. She was affectionate with him in the same way she was affectionate with her brothers, constantly adjusting their clothing, brushing off imaginary flecks of lint, touching a hand or a shoulder when she wanted to make a point, but try as he might, he was never immune. The simplest contact made him ache for more.

"*Gracias, niña*," he said, breathing in her unique, spicy scent and trying not to be too obvious about his sudden, overwhelming desire to crush her body to his.

She rolled her eyes. "For God's sake, Enzo, I'm nearly thirty. When are you going stop calling me *niña*?"

He laughed, relaxing into their customary banter. "Never,"

he said. He leaned against the bar. "Anyone good here tonight?"

She shrugged. "The usual crowd. Rich, beautiful, famous. Sometimes all three at once."

"I saw you send Dax Lewis packing," he said. "What did you say to make him look so unhappy?"

She frowned. "That was Dax Lewis? I thought he was one of Sebastian's old drinking buddies."

Enzo laughed. "Well, I suppose there's a good chance he is, actually."

They stood side by side for a moment, sipping their drinks and watching the crowd.

Enzo saw Pilar Del Campo enter, followed by Sebastian and Alejandro with their wives on their arms. All three women were wearing jewels so large—a choker for Pilar, a pair of dangling earrings for Kat, a bracelet for Georgia, who was heavily pregnant again—that Enzo could see them glittering from across the room. Half the women in the club turned to look at the handsome brothers, and not a few men hungrily eyed their beautiful wives.

Lord Henderson hurried over to greet them, kissing all the women hello and then taking Pilar by the arm and leading her into the crowd. There was something proprietary about the way he shepherded her that made Enzo pause for a moment and take a second look.

"Huh. Hendy and Pilar," said Antonia, echoing his thoughts. "That's new."

Enzo watched the dapper older man as he slid his hand to the small of Pilar's back.

You sly old dog, he thought, and smiled. "I like them together," he said. "That should have happened ages ago."

Noni shrugged. "Well, good luck to Hendy, anyway," she

said, wryly toasting the couple before taking another sip of her drink.

Enzo turned to her, mildly exasperated. He understood how Antonia felt about Pilar, but he wished the two women could find a way to bury the hatchet. They were more alike than either would ever admit.

"Is that what made you so mad this afternoon?" he asked. "Another run-in with Pilar?"

Noni flushed and buried her face in her drink. "It was nothing," she murmured; then she looked up at him sharply. "How did you know about that, anyway?"

It was Enzo's turn to look away. "I noticed that you seemed upset as you were leaving."

He could feel Antonia's questioning eyes on him as he resolutely kept his gaze on the dance floor.

"You notice a lot," she finally said.

"Well, you stomped off the pitch and then drove away from the farm like a bat out of hell," he said. "Hard not to notice."

She snorted. "I did not. I was maybe doing twenty-five."

"You're supposed to do fifteen. What if you hit a horse?"

She threw her hand up, laughing. "No one does fifteen. You never do fifteen! And how am I going to hit a horse? Give me a break."

Enzo opened his mouth to argue further but was interrupted by Hendy, who had commandeered the DJ booth, Pilar by his side.

"Hello?" Hendy said into the microphone. "Hello? Hello?"

The room quieted as people turned their attention toward their host.

"Ah, yes," said Hendy in his posh British accent, "um,

well, I just wanted to say welcome to you all. And thank you very much for attending."

A few people shouted "thank you" back at him.

He nodded in return. "Yes, you're very welcome, of course. My pleasure, you know, so happy to see everyone here celebrating what was a most excellent and winning season...um..."

He trailed off for a moment, and Pilar reached out and took his hand. He smiled at her gratefully and took a deep breath.

"So, since you're all here anyway, I have something of an announcement to make..."

The crowd got even quieter. Enzo glanced at Noni, who looked concerned.

"I'm afraid that this party isn't just an end-of-the-season gala. It's actually a retirement celebration as well. Because, uh, I am quite sad to announce, this polo season has turned out to be my last on the pitch."

There was an audible gasp from the audience. Enzo looked over at the Del Campo family, who looked somber but not surprised.

"Did you know?" he whispered to Antonia.

She shook her head in return.

Hendy cleared his throat. "Yes, well, I know I have always said they would have to carry me off the field, but, unfortunately, my doctors seem to feel that is exactly what will happen if I continue to play. The old knee simply won't take it any longer. So, I thought it best to spare you all the sight of me limping about and just go out on one last, winning season."

He smiled shakily, and his voice grew deep with emotion.

"I don't want anyone feeling sorry for me. I have, of course, been a lucky, lucky man to have been able to play the game I love for all these years. And I have been particularly lucky in this last decade to have played on the Del Campo family team, La Victoria."

He stopped for a moment and cleared his throat.

"To put it plainly, it has been the most extraordinary part of my rather extraordinary life. I have had the chance to be on the field with the kind of world-class players that only come along once every few generations. I've also had the extreme good fortune of calling these men my friends. Alejandro, Sebastian, Rory"—he raised his glass to his teammates—"I thank you so much for putting up with this old man all these years. Truly, it has been an honor and a privilege."

His teammates solemnly raised their glasses in return.

Hendy quickly dashed the tears from his eyes. "And don't think you'll be rid of me altogether! I shall, of course, stay on as patron, if you'll still have me."

"As long as you wish, my friend," said Alejandro. "We would not be the team we are today without you."

"To Hendy!" called out Sebastian. "Hip hip!"

"HOORAY!" the entire room called in response.

Just as Enzo raised his glass, Antonia put down hers and rushed out of the room.

* * *

Antonia had veered into the alley behind the nightclub, desperate to get away from all the curious glances on the busy sidewalk, when Enzo caught up with her.

"Noni?" he said, putting a hand on her shoulder. "Are you all right?"

She wiped the tears from her eyes, embarrassed to be caught crying. "I'm okay," she said, turning away from him.

"*Niña*," he said, "I know you love Hendy—we all do—but it's just retirement. He will be fine."

"It's not that," she said. "I mean, I'm sad for Hendy. I know it will be hard on him not to play, but..." She trailed off.

He kept his hand on her shoulder. "What, then?"

She kept her face averted. "It's nothing. It's silly. I probably had too much to drink."

He smiled at her. "What, your two sips of whiskey and water? I've seen you slam back six shots of Patrón and stay standing."

She shook her head. "I just...I had these stupid plans. I thought I would..." She stopped herself. She didn't want to talk about it. She felt like a fool.

He slid his hand down her arm and covered her hand in his. "You thought you would what, *querida*?"

His fingers were so warm wrapped around hers. She looked up and saw real concern in his soft brown eyes. "I just hoped that maybe tonight would be different," she whispered.

"How so?"

"It's just...they all knew."

"Who knew what? I don't understand."

"The Del Campos. The family. And the team. All of them. They already knew what Hendy was going to say."

"Yes, so?"

"So?" She shrugged, miserable. "So, no one told me."

He shook his head. "I still don't—"

"It's just proof, once again, that I'm not really part of the family."

He blinked, confused. "Of course you are part of the family. You're a Del Campo, aren't you?"

She dropped his hand and stepped away from him. "That's the point. I'm not a Del Campo." Her voice slightly trembled. "I'm a Black. And they never let me forget it."

He reached for her, pulling her back toward him. "*Niña*, why do you need this so much?"

She sighed and leaned against him, taking in his clean, musky scent. "Did I ever tell you about how I first learned to ride?"

He shook his head. "I don't think so."

She wiped her eyes. "You know that my mom and I never stayed in one place for very long when I was a kid, right? We were always moving. Usually in the middle of the night to avoid paying back rent. But for six months, when I was ten, we stayed in this tiny adobe house in New Mexico."

He nodded, and she felt him slightly tighten his grip on her.

"I loved all sorts of things about that house. It was small—only two bedrooms—and snug. It had a red clay roof, and beautiful bright blue tiled floors, and an old claw-foot bathtub so deep I felt like I could swim in it, and the window in my room looked out over the hills. At night, the breeze would come in from the desert and it smelled like sage, and warm sand, and the enormous hedge of rosemary that grew out back."

"*Qúe paz*," he said.

She nodded and smiled. "It was." Without thinking, she settled in a little closer to him. "Anyway, what I loved most of all was that just down the road, there was an enormous ranch. And they kept horses. A whole herd of scraggly, half-wild little mustangs that were basically allowed to roam free from sunup to sundown, feeding on scrub brush. In fact, I don't think I ever saw them get called in. I used to go down there every day after school. My mom was always either painting—that was her 'red period' as she called it—and didn't want to be disturbed, or sleeping, because she was usually out all night."

"She left you alone?" said Enzo. "But you were so young. Weren't you scared?"

She shrugged. "I was used to it. Anyway, I'd always bring some carrots or an apple to the ponies, and at first I'd just stand at the fence, hoping the horses would come to me, but they were skittish, you know? I couldn't get them to trust me, so I'd throw the food over the fence and watch them eat from afar. But one day, this little black and white spotted mare came up close enough to grab a carrot and run, and then after that she came back for an apple."

Enzo smiled. "The smartest one, eh?"

Noni nodded solemnly. "She was, for sure. So I fed her every day for about a week, and pretty soon she was letting me pet her and scratch her, and then, not long after that, she'd actually come running every time she saw me walking down the road."

Enzo smoothed a lock of hair from her cheek and tucked it behind her ear. It immediately slipped back.

Antonia smiled, remembering.

"I'd never had anything that . . . needed me like that, you know? My mom had a life of her own that had nothing to do with me—her art, the men. I couldn't have any pets because we moved around so much, and I never really made any friends because I never lived anywhere long enough to get over how shy I was. This little horse, I felt like she had singled me out. She made me feel special. Maybe for the first time in my life..."

Enzo nodded. "Horses are good at that."

"Anyway, one day, I couldn't stand it anymore. I wanted to ride her so much that it hurt, so I slipped under the barbed wire and came over to her side of the fence."

Enzo chuckled. "Somehow I knew this part was coming."

"She was a bit surprised, I think. And then even more surprised when I basically scrabbled up her back and grabbed hold of her mane. I'd never been on a horse. I had no idea what I was doing. But I was determined to try."

"And she bucked you right off, correct?"

Noni grinned. "Close. She ran to the nearest tree and scraped me off. Knocked the wind right out of me."

He laughed. "Of course."

"But I didn't care. I got right back on. And then I fell off again. But then the next day I did it again. And again, and again, until I was finally able to keep my balance, and she finally let me stay on, and then I was really riding."

She looked up at Enzo, smiling. "Oh, Enzo," she breathed, "it was the best feeling. Bareback on a pony that you love. I felt like it just erased all the bad stuff in my life. I didn't worry about whether or not my mom had spent our grocery money on art supplies again or if the kids at school were going to notice that I was wearing the same outfit every day because I didn't have anything else. I didn't wonder why my father never came to see us. I didn't think about any of the stuff that I usually spent all my time worrying about, you know? I just...flew. I just flew away from all of that rotten stuff when I was on that little mare. She made everything okay."

She shook her head, momentarily lost in the memory.

"And so, when my mom woke me up one night and told me to pack...I knew the drill, you know? I'd done it dozens of times before. Stay quiet, only take what could fit into our little car, and get out fast. But this time...I couldn't do it. I didn't want to leave. I panicked. When my mom went into her room to pack, I slipped out the door, in my nightgown, and ran down the road..."

She gulped, trying to hold the tears back.

"I still remember what it felt like. The road was so rough and warm under my bare feet. I fell down and skinned my knee and hands, but I got right back up. I didn't care. I just kept running until I reached the fence. I was so sure...so sure that the little mare would be there. I mean, it made absolutely no sense at all. It was the middle of the night. I just had it in my head that I would be able to say goodbye."

Enzo tightened his grip.

She took a deep breath and nodded. "But of course she wasn't there. I stood there and called and called, thinking she'd hear me, but she didn't. I would have just stayed there until morning, waiting it out, but my mother came down the road in our car—everything all packed up, though God knows she left most of my stuff behind—and she told me to get in.

"I said no. She was totally shocked. I never said no to her. So she said it again. And again I said no. Then she got mad— like really mad—and she got out of the car and picked me up as I was kicking and screaming and threw me into the backseat and slammed the door behind me. I immediately scrabbled over and jumped out the other side and ran back to the fence.

"And my mom, she looked at me and she said, 'Fine. You don't want to come with me? Then you can just stay here, goddammit.' She got into the car and drove away."

Enzo made a soft sound of dismay.

Noni smiled ruefully. "I know. She was a shitty mom. She still kind of is. Anyway, I think she probably just went down the road to the nearest bar and had a drink—killed enough time to make sure I was good and scared. And I was. I was terrified. I forgot all about the horse and started sobbing in a blind panic. I honestly didn't think my mom was ever coming back. I didn't know what I was going to do if she didn't."

Enzo drew her even closer. "*Querida*," he said.

She held up a hand. "Wait," she said. "Just listen. So I was standing there, on the side of the road, crying so hard I thought I was going to throw up, trying to see through the darkness, wondering if I should try and run after the car, when I felt a little nudge on my shoulder. I whirled around, thinking monsters and bears, but it was the mare. She'd found me. I slipped behind the fence and hugged her, and suddenly I didn't care if my mom came back or not. It was all okay again. I knew I'd be okay, too, you know? I knew that one way or the other, I'd figure something out."

Enzo stiffened. "But your *madre*, she came back, right?"

"Yes, she came back. But not before I rode the mare one more time. Not before I had the chance to really say goodbye."

She sighed.

"For years after, I would put myself to bed at night, no matter where I was, just by remembering how it felt to be on her back. That gait and sway, you know? I would just imagine myself riding in the desert sun on a slow walking horse, and I would be able to let go and finally sleep."

They were silent for a moment, listening to the sounds from the street, the thumping bass coming from the night-club. Suddenly Antonia realized just how long she had been in Enzo's arms. She looked up into his light brown eyes, watched them turn dark with something that she didn't entirely recognize.

"Antonia," he murmured hoarsely.

"I . . . I . . . ," she stuttered, "I haven't been that happy since, Enzo. Not until—"

"You came here," he finished for her.

She nodded, mesmerized by his sexy, generous mouth, by the way his strong arms were gripping her around the waist, his fingertips pressing softly into her flesh . . .

She closed her eyes for a moment, trying to shake off the sudden wave of desire she felt crash over her. "Enzo?" she whispered.

"*¿Sí, niña?*"

She opened her eyes again. "I need your help with something."

He smiled at her. "Anything."

She looked up at him, nervous. Took a deep breath. "I want to play on the team," she said in a rush.

He knit his eyebrows, confused. "You want to . . . ?"

"Play polo. On La Victoria. They're going to have to replace Hendy. I want to be the replacement."

He shook his head. "But can you even—"

"I can ride. You know I can ride."

"*Sí*, yes, but riding is just part of the game."

"I know that. I'm not stupid. That's why I've been practicing."

"How?"

"I joined a weekend league. Just low-goal. I go every week. I'm getting better. I think maybe I'm pretty good, actually. But I think I need to get to the next level before I can tell Sebastian and Jandro about it, you know? I need to get good enough. I figure I've got at least this summer before they'll find Hendy's replacement. And we leave for the Hamptons in a few days, and you know we're never as busy up there as we are down here. That's where you come in. I need you to teach me while we're there."

He took a step back, shaking his head. "Antonia, we are talking about high-goal polo. La Victoria is the very best. I mean, a weekend league is all well and good, but playing on your brothers' team...that seems a bit...improbable, don't you think?"

She folded her arms in front of her, suddenly cold. "Can you at least see me play before you shoot me down?"

He raised his hands. "Hey, I am not shooting you down. I just don't understand why you would—"

"It's the family team," she interrupted, pleading. "My family team. Maybe this sounds childish, but I just feel like if I was on the team, I would be in..."

"The family," he finished for her.

"I just don't want to lose them," she said.

He shook his head. "But you won't, *niña*."

She shook her head, feeling panicked. "You can't promise me that. You don't understand what it's like to lose people."

He smiled ruefully. "I wouldn't be so sure about that, Noni." He sighed, rubbing his forehead. "Of course I will help you."

"Oh, Enzo, thank you!" And before she could think, she threw her arms back around him and kissed him square on the mouth.

Chapter Six

It was like fire.

The moment her lips made contact with his, every dismissed fantasy, every tamped-down craving, every hidden passion came roaring to the surface. Years of being careful, turning away, keeping her off-limits were swept aside. Something unrelenting and primal surged through Enzo's blood and pounded through his body like a drum. He was no longer capable of holding himself back.

Her kiss was spontaneous and innocent; he knew it was probably meant to be over almost as fast as it was given, but Enzo finally had Antonia in his arms, her lips were on his, and he was not going to let her slip away.

He felt her gasp as he took her head in his hands, knotting her silken hair around his fingers, refusing to break contact. Her lips were plush and firm, and he broke their seal with his tongue, tasting the lingering, smoky hint of whiskey, losing his breath as her tongue met his, flicking tentatively and then retreating as he pushed deeper still.

He pulled her supple body to his own, feeling her breasts push up against him as she ground her hips to his. He freed one hand from her hair and trailed it down the curve of her waist, cupping her firm behind and pulling her closer still.

He couldn't stop kissing her. He swept her mouth with his tongue, savoring her heat and taste, bringing his hand around to touch her cheek and the edge of her jaw, to feel the velvet softness of her neck. He finally broke loose of her mouth, following his hand, kissing the corner of her jawline and down her throat, at long last tasting the flesh he had dreamed of knowing for so many years.

He slipped his hand under her jacket, finding a perfect breast, just large enough to fit into his hand. His lips chased after, and he only stopped short of taking her nipple into his mouth when she gasped his name.

"Enzo," she breathed.

He pulled back, dazed, searching her face. Her slanted black eyes were downcast, her long lashes making crescent shadows on her cheeks. Her face and chest were flushed; her mouth was swollen and wet. She slowly raised her dark eyes to his and pierced him through with their heat.

He took a step back, indecision starting to creep in.

"No," she said swiftly, grabbing hold of his lapel. "No. Don't do that. We're going back to my place. Now."

* * *

Antonia drove with one hand firmly on his thigh, not trusting that he wouldn't still change his mind. She had seen the flash of doubt on his face when they broke contact. But just seconds before that, she had felt the unbelievable urgency of his kiss, the way his hands had fully claimed her as his, the adamantine strength of his desire. He wanted her. He wanted her more than she had ever dared dream. And she wasn't going to let him turn away from her.

"I didn't know," she said softly, almost to herself.

He kept his eyes on the road. "You didn't know what?"

She felt her face flush an even darker red. "I mean, I didn't know that you...thought of me that way. I thought you saw me as a...little sister or something."

He turned to her, surprised. "Antonia," he said. His voice was husky with longing, his mouth slowly curled into a smile, and his caramel-colored eyes gleamed. He gently unhooked her hand from his thigh and lifted it to his lips and kissed it. Then he ran his lips over the palm of her hand and up to the tip of her index finger and sucked, bringing it into his warm, soft mouth and biting down gently before pulling away and carefully placing her hand back down on his thigh.

"I have never," he said, his voice lit with amusement, "thought of you as any kind of sister."

Antonia felt herself melt and was wildly glad when she finally reached the turnoff to her house.

She pulled the truck into her driveway, and as soon as she put it into park, Enzo was out and around to her side, swinging the door open and pulling her into his arms. She wrapped her legs around his lower back and slid down halfway out the door to meet him. They paused that way for a moment, her sitting on the edge of the truck, her legs hooked around his hips, staring into each other's eyes. She ran her fingers through his straight black hair and felt him inhale, his nostrils flaring and his eyes half closing in pleasure.

He was such a beautiful man, she thought. Not the kind of man you noticed instantly—not model handsome like her brothers or how her father had been—but the kind of man whom you get to know over time, admiring his goodness, his quiet strength, the way you could always depend on him to get things done before you even have to ask.

And then, one day, you suddenly realize that his smile is slow and sleepy and white-hot sexy against his smooth, dark brown skin. And then the next day, you realize his shoulders and chest are incredibly wide and strong. And then, as he lifts a bale of hay, you see the muscles in his arms flex, and the breath catches in your throat for a moment as you watch his biceps bulge so much that they look as if they are about to tear the sleeves of his shirt open. And then you see him handling a pony, and he is so strong and tender with the animal, his voice is soft and reassuring as he gentles the beast, and his hands are both calming and firm as he trails his fingers along the horse's neck...

Noni closed her eyes and let herself just feel him for a moment, so glad to finally have him under her hands. Moving her fingertips down over the sides of his throat, over his shoulders, sliding them under his jacket, working a finger between the buttons of his shirt, feeling the heat of his skin and the rough texture of his chest hair.

He let out a hiss as her skin touched his, leaning into her hand for a moment and then pushing her back and flipping open the buttons on her jacket, easing it off her, leaving her bare from the waist up.

She gasped as the cool night breeze slipped over her skin. His gaze met hers, his light brown eyes gone nearly black with desire.

"Are you sure about this, Noni?" he said. His voice was rough and shaking. "Because if I touch you again, I don't know if I can stop this time."

She smiled, throwing her head back, arching her chest, and thrusting herself toward him. "Please," she said. "Please, please."

* * *

Dimly, somewhere in the back of his mind, a warning bell sounded. Enzo knew he was stepping over the line, doing something he'd never be able to take back, and for the briefest instant, he hesitated.

But then his eyes fell hungrily upon the sweet pink blush of desire that stained her cheeks and chest, and he heard the way her breath came in little stutters and gasps, and then her dark gaze met his with a liquid fire, and he knew that even a much stronger man would not be able to turn away from this moment.

He cupped her jaw under his hand, bringing her head back toward him, and bent hungrily to her mouth, exploring the silken interior of her lips and tongue. He ran his hands down her bare back, thrilling at the strange, intense heat she emitted. She was blisteringly hot and smooth. She had once told him that she naturally ran a few degrees warmer than most people, a strange little medical anomaly. Suddenly, he needed to press himself against her—wanted to feel that feverish heat against his skin. He continued to kiss her as he loosened his tie, ripped off his jacket, and started to work at his shirt.

She reached up and stilled his hands, brought them back to her, leaving them to cup her breasts as she slowly took over unbuttoning his shirt.

She gasped as he slid his fingers over the tips of her breasts, filling his hands with their firm softness. Her own hands were fixed for a moment, the buttons on his shirt seemingly forgotten, her chest heaving, and then, swiftly, her hands trembling, she was pulling open his shirt and tossing it aside as she pressed herself to him, skin to unbelievably hot, soft skin.

He groaned. "Oh God, what you do to me."

She sighed in response and pushed herself even closer.

He ran his hands down the curve of her waist, working at the clasp of her trousers. She lifted herself so he could pull them off, kicked off her sandals.

He paused a moment to take her in. She was lit by the moon and the dashboard lights, all muscle and curves, wearing nothing but a pair of translucent, buff-colored panties, a long gold necklace, and a pair of thick gold bracelets. Her hair was silvery in the moonlight, trailing over her shoulders and down her back. Her skin was cream and pink. Her small breasts were perfect teardrops, crowned by dainty, blush-colored nipples. Her eyes were gleaming and radiant, infinite in their beauty and filled with a searing desire.

He took a deep breath, steadying himself against her over-whelming allure, trying not to be too greedy. "Should we go inside?" he asked.

She shook her head, met his eyes. "No. I want you now," she whispered.

He felt his whole body throb in response. It was like every dream he'd ever had of her. Except reality was better in every way. Her skin was softer, her hair silkier, her hands seeming to trail sweet fire wherever she touched him. No fantasy had ever matched the desire that sparked between them in this moment.

She groaned, deep and urgent, arching toward him.

He bent and took a rosy nipple into his mouth, sucking and licking, teasing, until it was stiff under his tongue. He moved to her other breast, lavishing it with the same at-tention until she squirmed against him, desperate. He slid his hand down her stomach, through her silky blond curls, searching for the wet, hot core of her. He closed his eyes when he touched her. She felt so good, so ready for him. He kissed his way down her belly, lifting her back onto the truck's seat and then spreading open her thighs with his hands. Her breath came in short gasps now as she slid her legs over his shoulders.

He took in her scent first, savoring the brine and spice smell of her, before kissing and then tasting her—sweet and salty and delicious. She sighed his name and he moved deeper, kissing and licking, thinking that he would never, ever get enough of this woman.

Without taking his mouth away, he reached and slid a finger inside her and she gasped and started to shake. He could feel the rush of her climax as it overtook her, her muscles contracting around his finger, her body trembling, and then her hips greedily writhing against him, and she peaked, calling out his name, and then peaked again, and then once more, until he couldn't wait any longer.

He stood and took out his wallet, hastily extracting a condom as she fumbled at his pants, frantically pulling them open and pushing them and his boxers halfway down. He unrolled the condom onto himself and then brought her legs around his waist, lowering her slowly down, sheathing himself in her. She was exquisitely hot, plush, and still pulsing, and he almost lost control right then and there; she felt so completely right.

He forced himself to go slow, to savor the beauty and pleasure of the moment. He looked at her face; her eyes were half shut in pleasure as he ran his hands over her muscular body. He felt her scars with his fingertips and whispered her name, barely able to control his need to tell her how much he loved her, how there was and would always be no one but Antonia.

He lifted her again and then slowly eased her back down,

and then they were moving in concert, faster and faster, harder and harder.

She clasped her hands behind the back of his neck and bent her head to his shoulder, letting her hair slide down over his chest and back. He could sense her building anew, could hear her breath start to quicken to short, jagged bursts, could feel her almost purring under him, and then, when he felt completely surrounded by her, so deep into her that he could feel nothing but her, he kissed her, hard, and reached to touch her. Suddenly, it was happening again, wave after wave as she clenched and unclenched around him and cried out in pleasure against his mouth.

And this time, for the first time in a long time, he let the waves take him, too.

Chapter Seven

Somehow they made it into the house, Noni giggling and wearing only his shirt, never happier about the fact that her little cottage was sheltered and private on all sides. Enzo had pulled his trousers back on, but his magnificent sculpted chest was still bare.

As soon as they opened the door, the dogs came slipping out, making happy, whining sounds of greeting and brushing in circles around their legs. The sisters knew and loved Enzo almost as much as they did Noni, but when they turned their ice-blue eyes up at him and grinned their wolfish grins, it seemed to Antonia that they were exceptionally pleased to see him this evening.

"Shhh," soothed Enzo as he bent to pet them. "*Quieta, tranquilas*. Shhh, shhh."

Noni moved inside the cottage, inwardly groaning at just how messy it was. Even though Enzo had seen it in this state hundreds of times over the years and she had never cared before, there was something different tonight. She felt shy all of a sudden and wondered if he might think less of her due to her apparent inability to pick up after herself.

She decided he didn't care after he followed her in and

then immediately folded her back into his arms. "*Mi corazón*," he breathed as he kissed the top of her head and then her cheeks and then her mouth again.

God, she'd known he would kiss like this. Like he did almost everything, with utter care and precision and mastery. She felt absolutely melted by his expertise. She had actually lost track of how many times she had just climaxed, and here she was, mere moments later, wanting him all over again.

He broke the kiss and looked at her, gently sweeping her face with the palm of his hand. She gazed back, noting his straight glossy black hair, just slightly long and jagged at the edges. She traced his angled black brows with her thumb and looked into his hooded caramel-colored eyes, admiring the faint laugh lines that radiated from their corners, the length and thickness of his lashes. His skin was polished and gorgeous, the color of dark brown sugar. His cheekbones were high and sharp. His nose was strong and hawkish, in contrast to his full, sensuous red mouth. His jaw was pronounced and just slightly shaded with stubble. She knew from experience that even after his closest shave, the five o'clock shadow would return within hours.

She sighed to herself in admiration. "Are you hungry? Thirsty?"

He shook his head and smiled at her. That sexy smile that unfolded so slowly over his face.

"Let's go to bed," he said gruffly, pulling her closer. "I'm not done with you, *mi amor*."

Her knees practically buckled and she knew that to be taken to bed was all she wanted as well.

She led him to her bedroom, pushing aside the piles of clothes, glad that she had at least changed the sheets recently.

He started to lay her down under him, but she shook her

head and pushed him onto the mattress first. He smiled and rolled onto his back, watching her with a hooded gaze as she primly took off his shoes and socks and then reached for the button on his pants and shimmied them off him.

Her breath caught. This was the first time she had seen him fully naked, and she couldn't help but stare. He was extraordinary. He smiled at her, perfectly at ease, and put his arms behind his head. She had to keep herself from laughing out loud with joy and wonder. *Finally*, she thought. *Finally he is here.*

She had dreamed of this moment so many times, never really believing that it would actually happen.

He stirred, and his muscles stretched and flexed under his golden brown skin. She reached out to touch him, tracing the width of his shoulders and chest and the way his body tapered to his narrow waist and hips. She followed the hair on his chest, down the treasure line on his stomach, and wrapped her hand around his hard, pulsing length.

His breath stuttered, and he closed his eyes for a moment. She dipped down and took him as far into her mouth as she could, loving the slight taste of herself on him, loving the way he got even harder, the way his breath hissed out, and then he groaned with pleasure as she sucked and licked the length of him.

She climbed up on the bed and straddled him, dragging her borrowed shirt over her head and then leaning down to kiss him. He reached up and tangled his hands in her hair, answering her kiss with his own, pulling her down on top of him.

He wrapped his arms around her, and she wriggled against him, neatly fitting her body to his. She lay her head upon his chest, listening to the loud and steady beat of his heart. His skin was soft over the rigid planes of his muscles, his chest hair scratched pleasantly against her cheek, and he smelled of sweet hay and salt. She smiled when she recognized a trace of her own scent on his skin. His hands wandered down and cupped her rear, pushing her more firmly against him.

She pressed herself to him for a moment, savoring the way his skin against hers sent flares of pleasure throughout her body. She propped herself up on one elbow and fumbled in her nightstand for a condom, ripping it open with her teeth and unrolling it onto him. She lay back on top of him again, pushing her body against his, and then she opened her legs, and he slid into her.

That first thrust sent sparks of heat blazing through her body, making her stomach clench, her cheeks burn; even her hands and feet tingled with pleasure. She felt him every-where. It was like she was home. He filled her in a way that no man ever had.

They moved together, slowly at first, and then faster, and then, without breaking contact, he rolled her over onto her back and hovered over her, his eyes searching hers. They were silent, lost in each other, the intensity of the moment only building. He rained kisses on her forehead, her cheeks, her mouth and jaw. She raked her nails over his back, grabbing his hard, muscular behind and pulling him even deeper still.

He shuddered, obviously fighting for control, and she locked eyes with him and then slowly reached down to touch herself.

They were carried away together. She was slammed with a flood of sensation, even stronger than the first time. She felt him pulsing into her, heard his voice calling out her name, closed her eyes and saw stars. Hot, electric pleasure flowed through her, cresting and subsiding and then crashing into her with even more strength. She felt herself lost in the waves, taken over by the frantic bliss, as if her heart and head might burst. She climaxed one last time just as Enzo groaned her name and then collapsed, spent, atop her.

They lay there unable to move, breathing in tandem, their hearts slowly coming back to their normal paces, their skin cooling as the night breeze swept through the windows.

Enzo rolled off her but immediately pulled her into the shelter of his arm, kissing the top of her head and stroking her back. Noni was as relaxed as she'd ever felt, her mind filled with a pleasurable humming blankness.

Luna nudged the bedroom door open with her nose and padded into the room, closely followed by Mojo. They both leaped lightly onto the bed and curled up at the bottom of the mattress, raising their heads in unison and looking curiously at Enzo. He laughed and started to get up.

"Okay, girls, I can take a hint."

But Antonia grasped his arm and pulled him back down. "No," she said softly. "Stay. Sleep."

Chapter Eight

The room was awash in moonlight when one of the dogs nuzzled her cold nose against Enzo's ankle and woke him up.

He turned his head and looked at Noni, who was burrowed against him, her strange heat radiating about him, her breath warm against his shoulder, her hair and skin gleaming in the pale silver light. He reached out and gently ran his hand over the curve of her hip and almost laughed when he felt himself tighten and throb all over again at the feel of her velvety skin under his fingertips.

She murmured in her sleep and moved closer to him. Unwilling to wake her up, he moved away and slipped out of bed, pulling on his boxer shorts. The dogs raised their heads and watched him with glittering eyes as he left the room. He stepped out onto the back porch, which overlooked a small cove of bright white sand and, beyond that, the vast and silvery sea.

It was a warm and sticky night, and Enzo was perfectly comfortable in his scant clothing. He stood and watched the water, listened to the sound of the waves hissing in and out, and tried to take measure of how he felt about what had just happened between him and Antonia.

He was, he had to admit, flushed with contentment. There was no doubt that being with Noni in this way made him happy, fed some part of him that he had purposefully been starving for ages.

But, he reminded himself, he'd thought himself happy before, and that had ended disastrously for everyone involved. Keeping his distance had never been just a whim. He had starved this need for a reason.

He had been ready to leave, but how could he now, after all this? He inwardly cursed his weakness. More than anything, he never wanted to hurt her, but what had happened between them tonight was all but certain to lead to someone getting hurt.

The screen door slid open behind him and he turned to see her standing there, wearing a black cotton kimono and sleepily rubbing her eyes.

"There you are," she said with a shy smile. "I woke up and you were gone." She joined him on the porch, leaning her back against his chest and sighing contentedly when he wrapped his arms around her.

They silently watched the moon on the sea for a moment. He took in her warm scent and fought the urge to slip a hand under her robe.

"Just think," she said, teasing, "of all the time we wasted. We could have been doing that for years."

He kissed the top of her head. Remained silent.

She burrowed closer to him. "We'll have to make up for all those missed opportunities."

He kept his eyes on the sea. He clenched and unclenched his fist. "I'm not so sure, Noni," he said softly.

She looked at him. "What do you mean?"

"You know I was married before, right?"

"Yes. You told me."

"I made mistakes, *niña*."

"Meaning what?" Her voice suddenly lost its brightness.

"Meaning I swore that I would never make those same mistakes again."

She turned to him, her eyes flashing. "Are you saying that what we just did was a mistake?"

"No," he said. "I mean, I don't know. Maybe."

She broke away from him, crossing the balcony and turning to face him. She stood silhouetted against the ocean, with her silvery hair drifting in the breeze.

She was so beautiful, it made his heart hurt to look at her.

He frowned, quiet for some time, thinking. Then he took a deep breath. "My father managed the horses for the Flores family. They lived on a ranch outside Buenos Aires. I spent most of my childhood on their farm. My *papá* taught me everything I know about the ponies."

She raised an eyebrow. "He must have been very good, then."

"*Sí*. He was. But he died when I was sixteen."

"Riding accident?" she said quietly.

He shook his head. "Auto accident, actually. A truck driver lost his brakes and smashed right into him."

She flinched. "I'm so sorry."

He swallowed. "My younger brother was in the car as well. He was thrown through the window. He ended up in a wheelchair, quadriplegic, but at least he survived."

She exhaled and crossed back to him, taking hold of his arm. "Oh, Enzo. I didn't know."

He nodded, watching the sea. "Anyway, after my father died, it was on me to support my family. My mother had to stay home to take care of my brother, and the medical bills just kept coming. So I dropped out of school and started working full-time for the Flores family.

"They were good to me. I'm sure they helped out my mother even more than I knew. And they had a daughter..."

He felt Antonia's breath hitch.

"Her name was Agustina Flores. She was a year younger than me. From the beginning, she was determined that we would be together..."

"Was she very beautiful?" asked Noni.

He shrugged his shoulders. "Oh, *sí*. And very spoiled and strong willed. She was used to getting whatever she wanted."

"And she wanted you."

He laughed harshly. "For some reason, yes."

He felt Noni tighten her hand possessively on his arm. He smiled. "Believe me, *niña*, she couldn't hold a candle to you. What woman could?"

Antonia snorted. "You don't have to flatter me. Go on."

"We were married by the time I was nineteen. I think her family would have chosen someone else for her if they were able to—I was not of their class, you see—but they knew how hardheaded their daughter was. They were a bit afraid of her, really. So they made the best of it and accepted me as one of their own."

"Did you love her?"

He paused, tracing his finger across the scars on Noni's hand. "I don't know. I very much wanted to. Even if I wasn't entirely sure"—he sighed—"how could I say no when it meant that my brother and my mother would be taken care of? I was so young, and the weight of my responsibilities seemed very heavy.

"My father-in-law brought me into his import business. After all, his daughter's husband couldn't very well be a hired hand anymore, could he? And it turned out I was good at it. I had a head for numbers. Within the first two years, I nearly doubled the revenues. Señor Flores was delighted. He promised me that if I kept it up, I'd be made partner by the time I was twenty-five and that I would inherit the entire business once he retired."

"But the ponies...Did you get to—"

He shook his head. "No. I probably could have played polo—but there was no question about me ever going back to the *piloto* path. I didn't have the time to do what I really loved, what my father had taught me—the training and the day-to-day caretaking. I worked all the time. I was at the office from morning until night, and if I wasn't working, I was attending parties and dinners and fund-raisers. The Flores family was very prominent. I needed to help keep up appearances."

He paused for a moment, leaning toward the sea.

"I was a millionaire many times over even before I was made partner. I had everything anyone could ever want. A beautiful house, a wife any man would envy, my mother and brother were taken care of for life...All I had to do was keep pretending to be someone I wasn't. To be the man that Agustina and her family wanted me to be..."

She nodded, understanding. "You were—"

"Miserable. I was miserable. And I was trapped. Every day felt the same—put on a suit, go to the office, stare at numbers, go home, put on another suit, go out, make small talk with people I barely knew, go home, say good night to my beautiful wife—who, to be honest, I had nothing to say to—go to sleep next to her, and then wake up in the morning and start all over again. The only time I felt free was when I could sneak down to the stables, spend a little time in the barn, just smell the hay and the horses, you know? Get my hands a little dirty and drink *maté* with the other grooms."

She smiled.

"I would go back home—to my mother and my brother— every Sunday. And I would talk to my little brother. Diego, his name was. He was a funny kid, always joking about being stuck in the wheelchair. Never complained, though. And he could see that I was unhappy. He tried to bring it up many times, but I'd always brush him off. I never wanted him to feel guilty. I mean, compared to his life, what was so very hard about mine, right?"

Noni shook her head. "There are a lot of different ways to be trapped."

He smiled ruefully. "That is true." He took a deep breath. "In spite of all the best medical care, in spite of everything I could pay for, Diego was still weak. His health was always precarious. He could catch a head cold and it would turn into pneumonia within a day. He had no resistance left..."

He swallowed the sudden lump in his throat.

"He died the year I turned twenty-five. The year I made partner. He developed a sore on his back—one he couldn't feel—and it got infected and..."

He stopped talking for a moment, clenching his jaw. Noni slipped her arms around him and held him tight. He bent his face to her head for a moment, took a deep breath of her scent.

"Before he was gone, though, he made me listen. He told me that he was sick of seeing me so unhappy, that I couldn't keep living the way I was living. That our father would have been so disappointed to see me this way. That I had to prom- ise him that I would try to change things..."

He cleared his throat. Was quiet for a moment.

"I tried. After Diego was gone, I told Agustina that I didn't want to work for her father anymore. That I wanted to work with the ponies again, that I needed to. She laughed and thought I was joking. When she realized that I wasn't, she threw a temper tantrum and said that I would have to choose between her and the horses. So...I did."

"I would have made the same choice," whispered Antonia.

He looked away from Noni, remembering the expression on his young wife's face when he told her he was leaving. The look of heartbreak and bewilderment. The tears. The shock and recriminations from his in-laws...

He shook his head. "It was a selfish thing, *niña*. Nothing I am proud of. I hurt that family. I hurt my wife. It was not their fault. They had brought me into their circle and offered me everything they had. They had done nothing but love me in their way. They couldn't understand why I had to leave. But I felt that I was slowly dying there. I didn't recognize myself any longer. I knew that I would never survive in their world."

Noni lay her head against his chest. "I understand," she said. "I really do."

"I suppose I could have taken half of everything. I had earned a lot of money for the company by that point. Agustina and I had made sound investments. We owned many properties. But I didn't want it. I didn't want any of it. I had just enough money left to make sure *mi mamá* would always be taken care of, and then I left town.

"For a few years, I hired on at whatever ranch would take me, until I knew enough so that when I landed at the Del Campos', I was ready to be a *piloto* like my father had been." He smiled at her, touching her face with his fingers. "Then, of course, I met you. And now I am in trouble."

Antonia stared up at him, chewing her lip. "Of course, I'm...I'm glad you told me all this, Enzo, but I still don't see what it has to do with us."

He stroked her hair. "*Niña*, there are rules. Alejandro is very clear about what is acceptable for those who work for him."

She made an exasperated sound. "That's ridiculous. What about him and Georgia? He hired her himself and then he ended up marrying her. Besides, Alejandro is my brother, not my father. And I'm a grown woman. Why would my brother tell me what to do?"

"But that's just it. He is your brother. In little more than a month, you are about to inherit hundreds of millions of dollars. Everyone knows this. Whether you can admit it or not, you *are* a Del Campo. You are part of a family so powerful and wealthy that they make the Flores clan look like *peones* in comparison. You are destined to be part of the exact same world that I left behind."

"What are you talking about?" said Noni. "The Del Campo world revolves around horses. You of all people know that. It's not the same at all. You're not making any sense."

He shook his head and stepped away from her, quiet for a moment. "Why should you trust me?" he finally spit out. "I just told you what I did to Agustina and her family. Why should I get another chance? What if I hurt you the same way? I made a mistake tonight. I never should have..."

She turned her huge, dark eyes on him. Her face was livid was anger. "You never should have what? Been with me? Don't play stupid, Enzo. I know you felt what I felt. I also know that it's not always like that. That it's almost never like that. That people can go their whole lives looking for something like what we just felt between us—and die never finding it. We are best friends—and we can make each other feel like that? Do you know what a gift that is? That is not something you throw away. I don't care what happened in your past. I am not Agustina Flores. And you are not that same trapped young man. Everything is different now. You've changed."

He couldn't take seeing the hurt and anger in her dark eyes. He turned his face away from her. "But what if I haven't? You've gone through so much. I don't want to—"

"Stop," she barked. "You don't have a clue what I've gone through. You don't have any idea. Don't you dare try to tell me that you're just protecting me or whatever ridiculous excuse you have ready. I want you, and I know you want me. So you can just cut the bullshit and accept what I'm offering with your arms wide open."

She stepped toward him and stood up on her tiptoes, taking his face in her hands. "Kiss me," she demanded.

He could not help himself. He kissed her. And she was hot and sweet and made him dizzy with need.

She broke the kiss with a gasp and stared up at him, her eyes burning with equal parts righteous anger and desire. "Did you feel that?"

He stared back. "*Sí.*"

She nodded. "And did you ever feel that with Agustina? Have you ever felt anything like that with anyone before?"

He looked at her. "No," he said roughly.

"Exactly," she whispered.

And she kissed him again.

Chapter Nine

Noni woke the next morning to a note on her pillow:

Niña, I went to fetch breakfast. Your refrigerator is a disgrace.
—E

She smiled to herself and rolled over in bed, stretching extravagantly. She felt a delicious soreness all through her body. After she had thoroughly kissed Enzo last night, demanding that he acknowledge what was between them, he had swept her into his arms, carried her back to her bed, and made love to her again for hours. It had been almost hallucinogenic in its intensity. He had teased out reactions from her that she didn't even realize she was capable of.

She got out of bed, slipped on her robe, and headed down the hall into the kitchen. Maybe she only had a six-pack of beer and an ancient jar of dill pickles in her fridge, but she knew that she most definitely had a bag of coffee beans in her freezer and figured the least she could do was make a fresh pot before Enzo returned.

She froze as she entered her kitchen, looking around, confused. It was...clean. Immaculate, actually. Every surface sparkling in a way that it hadn't since she had first moved into the place.

She sniffed. Lemon cleanser and—yes, there it was—coffee. A full pot, already waiting for her.

She poured herself a cup and wandered into the living room, bemused to find that it had also been made spotless. She looked into her bathroom and office and was mortified to see that it looked like a professional maid had swept through.

"What time did he even get up?" she muttered to herself as she gazed at the neatly stacked papers and mail on her dining room table. It had been months since she'd seen some of the surfaces he had unearthed and then apparently wiped down and dusted. The only room that hadn't been cleaned was her bedroom—and that was only, she assumed, because she had actually been sleeping in it.

She sank down at the table, distracted by a back issue of *Hoof Care and Lameness* magazine that she'd forgotten had come in the mail, when she heard her kitchen door open.

"Enzo?" she called, padding back into the kitchen.

He stood in the doorway, four bulging bags of groceries in his arms, her dogs trailing after him, panting happily.

She shot the animals an amused look. Traitors.

He put the bags down on the counter and grinned at her.

Damn, but he was good-looking.

"*Buenos días, mi corazón,*" he said as he started to unload the bags.

"That's a lot of food," she observed. "Are we having guests?"

He shook his head. "I know it looks like I went a bit overboard, but you literally have nothing to eat in this house."

Antonia raised an eyebrow. "I don't really cook."

"Luckily, I do," he said cheerfully, and tossed her what looked like a perfectly ripe peach.

She put it down on the counter and then, catching its sweet scent, changed her mind and picked it back up. She bit into it and the juice ran down her chin. Sputtering, she wiped at her mouth with the back of her hand as Enzo laughed.

"Good, no?" he said. "I'm going to make you sour cream peach pancakes. How does that sound?"

She put the fruit back down. "Enzo," she said, "you don't have to do all this."

"All what?" he said as he lined up his ingredients and opened her cabinets, searching.

"Cook," she said. "And clean. Especially not the cleaning."

He turned back to her. "Antonia," he said, "do you know how many years I have been waiting to get my hands on your house?"

She blinked, thinking of his small apartment above the Del Campo barn. She had never seen it anything less than immaculate.

"My place is not always *that* messy," she said defensively. "I mean, maybe I'm not compulsive like you but—"

He raised an eyebrow and smirked. "It's always that messy, *querida*. You live like a teenager."

"I'm busy," she protested.

"You are," he conceded, "but you're also lazy." He took a mixing bowl down from the shelf. "At least when it comes to housekeeping. And believe me, that is fine. I know you have better things to do with your time. However, if I'm going to make you breakfast, I need a clean work space. Now, where can I find a whisk?"

"But you didn't have to clean my bathroom," she grumbled.

He gave her the eye. "Oh yes. I did."

He marched over to her and kissed her firmly on the mouth. "Now. The whisk?"

She laughed, giving up. "I don't have a whisk. Use a fork, you clean freak."

* * *

They ate outside on her back porch, enjoying the unusually crisp breeze blowing up from the ocean. Enzo watched Antonia as she took a bite of pancake. She closed her eyes and sighed.

"Oh my God, you weren't kidding. These are amazing."

He laughed. "*Gracias, niña.*"

She took another bite, a look of pure bliss on her face. "Actually, I think this is the first time anyone has ever made me pancakes."

He blinked, surprised. "No. Really?"

"Really."

What about your *mamá*?"

She snorted. "Definitely not." She reached out and touched his hand. "It was worth the wait. Thank you."

He smiled at her and raised her hand to his lips and kissed it. "*De nada,*" he said. He tightened his grip, bringing her hand to his mouth again.

She met his eyes and laughed, snatching her hand away "Oh no. Don't you start again. I'm starving. I need to eat!" she protested.

He laughed, too. "All right. Fair enough. We'll eat first."

He watched her clear her plate, dab daintily at her mouth

with a napkin, and then lean back with her cup of coffee in her hands, sighing happily.

"What day are you leaving for the Hamptons?" she asked him.

"Next Monday. Same as the Del Campos."

"Where are you staying this year?" she asked him.

"I took a studio in Hampton Bays. Nothing fancy, but it's close to the beach and not far from the farm if the traffic isn't bad. What about you? Did you rent that little cottage on Shelter Island again?"

She frowned. "No," she said. "I called too late. Someone had already taken it."

"So what are you going to do?"

Her face flushed as she shifted and looked away from him. "Actually, Alejandro offered to let me stay on the yacht. They're bringing it up to get a little work done, but the family will be staying at the main house in Southampton, so he thought I might as well take it."

Enzo felt his smile twist bitterly. "Ah, the good ship *Pilar*, eh? How luxurious."

She looked at him. "Don't," she said. "Don't make it like that."

"What?" he said, shrugging. "I'm sure all the best farriers stay on yachts, no?"

Her eyes glittered. "A day ago you would have laughed and told me to enjoy it. Nothing has changed."

He raised an eyebrow. "Nothing?"

She sighed, exasperated. "Okay, some things have changed—but whether I'm staying on the Del Campo yacht or not shouldn't matter."

He frowned and took a sip of his coffee, avoiding her eyes.

She touched his hand. "Listen. I have an idea. I have to go

to New York City first. My mom has a show at a gallery in the East Village. Why don't you come with me?" She smiled at him. "We could make it a long weekend."

He considered this. It had been a long time since he'd been to the city. The last time he had stayed had been years ago, at the Del Campos' expense, when they had asked him to go up and attend a seminar on some new breeding techniques for the ponies. They had booked him at the St. Regis Hotel, and he remembered his hushed, elegant suite, the deep marble bathtub. He felt a shiver run down his back, imagining Antonia stretched out, naked and beckoning, across the snowy white linens of one of those large and sumptuous beds...

"All right, *sí*," he said. "But I will book the hotel, okay?"

Chapter Ten

Antonia clutched Enzo's arm as they stood outside the tiny, shabby gallery in the Bowery. She felt sick to her stomach. "This was a mistake," she said. "You should have stayed at the hotel."

He squeezed her hand reassuringly. "Of course not," he said.

She shook her head. "My mother—" she began.

"I know all about your mother," he reminded her.

"No. I mean, I know, but when I told you about her, you weren't my...I mean, whatever you are yet. You know?"

"*Sí*," he said. "I understand, but surely we don't have to tell her anything yet if we're not ready."

"She'll know," Noni whispered. "She always knows. She'll smell it on us." She turned to him. "Let's just go back to the hotel. I'll tell her I got sick. She'll understand. She's a total hypochondriac."

He smiled at her. "Surely it won't be that bad. Come on now, just in and out. It will be over before you know it."

She shook her head, defeated, as he opened the door for her. "You really have no idea what we're getting into."

The space was small and crowded, with a mass of people

milling around, drinking wine and examining the brightly colored, enormous canvases hung on the wall. Most of the people seemed close to Antonia's mother's age and were wearing head-to-toe black.

Noni scanned the room, looking for her mother. "I don't see her," she said to Enzo. "Maybe we can leave early."

"I'm just going to pretend I didn't hear that, darling," came a raspy voice from behind her.

Antonia turned to face her mother, who had come up behind her without them noticing.

Benny Black looked gorgeous, as always. She wore a long figure-skimming bright red dress, cut shockingly low in the front, her blond hair braided into an intricate crown on top of her head and beaded earrings so large and heavy that they almost grazed her shoulders.

"Mom," said Noni, and gave her a hug.

While Noni was growing up, people would constantly remark upon the resemblance between herself and her mother, but Noni could never see it. Her mother was a thousand times more striking and glamorous, and, of course, she had those enormous turquoise eyes, something Benny always made a point of mentioning when people said they looked alike.

Except the eyes of course. Noni has her father's eyes.

Her mother extracted herself from Noni's arms. "Darling," she said, squinting at Enzo with interest, "you didn't tell me you were bringing your...?" She let the sentence dangle, waiting for Antonia to finish it.

"Friend," said Noni with alacrity. "Mom, I told you about my friend Enzo Rivas, remember?"

Benny smiled her brightest smile. "Of course," she said. "You're a groom, I think Noni said?"

"No, Mom, Enzo is the *piloto*," said Antonia. She was already beginning to feel exasperated.

Benny's smile faltered. "*Piloto*? Now what is that again?"

"He trains the horses, Mom. He runs the barn. He manages just about everything for the Del Campos."

"Oh," said Benny, and her voice took on a knowing tone. "Oh well, that must be a difficult job. I mean, from everything Carlos used to tell me about Pilar—she was basically impossible to satisfy. I imagine any sons of hers would be the same, no?"

"Mom!" hissed Antonia.

Benny turned to her, all wide-eyed innocence. "What?" She smirked. "Oh, get your mind out of the gutter. I didn't mean it that way."

Enzo cleared his throat. "It is very nice to finally meet you, Mrs. Black."

Benny turned her smile back on to Enzo and offered her hand. "Please, call me Benny."

Enzo took her hand and nodded. "Your show is very impressive, Benny."

"Well," she returned, her voice full of false modesty, "it's not as good as it could have been. I just sort of slapped it together at the last second, to be honest."

Noni fought the urge to roll her eyes.

"Then I am even more dazzled," said Enzo. "You are very talented."

Benny leaned in closer. "Really," she confided, "my time should be past. I expected by now that it would be Antonia having the shows and taking the art world by storm, you know?"

"Oh?" said Enzo, looking back at Noni.

This time she did roll her eyes. Her mother never gave up. "Except that I'm not an artist, Mom," she said.

Benny made a little moue of exasperation. "Of course you are. You just haven't found your medium yet."

"Actually, I really like what I do now."

"Oh right," said Benny, waving her hand, "I forgot that shoeing horses is now your calling." She turned back to Enzo, shaking her head. "She obviously gets this from her father's side of the family."

Enzo raised his eyebrows. "Noni is very, very good at what she does. One of the best I've ever seen."

"Of course she's good at it—she's good at nearly everything she does, but that doesn't mean she should just settle, does it?"

Enzo's smile suddenly faded.

"Mom," said Noni sharply, "cut it out. I'm not settling for anything."

Benny shrugged and took Noni by the arm, pulling her forward into the crowd. "Anyway, darling, I have a surprise for you. Come with me." She looked back at Enzo. "You don't mind, do you? I just have to borrow her for one teeny moment."

"Be my guest," said Enzo.

"Mom," protested Antonia as Benny dragged her through the crowd, "what are you doing?"

Benny squeezed her arm tighter. "Now, don't be mad at me, darling. He was in the city anyway, and we just happened to run into each other. And really, he has every right to be here."

"What are you talking about? Who has—" She stopped midsentence, suddenly seeing whom her mother was towing her toward. Her mouth went dry, and she thought she might throw up.

Jacob.

Chapter Eleven

Enzo smiled politely as a young redheaded woman in a tight black dress questioned him about polo. They had nominally been looking at the same giant painting of a hair dryer, though really, Enzo had been watching Noni stand next to her mother and a tall handsome man with shaggy blond hair and a neatly trimmed beard.

The man was a little closer to Noni than Enzo was comfortable with.

"Isn't it awfully dangerous, working with horses like you do?" said the redhead. She leaned close and Enzo smelled cigarettes and an overly sweet, fruity perfume.

"It can be sometimes," he said, leaning away.

He glanced at Antonia, noticing that her cheeks were flushed a bright red and her eyes were fixed on the floor. The blond man laughed, and Noni's shoulder hunched. She looked miserable.

The redhead tracked his gaze.

"Oh," she said, "Jacob Van Dyke. It is sort of amazing that he's here, don't you think?"

He turned to her. "Why?"

She shrugged and swept her hand around, indicating the

paintings in front of them. "Well, these are all right, I guess, but they certainly aren't up to his standards. I mean, I heard he was this close to a MacArthur fellowship last year."

He looked back at him. "What kind of art does he make?"

She laughed, surprised. "You don't know? He's a sculptor. Metalwork, mainly."

Enzo nodded slowly, not taking his eyes off him. "Does he live in New York?"

"No," she said, "he's based in Berlin."

The bearded man had stepped even closer to Noni and was talking intently to her. She continued to look away from him, and when he reached out and touched her shoulder, Enzo watched her flinch.

That was enough.

"Will you excuse me, please?"

He was halfway across the room before the woman could answer.

He made his way through the crowd, slipping in next to Antonia and taking her arm.

She turned and looked at him, and he saw that old trapped and feral look in her eyes that he'd once known so well.

"Are you all right, *querida*?" he murmured.

Benny broke in before Noni could answer. "Enzo, this is Jacob Van Dyke," she said. "He's an old friend of Antonia's."

Noni flushed an even deeper red. Jacob stuck out his hand.

Enzo gazed at him for a moment and then slowly took his hand. "Nice to meet you," he said.

Jacob squeezed, flashing a lupine smile and dazzlingly white teeth. "You as well," he said in return. He looked at Noni. "How do you two know each other?"

Benny cut in again. "They work together." She shot Jacob a knowing look. "For the Del Campos."

Jacob shook his head. "More horse people, eh? I still can't believe you're doing smithy work, Noni. What a waste of talent."

"That's exactly what I just said!" crowed Benny.

Antonia turned to Enzo. "I'm not feeling well," she announced. "I think we should go back to the hotel."

Benny's smile froze on her face and she gave Noni a searching look. "Oh? You're at the same hotel?"

Antonia looked her mother right in the eyes. "Sharing a room, actually. At the St. Regis."

Benny's face flushed in a way that strongly reminded Enzo of Noni right before she lost her temper.

Jacob suddenly looked at Enzo with a new light of consideration in his eyes.

Noni kissed her mother briefly on the cheek. "Good night, Mom. Congratulations on the show." Her eyes flicked to Jacob and she gave him a barely perceptible nod. "Jacob."

"It was so good seeing you, Noni," said Jacob as he closed the space between them and pulled her in for a hug. Enzo took note of the way Antonia stiffly endured it, not even pretending to hug him back.

Jacob finally let her go. "We'll see each other soon, okay? Who knows, maybe I'll make it up to the Hamptons."

Antonia didn't respond. Just took Enzo's hand and led him out of the gallery.

Chapter Twelve

Noni was silent on the cab ride back to the hotel. She kept her eyes on the window, her body slightly turned away from Enzo. She didn't want him to look her in the face.

He rested a warm hand on her knee. "Antonia," he said.

She bit her lip. Enzo calling her by her proper name felt like an insurmountable distance had just sprung up between them.

"It's not what you think," she said hoarsely. She turned her body toward him but didn't meet his gaze.

He waited.

"He didn't beat me. Or mistreat me. He's not a terrible person. He just..." She flicked her eyes up to Enzo's. "He just left."

Enzo nodded. "You loved him." It wasn't a question.

She laughed. Even to her own ears the sound was forced and harsh. "I don't know. I thought I did. He took...I felt like he took everything from me when he left. I thought I would die without him."

"But you didn't," said Enzo softly.

"But I didn't," she agreed. "Thanks to Alejandro and Sebastian and"—her voice was shy—"you."

He smiled at her.

She took his hand. "Let's not talk about it, okay? We only have one more night in the city. I'm not going to ruin it thinking about him." She shook her head. "Or my mother, for that matter."

"Your mother..." He laughed. "I do not think she liked me."

"Oh," she said, "don't take it personally. She has never liked anyone I've introduced her to. Including Jacob. Until now, I guess. She was all over him tonight. I wonder why?"

"He is a big deal in the art world, apparently."

Noni wrinkled her nose. "Is he? Well, that's new. He was basically a starving artist when I knew him. If he's doing well, that would definitely raise his stock with my mom."

"Apparently he almost won a MacArthur fellowship last year."

Noni laughed. "Who told you that?"

"Some woman I met while looking at your mother's enormous painting of a hair dryer."

Antonia tapped him on the arm playfully. "I saw that woman. A tall and very pretty redhead."

He shrugged. "She smelled like cigarette smoke and overripe strawberries. It was not a good combination."

She smiled and scooted closer to him. He pressed his face to the top of her head and inhaled. "Not like you," he said gruffly. "You smell *rica*."

She turned her face up toward his. "Yeah?" she said. "What does *rica* mean, exactly?"

He bent to smell her again and closed his eyes. "Delicious. You smell like heat and spice and"—his voice grew hoarse as he opened his eyes and looked directly at her—"sex, *mi corazón*. You smell so good, it's all I can do not to tear your clothes off and bury my face between your legs right here in the back of this car."

Her breath caught, and suddenly her whole body was aflame.

He kissed her then. There was nothing skilled or nuanced about this kiss. It was just blunt, searching need. He kissed her like he was claiming her as his own. And she responded instantly, tangling her tongue against his, twining her arms around him and pressing as close as she could, melting against him, desperately trying to quiet all the feelings that were still churning inside her.

She ran her hand up his tensed thigh, feeling the bulge under his jeans. She felt his breath catch as she touched him, heard him stifle a groan of pleasure against her mouth. She broke their kiss and moved her lips to his throat, dragging her cheek along the delicious scratch of his stubble, licking and kissing, wiggling herself onto his lap.

"Ahem." The taxi driver loudly cleared his throat. "We're here, my friends."

Noni softly laughed and slid off Enzo's lap. "Sorry," she murmured to the driver as Enzo ran his credit card through the machine and added a very large tip.

The driver shrugged. "Eh, I've seen worse. At least you kept your clothes on."

* * *

The hotel room at the St. Regis was just as Enzo remembered, elegant and sexy and luxurious. The room was done in cream and gold with soft lilac accents. The bed was vast, with pristine white linens, a mountain of fluffy down pillows, and a tufted headboard made of lavender silk. A cream-colored love seat and two plush armchairs clustered around a fat lilac ottoman. The opulent drapes hid a rooftop view and filtered the late afternoon light to a dusky, golden glow. There were shapely white vases of purple roses scattered about the room, reflected in the enormous baroque gold-framed mirrors that served as the only ornamentation on the walls. The bathroom was equipped with a deep marble soaking tub that easily fit two.

Despite her scars and tattoo and tough attitude, Noni fit right into this room, thought Enzo. She was wearing wide-legged linen pants and a black silk tank top that showed off her defined arms and shoulders, but even if she had been dressed in her usual faded jeans and tattered T-shirt, her radiant beauty would have still matched the elegance of this room. She was, without a doubt, the most naturally stunning woman Enzo had ever seen.

She looked like her mother in a way, he mused. They both had the same creamy coloring and striking Nordic bone structure, but whereas Benny's big blue eyes made her seem like a generic, pretty Californian blonde, Antonia's sloe-eyed gaze was filled with sparks and fever and lent an enigmatic depth to her nearly perfect face.

He could search those eyes forever and still not know everything there was to know about this woman.

They had been inseparable this last week in Florida. He had spent every day with her at the barn, every night at her cottage. He couldn't seem to tear himself from her side. And with every passing moment, he'd begun to tentatively believe that she was right. That none of the things that had held him back from her over the years really mattered after all. That this time maybe it would be different, that he could be trusted with another woman's heart. That the world that he and Noni made together was one he could happily live in...

And now, realizing how badly she had been hurt before only made him more determined to handle her with care.

He watched her slip off her black ballet flats and turn back to him, pressing her body against his and twining her arms around his neck.

"Where were we?" she breathed.

He slid his hands over the muscular curves of her body. She was so tiny but iron-hard, made strong by all her hours working with the horses and in front of her forge, hammer in hand.

She lifted herself onto her tiptoes and kissed him feverishly, and he responded, pulling her closer, feeling her soft lips against his. He groaned and kissed her harder, feeling her twist against him in what at first he felt as desire, but then... he slowed.

There was something wrong. Something almost frantic in her response to him, something not altogether willing or natural...

She's trying to escape, he thought, *to forget.*

He gently pulled away and looked down at her; indeed, there was a desperate agitation in her ebony eyes that sent an icy shiver up his spine.

"*Niña,*" he said softly, not wanting to spook her further, "let's slow down a bit, eh? No need to rush. Why don't you go take a nice hot bath, and I will call room service and order us some dinner. We can eat here and never need to leave the room at all tonight if we don't care to."

He did not think he imagined the ghost of relief that passed over her face.

"Yes, okay," she said, biting her lip. She leaned her head against his shoulder for a moment. "That sounds nice."

"What would you like for dinner?" he asked as she retreated to the bathroom.

"Surprise me," she called over her shoulder, and then shut the door between them with a quiet little click.

* * *

He over-ordered, somehow hoping that crab salad and roasted chicken, risotto with wild mushrooms, smoked baby beets and goat cheese, a kale Caesar salad, chocolate and lemon tartlets, and a bottle of Veuve Clicquot Cave Privée would soothe whatever it was that was making Noni ache so badly.

He hadn't spent this kind of money—on the hotel room, the cabs, room service—for ages, and it felt odd but not entirely unpleasant. He could afford it. The Del Campos paid him very well, and besides the monthly allowance he sent home to his mother, his expenses were low. He had savings, and he certainly didn't mind splurging when it came to Antonia.

Still, he thought, he could never keep up this kind of lifestyle in any kind of permanent way. And wasn't that what Noni would expect? Maybe she hadn't grown up with this kind of luxury like the rest of the Del Campo children had, but there was less than a month until she came of age and inherited her third of the estate. Wouldn't she want this kind of life all the time once she could afford it?

But, he thought to himself as the room service waiter wheeled in their dinner on a multitiered cart, it would be different with her. He knew that Antonia would never want him to leave the horses, and he knew that she would always work with the ponies, too.

Then again, he reminded himself, she wanted to play on the team. That was something altogether different than being one of the barn staff. And what would her brothers think? Their little sister getting involved with their *piloto*?

He tipped the waiter as he left, then knocked softly on the bathroom door.

"*Niña*," he said, "our dinner is here, and I'm afraid I got a bit carried away. Not even you will be able to eat so much."

He leaned closer, listening to the soft hush of running water. "Noni?" he called.

No answer.

He knocked harder. Still no answer.

He tried the door. It was locked. His heart beat a little faster.

"Antonia?"

Nothing.

"Antonia, I am coming in!"

He threw himself against the door, and it flew open with a crash. Noni was hunched in the bath, the water running, her face in her hands, her long blond hair bedraggled, the ends floating in the water around her, her whole body in a spasm of sobs.

Enzo froze. He had never seen her like this before. Even at her worst, at her darkest. She had been angry, she had been distant, fierce, lashing out at anyone in her way, but he had never seen her so purely sad.

"Noni," he breathed.

She brought her knees up out of the water and hugged them to her chest, ducking her face down out of sight.

"*Que te pasa mi reina*" he said, and without thinking, he got into the water with her, pulling her toward him.

She looked up, shocked out of her misery. "Wha-what are you doing?"

He looked down. Socks (thank God he'd removed his shoes earlier), jeans, his button-down shirt, all soaked. Fully dressed, in the bath.

He didn't care. She needed him.

Her face was red and swollen, but she laughed through her tears. "Are you crazy?"

"Tell me what's wrong," he said huskily.

The smile vanished from her face. She shook her head and closed her eyes.

"I'm sorry, but I can't talk about it," she said softly. "I just...can't."

He touched her face, smoothed the wet hair back from her eyes. "You said he never harmed you. What did he do, then? This seems so much more than a broken heart. How can he still have this hold on you?"

Her bottom lip trembled. She opened her eyes and looked at him, tears clinging to her long lashes. "Maybe you were right before," she whispered, "when you said that this was a mistake."

He reared back as if she had hit him. He felt a red-hot pain rush through his chest at her words.

"What do you mean?"

She looked away and swallowed. "I just mean...maybe you were right. We're from two different worlds. We were so good as friends—maybe it was stupid of us to jeopardize what we had..."

Suddenly, Enzo was sick with jealousy. He could barely see straight. He pushed back and away from her, sloshing water over the sides of the tub.

"Because of that man?" he said. His voice shook. "You see him and suddenly we are a mistake?"

"No," she said, "no, not like that. I mean, yes, some of it is seeing him, but—"

Enzo stood up, water streaming down him as he climbed out of the tub. "That's enough," he said. "I don't need to hear any more."

She looked up at him, her dark eyes stricken. "Enzo."

He waited.

She opened her mouth, but nothing came out.

She closed her eyes; a sob started to shudder through her body. "Just go," she said. "It's better if you go."

He left while her eyes were still closed.

Chapter Thirteen

Noni took the jitney up alone the next day, and Sebastian met her at the station in Westhampton.

As they drove to the dock, Noni only half listened to her brother's cheerful chatter. She was still incredibly raw from the events of the day before. Seeing Jacob after all this time, it had brought everything rushing back. The pain. The loss. The way he'd left her feeling so beaten down and hopeless...

And all her brave words this last week to Enzo about how things between them were going to be different than anything that had come before. How he needed to let the past go and trust himself with her. She was such a hypocrite. She'd convinced herself that she'd changed, healed, become stronger and managed to leave her old, broken self behind, but all it had taken was one short encounter to send her right back to where she used to be.

And then the fight with Enzo... She knew she should have explained herself, but she just couldn't force the words out. She's been so ashamed that he had seen her that way—scared and sobbing. She had worked so hard to be the strong, independent person he thought she was. She had pretended so much over the years that she had really started to believe that she was a new person. But now he knew. She was just the same old mess. She was still in jagged, splintered pieces. She simply hadn't been able to bring herself to explain. Too many secrets kept for too long. She was sure that if she had told him the truth, Enzo would have never felt the same way about her again. It was surely better for both of them to just cut things off.

She sighed and closed her eyes for a moment behind her sunglasses. She hadn't slept at all last night...

"Noni?" said Sebastian. He sounded very far away.

Her eyes flew open with a jerk.

Her brother shot her a look of concern. "We're here, darling. Did you hear me about your truck and the dogs? I said Alejandro would bring them both over later. They're at the farm."

She blinked, trying to get her bearings. She should be used to traveling from place to place by now. Polo players and their entourages followed the game, and she'd been working for La Victoria for years. No sooner did the season end in one place than a new one would open up in London, the Hamptons, Argentina, snow polo in Aspen... They traveled the world, chasing the stick and ball. But there was always a moment of adjustment for Noni. Especially when she left her little cottage in Florida.

And this year, her displacement felt worse than ever.

She followed Sebastian onto the yacht, trying to shake her terrible mood.

Noni had been on *La Bonita Pilar* once or twice before, but just on the upper levels. She'd eaten up on the deck, seen the view from the balcony, spent some time in the twelve-person Jacuzzi, but this time, as Sebastian led her downstairs, Noni was seeing parts of the boat that she'd never even known were there.

She looked around, momentarily stunned out of her funk. "Seb, this is bigger than my entire cottage," she said to her handsome green-eyed brother.

Sebastian grinned. "*Papá* liked his boats." He swept his hand around. "So this part is the lounge and the mess deck. Bar is over there," he said, indicating a fifteen-foot-long slate-topped structure crowned by an enormous glittering chandelier, "fully stocked, of course."

She arched an eyebrow. "Of course."

"Push the couches back and you have a nice dance floor," continued Seb. "Because I know you'll be having crazy parties every night, right, *hermanita*?"

Noni snorted as she looked at the gorgeous ocean view out the long bank of windows. "Oh yeah. Totally."

Seb smiled. "Just make sure you invite me if you do." He led her into a room off the lounge. "Through here is the galley."

It was a full-sized chef's kitchen. With a stainless Sub-Zero refrigerator, a six-burner stove, and tons of counter space and clever storage. The floor was a gorgeous deep red tile, and there was an island with room enough for six to sit around it.

"Since I know the extent of your culinary capabilities, I don't imagine you'll be cooking here much," teased Seb. "Which is fine, the staff will keep it stocked, and if you want anything special, you can let the cook know."

"The cook?" said Noni. "Oh no, Sebastian, I don't need the staff. I can take care of things on my own."

Seb laughed. "Um, no offense, darling, but you definitely do need the staff. You can keep your cottage however you like, but *Mamá* will flip her lid if she shows up here and sees the mess you and your dogs are bound to make."

"Why would Pilar come here?" said Antonia. "I thought she got seasick."

Sebastian shrugged. "She does. She hates this yacht. But you never know what she might take it in her head to do. The staff is for your own protection, *niña*."

Noni flinched, hearing the familiar nickname. A flash of the tortured look on Enzo's face just before he left swam before her eyes.

"There are four staterooms," said Sebastian, leading her out. "That's what we call bedrooms on the boat, and they all have en suite bathrooms, or 'heads' as they are known. The nicest stateroom is here."

He opened the door to a huge airy room done in nautical blue and white. The enormous pristine white bed reminded Antonia painfully of the bed at the St. Regis where she had ended up tossing and turning the whole night through.

Tears suddenly sprang to her eyes.

She turned away from Sebastian, hoping he hadn't seen, and busied herself at the windows, opening them to the sea breeze. "It's a beautiful view," she said tremulously.

Sebastian looked at her and cocked his head. "Are you all right, darling?"

She forced herself to smile. "Totally fine. Listen, I'm all set. I know you need to get back to the farm. Go ahead and I'll catch up with you there later, okay?"

He narrowed his eyes. "Are you sure?"

"Totally! Why wouldn't I be? Look at this beautiful place I get to live in for the summer!" She quelled her urge to literally push her big brother out of the room.

He looked suspicious but nodded slowly. "Okay, *bien*. I'll

see you later this afternoon at the barn, though, all right? Don't forget to find me. Jandro and I leave for London early tomorrow, and who knows how long it will be before we get back."

Noni's heart sped up a bit. "How many players are you seeing?"

He shrugged. "No way to tell. It's only the first stage of the search. We'll probably just watch a lot of games. See if there's any talent worth poaching."

"But if you see someone talented, will you just bring them on right away?"

He shook his head. "It's not as simple as mere talent. I mean, yes, talent is one thing, but we also need to like them, you know? And not just me and Jandro, but Rory and Hendy as well. We have to see if they have chemistry with the whole team."

Antonia forced her voice to sound casual. "Would you ever consider a woman?"

Seb looked at her for a long beat. She squirmed inwardly. "Of course," he said slowly. "I mean, our grandmother, Victoria, was a great player. She was the one who first taught me and Alejandro to play, you know."

Noni sighed. "I wish I'd met her."

He smiled a bit sadly. "Me too, *querida*. She would have loved you. She very much wanted a granddaughter. She was always teasing *Mamá* and *Papá* about having a third child." He shook his head. "What a crime that you were there all along and nobody knew."

"Except Carlos, of course," said Noni. She couldn't keep the bitterness from her voice.

Seb smiled ruefully. "*Sí*," he said, "except Carlos."

There was a moment of silence between the siblings.

"Anyway," said Noni.

"Anyway," agreed Sebastian. "Get settled in. I will see you at the farm later."

He gave her a quick kiss on each cheek, and Noni smiled as he left. She never got tired of affection from her big brothers.

But her smile faded as she turned back to the big white bed. She stared at it for a moment and then backed out of the door, determined to look at the other bedrooms and find one that didn't make her want to cry.

* * *

Enzo surveyed his flat as he slowly unpacked. It was just the right size for him. An attic studio, bright and airy, with soft yellow walls, a miniature kitchenette, and a full-sized old-fashioned cast-iron bed draped in a vividly colored patchwork quilt. There was a little wooden table and two chairs that would do double duty for desk work and dining. A small bathroom with a shower. The Juliet balcony was just big enough for one person and gave Enzo a tiny slice of a sparkling ocean view.

After he left the hotel, he had come *this* close to picking up the phone, calling Mark Stone, and taking the job as *piloto* to the new team. It would have been a clean break, an easy way to put needed distance between him and Antonia. He had only been stopped by the knowledge that he'd be leaving the Del Campos high and dry. Alejandro and Sebastian planned on spending most of the summer in London with their families, scouting new players, and they were depending on Enzo to take care of their ponies and keep the barn running. If he left with no advance notice, it would be a huge hassle for them, and whatever he felt about Noni, none of it was her brothers' fault. They didn't deserve to be left in the lurch.

Still, once they found their new teammate, once the summer season was over, Enzo thought he would probably move on—with Mark's team, if the job was still open—or somewhere else if it was not. He had learned his lesson. He could not be so close to Antonia and not expect to get burned.

In the meantime, there was no avoiding her—they would have to work together over the summer—but he was determined to get control of himself and keep the distance between them.

He sighed and slid his now-empty suitcase under the bed. He knew he should head for the barn and find Alejandro and Seb before they left for London. There was a long checklist of tasks to go over, but the idea of seeing Noni again, after the way things had ended, felt almost unbearable. Not a minute had passed since he had left that hotel room that he hadn't been thinking of her, wondering how she was doing, feeling suddenly overtaken by the image of her in his arms, under him, her dark eyes gazing into his, her silvery blond hair in disarray across the pillows, the way she would bite down on her lower lip when he would touch her...

He sat on the bed for a moment, sternly reminding himself that he had gone years without her. What was one more summer? He would keep himself busy. There were a million things to be done, even more so than usual since the Del Campo brothers would be absent from the barn, and Noni would surely be occupied with her own tasks. It would be a simple enough.

He clapped his hands together and stood, ready to get back to work.

Chapter Fourteen

Antonia probably shouldn't have brought the dogs to the farm, but she didn't quite trust the sisters on the boat yet, unsure of what they would do to keep themselves occupied while locked up on the lower deck.

The huskies were used to horses, of course, but they had long ago sworn themselves to be mortal enemies of Pilar's two calm and regal Rhodesian ridgebacks and would harass them nonstop whenever they met.

Noni felt it was something instinctual on her dogs' part. Some sort of class warfare. Unlike Pilar's pedigreed show dogs, Noni's pups had humble beginnings. She had found Luna and Mojo in a box by the side of a Florida road when they were puppies, half dead with hunger and dehydration. With the help of Alejandro's wife, Georgia, who was a veterinarian, she had nursed them back to health.

They looked mostly like huskies with their icy blue eyes and fluffy coats, but they were small and scrappy and wild, and sometimes, especially when they turned up their noses and eerily howled at sirens or the full moon, Noni suspected them of having some coyote blood mixed in there as well. In any case, they were most definitely mutts, and nothing like the pure-blooded and noble ridgebacks, who seemed completely taken aback every time they encountered the sisters and their bad doggy manners.

In fact, they were pestering the ridgebacks now, running circles around them, yapping, darting in and out and snapping at the bigger dogs like teasing children. Noni knew from experience that the ridgebacks would only take this for a limited amount of time before their patience wore thin and then they would erupt—roaring like the lions their ancestors hunted in South Africa—and a real dog fight would be on her hands.

Pilar knew this, too, and came rushing out of the house, calling her dogs in.

Noni whistled for her girls and caught them by their collars. "Sorry," she called to Pilar as Pilar herded her dogs back toward the house. "I didn't want to leave them alone on the boat."

Pilar turned back to her, a frown on her face. "You are keeping them on the yacht?"

Noni blinked. "Well, yeah. I mean, Sebastian said—"

Pilar rolled her eyes in exasperation and waved her off. "*Dejá, no importa*. Never mind. We were getting the floors refinished, but I guess I will postpone that until the end of the summer. No reason to fix the floors if they are just going to get all scratched up again."

Antonia started to point out that Pilar never came onto the boat anyway. What did she care what the floors looked like? But caught herself in time. She didn't want to pick a fight. Certainly not with Señora Del Campo.

"That's probably a good idea," she said instead. "Waiting until we're gone."

Pilar shook her head, shooing her dogs into the house. "As

if I have a choice," she muttered before she followed her dogs inside and shut the door a little louder than Noni felt was strictly necessary.

Noni let the girls go and they raced off toward the barn.

The Del Campo farm in Southampton was less grand than the estate in Wellington, but worth far more. There were twenty acres of fields and paddocks behind high stone walls, half of which was given over to a regulation-sized polo field. The house was a stately three-story colonial tucked away at the back of the farm, built in the 1700s and covered in the traditional silvery cedar shakes that were seen all over the Hamptons. The numerous twelve-over-twelve windows were original to the house, the glass panes thick, bubbled, and wavy. Noni loved the distorted underwater feeling she got when she gazed through them.

There were old-fashioned cottage gardens all around the house, filled with lilacs and peonies, roses and hydrangeas, daisies and bearded iris. The gardens were flanked by half a dozen enormously old and twisted black walnut and maple trees and a long, lush lawn that rolled down to meet the graveled circular driveway.

It was her favorite property that the Del Campos owned.

The Hamptons summer polo season was not as prestigious as the London summer season, and La Victoria usually played in England, but whether her boys were abroad or not, Pilar preferred to be in the Hamptons for her summers. The Del Campo brothers and their families took their jet back and forth from England for charity games to occasionally take part in the social whirl that was a Hamptons' summer and see their mother, but Pilar was content to stay put in Southampton, puttering about her garden and helping keep track of the ponies they kept quartered up here.

With the team scouting for a fourth player in England this summer, most of the ponies would be housed here while they were gone. She and Enzo would be kept very busy, indeed, thought Noni.

The Hamptons house was, more than any other property, Pilar's home. The house in Wellington was all Carlos—all about flash and presentation, designed to entertain the local horsey set. The *estancia* in Argentina was the family seat, owned by Del Campos for generations and generations. But the Hamptons house was something that Pilar had picked out for herself once she had realized that her husband would not be the husband she had hoped for him to be.

Carlos hadn't liked the Hamptons, which had been nothing more than a sleepy community of artists and farmers when they had first moved in. He much preferred the London season, but the story that Noni had heard whispered was that Pilar had insisted on him buying her the Hamptons house after she had found out about his first affair. That she had wanted a place that was solely hers, untainted by his betrayal, and she had threatened to take the boys and go back to Argentina if he didn't give it to her.

Sometimes Noni felt disloyal, loving the house that her father had liked least, the one that he had spent almost no time in. But that was, Noni mused, probably the exact reason she was attracted to the place. It felt like a safe harbor, unsullied by the poison that had seeped into Carlos and Pilar's long and unhappy marriage. Pilar had made it a refuge for herself and her sons, and that feeling of shelter was still so strong that Noni could sense its pull, even from the outside.

She turned toward the barn, nervous about seeing Enzo again. Out of the corner of her eye, she saw Pilar open the door and let her dogs back out, apparently satisfied that Noni's mongrels were safely away in the stables.

Antonia sighed, imagining the long hot summer ahead of her. With her brothers gone to London, there would be no buffer between her and Pilar. And she couldn't even think about how things were between her and Enzo...

She had a sudden flash of Enzo's eyes, dark with passion, as he pored over her body. She felt the heat rush to her face as she recalled the way his strong, rough hands had moved with such gentle assurance, teasing out reactions from her that made her squirm to remember.

She shook her head—trying to knock out the memories—and then looked toward the barn. She was sure he was already there. Maybe they could talk this through somehow...

* * *

Enzo sensed her presence before he saw her. He was alone in the office, looking over some new vendor information, when the air around him suddenly felt charged. He looked up, the skin at the back of his neck prickling in anticipation, and there she was, standing in the doorway, breathtakingly beautiful in faded jeans, work boots, and a low-necked gray tee. Her long silky hair tucked behind her ears. She was wearing mirrored aviator sunglasses, so he couldn't tell if she was meeting his gaze or looking past him.

"Hello," she said, excruciatingly polite. "How are you?"

He blinked. So she was going to play it like this. Pretend she didn't care.

Her face was blank. He wished she would take off her sunglasses.

He suddenly wondered if she had been back in touch with

her ex. He clenched his fists as he imagined her calling him from the hotel room, bereft, needing comfort, inviting him over...

He swore inwardly. If any of that had happened, he had only himself to blame, didn't he? He was the one who left her there, upset and miserable. He was the one who walked out.

But then again, she was the one who had told him to go...

All of his intentions to keep a distance between them were suddenly pushed aside. "I feel like hell," he said bluntly.

She finally took off her sunglasses, and the illusion of her being cool and in control was shaken by the dark circles under her eyes. She looked tired. And sad.

"Noni," he said urgently, "I need you to tell me. Do you still have feelings for that man?"

Her face went pale. She bit her lip and stared at him, silent. He could see her struggling.

He took a step toward her. She took a step back.

"I'm sorry," she said softly. She looked away. "I should get to work."

And she turned, shutting the glass door gently behind her.

He stood for a moment, imagining himself going after her, taking her into his arms, begging her to come back to him, saying all the things he had sworn to himself he would never say to her, truly making her *his*.

Instead, he allowed himself nothing more than a long moment of watching her walk away.

And then he turned back to the paperwork, more determined than ever to keep to himself.

Chapter Fifteen

After narrowly avoiding a bite from a temperamental stallion, Antonia desperately wished, yet again, that things had never changed with Enzo. She missed their old friendship, she ached to simply talk with him, and, at the moment, she needed their old work relationship as well. He usually helped her with the more sensitive ponies, holding their heads while she picked and shoed, soothing the horses that needed a little extra comfort.

But after what had happened in the office this morning, she could hardly ask for any version of his help.

She pulled the stallion's hoof up between her knees and sighed. She had wanted to throw herself into Enzo's arms when she had first seen him back in the office, tell him how sorry she was, what an idiot she had been. But just like in the hotel room, the specter of Jacob, and everything that had happened between them, had kept her silent and fettered.

She thought she was over Berlin. She thought she was over her ex. But seeing him again had brought it all back to the surface. Suddenly, wounds that she had convinced herself had healed were, once more, bleeding and raw. Feelings that she thought she had long ago buried had come clawing their way back to the surface.

And when Enzo had asked her point-blank if she still had feelings for Jake...she had realized that she truly didn't know. Because if she was really over him, why had she felt such a punch to the gut when she had seen him at the gallery? If she was past what had happened to her in Berlin, why did she end up sobbing in a bathtub while Enzo had to practically knock down the door?

Perhaps this was all temporary. Perhaps it would pass. In the meantime, it wasn't fair to Enzo or herself to stay so close. She needed to sort out just how deep this really ran.

She probed at the pony's hoof, expertly prying off his old shoe and digging out the dirt and trimming down the overgrown frog. Once she had exposed a nice, clean sole, she pulled out her clippers and tackled the outer wall of the hoof, trimming off anything that looked too long. She used her rasp to even the whole thing out, eyeing it carefully to make sure it was level. After that, she went to work on the inner hoof and then placed the pony's foot back on the floor, looking at it from every angle until she was satisfied that the hoof lay totally flat.

She ducked under the pony's neck, careful to stay well away from his teeth, and headed back to her truck where she kept her portable forge so she could heat up and shape the pony plate and hammer it to just the right size.

On the way, she was startled to see what looked like Pilar in an empty stall. Her back was to Noni, and she was, Noni realized, talking to someone.

Judging from the low murmur of Pilar's voice and her soft, throaty laugh, Noni didn't think it was either of her sons.

She paused for a moment, wondering if she should make

her presence known, but before she could say anything, Pilar swung around so that she was in profile to Noni, and the other person in the stall came into view—Sir Henderson, one hand on Pilar's waist, the other stroking her hair as he bent his mouth hungrily to hers.

Neither of them noticed her as Antonia stole away, feeling like a child who had left her bed for a drink of water and then accidentally walked in on her parents making out in the kitchen.

She had known they were something of an item. Their behavior at the party had made that fairly clear. But she had been truly surprised by the tender and passionate look on Pilar's face as she had gazed up at Hendy, the heat that was so obvious between them as he kissed her.

This was not just a comfortable alliance between two old friends. This looked like something much more.

Noni smiled to herself. As difficult as she found Pilar, she couldn't help but cheer her on. Having known the Del Campos as long as she had, Antonia was no longer under the illusion that she had been the only one who had felt hurt and rejected by Carlos's lack of attention. If Pilar had managed to find something sweet, and maybe even a little hot, in her golden years, well, good for her. The tough old bird had probably more than earned it.

She turned the corner and saw Enzo striding outside, heading for the paddocks, and she opened her mouth to call out to him, catch up, and tell him what she had just seen. She imagined the way he would laugh and tease her about the awkwardness of the moment.

But before she could utter a word, he seemed to sense that she was there. He glanced over his shoulder and met her eyes, and the look he gave her was made of ice and stone.

The smile faded from her lips and his name shriveled in her mouth. They simply gazed at each other for a moment, the hurt between them hanging almost palpable in the air, and then, with a slight shrug, he turned back around and kept walking.

Chapter Sixteen

Enzo dined alone in his flat that night, making a sandwich and heating up a tin of soup. He read a book at the table as he ate. It was a good story, a romantic thriller by Florencia Bonelli that his mother had pressed upon him last time he had gone home to Argentina. Not his usual style, but he'd been surprised by the way it immediately captured his attention when he flipped it open on the plane.

But tonight he found himself reading and then rereading the same sentence over and over again.

He put the book down, restless and annoyed, and pushed away his meal. He wasn't hungry either.

He stood and walked out to his little balcony, searching for the glimmer of ocean in the distance, but there was no moon tonight, and the sky was too dark to reflect on the water. He shivered a little in his thin T-shirt and jeans. It was still cool; the summer heat had yet to come roaring in.

He walked back in and stretched out on his bed, closing his eyes and hoping to discover that he was tired enough to sleep. Instead, images of Antonia, the way she had looked at him today as he left the barn, the smile freezing on her face as his eyes had met hers, swirled in his head. Then they shifted and suddenly he was seeing her half naked and astride him, her lips parted, her long platinum hair just barely obscuring her breasts, the mix of coal and stars in her gaze holding him helpless, pinned, bewitched...

He threw himself out of the bed with a groan. She was haunting him. He would never shake her.

As perfect as the little studio had seemed that morning, now it felt claustrophobic and confining. He felt like he might go crazy if he didn't get out. He shrugged into his jacket, pulled on his boots, and left, taking the stairs two at a time in his hurry to make his escape.

* * *

The dogs were curled into balls at the foot of Noni's bed, their heads buried under their tails, breathing peacefully. Antonia was wearing nothing but a long, thin T-shirt, but she was snug and warm under the plush down comforter. The boat moved slightly on the ocean current, just enough to make her feel pleasantly rocked.

She had picked a smaller bedroom to sleep in, but one that was just as luxurious as the master. Instead of the nautical blue and white of the bigger room, this one was done in silvery gray, midnight blue, and dusty rose—colors that Antonia imagined echoed the hues of a winter sunset over the sound. The view out her windows was all sky and sea—star spangled and dark at the moment—and Antonia had left the windows open so she could enjoy the sharp ocean breeze coming in off the water.

Noni still couldn't get over the extravagance of staying here. She had arrived home to find that the chef had left her dinner, still warm in the oven—salmon and some artfully prepared potato dish that managed to be both crispy and meltingly creamy. A fresh salad of local asparagus, pea shoots, and little bits of prosciutto was on the counter, alongside a warm strawberry-rhubarb pie with thick yellow cream to pour over it for dessert.

There was also a bottle of white Burgundy, already decanted and ready to drink.

She had taken her meal and a large glass of that wonderful wine up to the top deck, wrapped herself in a cashmere throw against the late spring breeze, and enjoyed the sunset over the sound. The dogs had lain attentively at her feet, hoping for a bite thrown their way; the seagulls had swooped and dived over the water, crying out over the sound of the hissing waves.

The staff had left for the night, after cleaning the boat from top to bottom, stocking the kitchen, unpacking her suitcase, turning down her bed, and doing Lord knows what else, thought Noni. What did it take to maintain a yacht? Surely much more than she imagined.

In little more than a month, Antonia would fully come into her inheritance. Three hundred million dollars. When that finally happened, she supposed that she could buy a boat just like this one if she wanted to.

But, as pleasant as it was, she couldn't imagine wanting to.

In fact, she had no idea what she would do with her money once it became hers. The generous monthly allowance her father had left her, plus the salary she made as a farrier, were already far and away more money than she'd ever had. She was happy with her little cottage in Wellington, with her old blue Chevy truck, with not having to look at a menu and automatically order the cheapest thing...

But the money was hers. The same amount that her brothers had inherited when they each turned thirty. She wondered if it had changed them at all but thought probably not, since they had grown up with money and took it for granted in a way that Antonia never could.

After the sun went down and Noni poured herself another glass of wine, she entertained herself watching *Bridesmaids* on the big screen in the media room. Then she took a long hot bath in the huge Jacuzzi tub off her bedroom, making use of the basket of hand-milled French soaps and bathing products and trying to ignore her dogs, who sat at the side of the tub and looked as if they just might try to crawl into the water with her if she gave them the slightest encouragement.

She had done a decent job of keeping her mind quiet. Food. Ocean. Movie. Bath. All these things provided enough distraction to keep darker thoughts at bay.

But now she was in bed. And the TV was off. And the dogs were asleep. And she wasn't hungry. And she'd had a little too much wine. And she had nothing left to turn her attention away from what she was missing, what she regretted, what she so desperately longed for...

She sighed, slipping down farther under the covers, feeling the soft, silky whisper of the sheets against her skin, smelling the captured scent of the clove and lilac soap she had used in the bath, moving her arms and legs out to their full stretch and still not even coming close to finding the edges of the mattress.

She was alone. And she was lonely. She realized that she didn't want to think about Jacob anymore. She had rehashed all the old memories and they had left her heartsick and mentally exhausted. No, it wasn't Jacob she missed. What she really wanted was Enzo. His hard, gorgeous, and comforting body curled around her. She wanted to turn over and be able to run her fingers through his sleek glossy hair; she wanted to listen to the soft, deep sound of him breathing next to her; she wanted to wrap herself in his arms, tangle her legs with his, smell his delicious earthy smell, feel him quicken and pulse against her, hear his low, rough voice calling her *niña, querida, mi corazón...*

She shifted restlessly, feeling her temperature rise. The dogs, annoyed at the movement, slipped off the bed with complaining little groans and settled themselves on the floor.

She thought of the way the slow drag of his cheek against hers felt—the raspy, rough, and thoroughly masculine feel of his skin on hers. She imagined how he would dip his mouth to the hollow of her throat and feel the rapid fluttering of her pulse. She wanted those strong, capable hands leaving trails of sparks and fire all over her skin; she wanted that mouth on her breasts, on her belly, finding the very core of her, parting her with his tongue...

She moaned and her hand drifted down her body as she remembered the way he had kissed her there, the way he had pinned her to the bed and taken his time, tasting her, teasing her, driving her wild.

She touched herself softly and then with more intent, captured by the memory of the way things had been between them, her mind spinning with echoes of all the pleasure he had brought her, the words he'd whispered, the amazingly skilled way he had handled her body, the way he had made her truly *his*.

She cried out, brought to her peak by the sudden and vivid memory of Enzo's face as he climaxed, the way his eyes had devoured her, the way the color had rushed into his cheeks, the hiss of her name on his lips as his big, hard body had moved against her, inside her. She writhed and twisted, calling his name in return, until she shattered into what felt like thousands of white-hot fragments and then collapsed, breathless.

After a long moment, she opened her eyes and stared out at the spangled sky. Even the sound of the tide seemed muted as she lay quiet and alone in the bed, moved only by the gentle to and fro sway of the sea beneath her.

* * *

Outside the yacht, at the edge of the dock, Enzo sat idling in his truck. After pacing the beach, walking the streets, and then driving from one island to the next, he had found himself here, studying the darkened boat, wondering if she was awake, or even there, wondering what she would do if he slipped on board and took her into his arms and declared himself to her. What she would say if he told her how he felt about her, how he had always felt, how he would always feel.

Suddenly a light came on in the lower deck. One of the windows glowed a soft yellow.

She was there.

He turned off the engine, put his hand to the car door handle, and then hesitated.

The boat bobbed gently in the dark water, an enormous, hulking mass. There were probably alarms, thought Enzo. Of course there were alarms. One couldn't just stroll aboard a multimillion-dollar yacht. Especially this late at night.

He glanced over at his phone, sitting on the seat next to him. He could call her. He could text. Ask her to meet him out here...

The light went out.

He breathed slowly, reminding himself of all the reasons

not to act. Reminding himself that he had already nearly put his heart into her hands and that she had refused him just in time.

He had dodged a bullet, he told himself. They both had.

He watched the window.

It remained dark.

He turned the key in the ignition, backed up, and drove away.

Chapter Seventeen

Noni woke early. She was still uncomfortable with the idea of being waited upon and was determined to avoid the staff on the boat if she could. She dressed in layers, expecting the morning haze and fog to burn off later. She wandered into the kitchen, took a few desperate moments to figure out the espresso machine, and then herded the dogs out for a quick walk on the beach, a foamy latte in hand.

The beach was glorious—all mist and wind and pearly sunrise—and, except for a few sandpipers bobbing around in the shallow water, she and the sisters had it to themselves. Noni unhooked their leashes and let them run ahead, and they quickly disappeared into the clouds of skittering fog.

Antonia trailed behind slowly, knowing that the dogs would come running back to her soon enough. She sipped her coffee and kept her eyes on the ground, looking for shells and stones and interesting effluvia that might have washed up the night before.

She had just pocketed a large piece of bright blue sea glass, the edges sanded to dull, rounded curves, when the girls circled back, nearly knocking her over in their exuberance. She laughed and then shook her head ruefully, seeing how dirty they had already managed to get—their long hair matted with sea foam and sand. It would take only a moment to hose them off before they set off for the barn. She turned back toward the boat and whistled to the dogs, and they followed obediently, with wide doggy smiles.

The staff was just arriving as they returned to the *Pilar*, and Noni awkwardly introduced herself before hosing down the dogs on the upper deck. The girls loved the water and snapped and bounced around in the sparkling, silver stream.

After, they shook themselves off before Antonia could get out of the way, and she got drenched in their spray, so she had to go back downstairs to change. On her way to her bedroom she ran into the chef—a woman maybe a few years older than Noni, with short dark red dreadlocks, café au lait skin, and warm brown eyes. Noni smiled apologetically as she dripped onto the kitchen floor.

"My dogs—" she began.

The chef laughed. "Say no more. I have an overweight Lab at home who wreaks daily havoc."

"I'm Noni." She stuck out her hand and then quickly withdrew it again when she saw how wet and sandy it was. "Oh, sorry. Ick. You don't want to shake that."

The chef laughed again. "I'm Liz." She looked at Antonia's wet clothes and shook her head. "Why don't you go change and I'll make you some breakfast? I have some strawberry muffins in the oven, but I can make you anything you like."

Noni took an appreciative sniff and smelled the sweet, caramelized scent of brown sugar and cooking fruit. "Those smell amazing. Just a muffin would be great. Thank you."

She slipped into her room and quickly changed—throwing her damp clothes in the hamper and pausing a second to think about how ironic it was that, if she had been home, she would have just left them in a puddle on her floor. Apparently having someone around to pick up after her finally made her want to pick up after herself. Next she slid into a pair of dry jeans and a black tank top. She traded out her damp tennis shoes for her riding boots. It was already warming up, so she left her jacket behind.

Liz handed Noni a warm muffin slathered in butter as she passed back through the kitchen. Noni stopped and took a bite, and her eyes practically rolled back in her head, it was so good. "Holy hell," she breathed. "This is amazing."

Liz smiled and waved her hands. "Thank you. The strawberries are so good right now. I'm trying to use them in everything. Now, do you have any requests for tonight's dinner?"

"Oh," said Noni, feeling awkward again. "You don't have to do anything. I can just pick up some takeout, you know. Like, a pizza, or something."

Liz shook her head. "I don't mean to toot my own horn, but I can make you a pizza better than anything you can buy on the island. Do you like clams?"

Noni must have looked mystified, because Liz laughed. "You've never had a white clam pizza before? It's amazing. If you eat shellfish, that's what I'll make, then. That and a simple green salad—the first microgreens are showing up at the farmers market these days. Are you okay with a balsamic shallot dressing? And how about strawberry granita for dessert?"

Antonia lifted her hands in surrender. "Sure. Absolutely. That all sounds amazing, but you really don't have to fuss over me like this. You know—this is my brothers' boat. I can just take care of myself."

Liz's lips thinned into a frown. "This isn't me fussing. This is me doing my job. With almost the whole Del Campo family in England, I only have you and Pilar to cook for, and Pilar hardly uses me at all. If you turn me away, too, I'll just be cooking for my dog."

Noni laughed and nodded. "Well, okay, then. I put myself into your obviously capable hands. Thank you. Oh, and thank you for last night's dinner. It was amazing, too. Where did you learn to cook like that?"

Liz shrugged. "Oh, you know, a couple years at the Culinary Institute of America. A few years in Italy. A few years in Morocco."

Noni raised her eyebrows. "I am obviously totally outclassed. And immensely lucky to be eating at your table."

Liz handed her a basket of the warm muffins, neatly wrapped in a clean, red-checked napkin. "Just in case you want more. Or want to share at the barn. And listen, I'm going to whip up some dog biscuits for your pups. There's no reason they should be eating that stuff out of a box."

Noni smiled and suddenly felt a knot in her throat. She blinked rapidly, holding back tears.

"Noni?" said Liz, a quizzical look on her face. "You okay?"

Noni felt herself flush, embarrassed. "God," she said, "yes. I'm fine." She rubbed at her eyes furiously. "I'm so sorry. I don't know why I . . ." She shook her head helplessly. "I think the muffin was just so good, probably."

Liz cocked her head and smiled doubtfully, and Noni took that as her cue to leave. "Anyway," she said, struggling to get herself under control, "thank you for breakfast."

She practically sprinted up the stairs, whistling for the dogs and heading for her truck, anxious to escape her embarrassment.

She loaded the girls into the back of her canopied truck

and then slipped into the front seat, taking a few deep breaths and wiping away one last stray tear.

What in the hell was wrong with her? Liz's simple kindness toward her dogs, of all things, had reduced her to a gibbering idiot. Seriously, she had to get a grip. She'd cried more in the past two weeks than she had in the past two years combined.

She should know better. If she had learned one thing from her childhood, it was never to get too attached. And after Berlin, she certainly should have known this lesson by heart. Instead, she had let herself fall into a family she scarcely knew—trying to claim them as her own. Then she had forced things between her and Enzo, and now look where she was—crying over dog biscuits.

Noni loved her dogs, but it was rare that anyone else saw their appeal. They were eerie, slightly feral, and always in trouble. People tended to yell at them, swear when they were around, and shoo them out of places. Only Antonia and Enzo had ever actually seemed to like the sisters.

They were basically as weird and unlovable as...as Antonia sometimes felt herself to be.

She shook her head. This would not stand. She had to get a hold of herself.

"Plus now that nice chef thinks I'm totally bonkers," she muttered as she threw her car into drive.

She reached into the basket next to her and grabbed another muffin as she drove.

Chapter Eighteen

The barn was quiet that morning. The Del Campos had left for London the night before, and the grooms were busy doing the morning feed before they started exercising the animals.

Enzo had spent the morning making a list of ponies who needed some special attention—young horses, green horses, a few that were recovering from various health issues. He liked to make sure that he personally dealt with the ponies that needed the most work.

He saddled up the first horse on the list—a bright red bay named Rosemary that had a wild streak which needed gentling. He was leading the pony through the barn when he saw Antonia a few stalls up, seriously sexy in skintight jeans, a black tank top, and black knee-high riding boots. She was grooming the little black mare Hex.

He paused to watch her as she led her pony out of the barn, wondering what she was up to. She was in early. Normally she didn't get here until after the morning exercise was over.

He stopped for a moment longer to put on his helmet and riding gloves and then followed Noni out.

Outside, the morning haze had burned off, and it was one of those perfect Hampton days. The sky was bright blue, with little wisps of white clouds floating around; the field was a vibrant spring green; there was a soft breeze; and the air was definitely warming up. More summer than spring, for sure, thought Enzo.

Noni was already at one end of the pitch, rolling Hex into a full gallop, a mallet in hand as she chased the little white ball across the grass.

Enzo caught his breath. He'd forgotten all her polo plans, forgotten that he had promised to help her train.

He wondered if she would still take his assistance if he offered.

Antonia raced forward, pulled back her mallet, and hit the ball with a mighty *thwack*. It spun up into the air—so high that Enzo had to squint to see where it had gone—and then came hurtling back down and hit the ground halfway down the pitch.

Enzo felt his mouth drop open. He had no idea that she could do that.

She came barreling down the field and curved under the pony's neck just long enough to take the ball up in her mallet, sending it ahead and then catching up in a few short strides, babying it down the pitch with constant tiny hits as she ran full speed alongside it. Until, with one sharp blow, she sent it sweeping through the goal.

She slowed the pony, leaned down to push the ball back out onto the field, and started all over again.

She was stunning on a horse. Natural and relaxed and joyous. She still had some rough edges here and there, but there was no doubt that she had her brothers' talents. Alejandro's doggedness combined with Sebastian's style. She caught the ball easily and sent it hurtling along, smiling to herself as she spurred the pony into an even faster gallop.

Rosemary snorted impatiently and nudged Enzo with her nose. He blinked and shook his head—he'd forgotten why he was even out here to begin with. He grabbed a mallet from the equipment shed, and then he swung up into the saddle and took the pony out onto the pitch.

Noni didn't notice them at first; she and Hex were at the other end, their backs to Rosemary and Enzo. But then she circled around, caught the ball, and sent it straight at Enzo.

"Oh shit!" she cried out as she saw him. "Watch out!"

He calmly backed up and hooked it—sending it right back at Noni.

"Hey!" she shouted, leaving the ball on the ground and cantering toward him. "You should have warned me you were on the pitch."

"I didn't have a chance," he said, smiling. "You were too quick."

She shook her head. "You're lucky I didn't hit that one harder."

"You're good," he said as she reached his side. "You're really good."

She waved him off. "I'm okay." But he could tell from the sudden flush of pink to her cheeks that she was pleased.

"No," he said, "you are way more than okay."

She fought to hide her smile. "You want to play?" she said. "Just a little stick and ball?"

In answer, he spurred Rosemary out toward the goal.

"Come on!" she yelled. "Cheater!" and came galloping after him.

He sent the ball straight up the pitch and chased it down the line of the ball. Noni came galloping up next to him, taking the other side of the line. They had a ride-off—the horses running neck and neck down the length of the field, bumping against each other, trying to push each other over the line.

Hex was a made pony, much more experienced on the field, but Rosemary had a wild eagerness that gave the little black mare a run for her money.

Noni reached the ball first, hooking it with a back shot and sending it down the pitch in the other direction even as she continued to ride forward. Enzo started after it, but Noni and Hex stopped almost instantly, going from a full-out gallop to completely still before making a hairpin turn and racing after the ball as well.

Hex caught up with Rosemary, and Enzo and Noni reached the ball at almost the same moment. Each leaned out with the same intent to hook the other's mallet away, crashing their sticks together in a tangle. The sound of wood on wood startled Rosemary, and she reared up.

"Whoa!" shouted Enzo. He barely kept his seat before pulling her back down again.

"Are you okay?" said Noni.

He directed Rosemary away from them, making her go into a tight and controlled trot. "*Estoy bien*," he said. "This girl needs work. Hang on."

Enzo posted across the field, quietly speaking in Spanish to the nervous mare until he felt Rosemary soften beneath him. He slowed her down to a walk. He glanced up and caught Noni watching him, her dark eyes even darker than usual.

"You always know what to do," she said softly.

He raised his eyebrows.

"With horses," she clarified.

He shrugged. "They tell you what they need. It's just a matter of listening."

Noni kept looking at him. He could see a flush of color creeping up her chest and neck.

He felt an answering rush of heat move through his body.

"We should take them back in," said Noni breathily.

He nodded. "Lead the way," he said.

She turned her pony and started back toward the barn. Watching Noni's tight little rear jounce in the saddle ahead of him made him dizzy with desire. He swore softly and kicked Rosemary into a trot and followed.

* * *

They tied the horses up in adjoining stalls, silently removing the tack and rubbing them down.

Noni had always loved watching Enzo work with the ponies. He was magical with the animals, never got angry or lost his patience, was able to intuit what they needed as if the horses spoke to him directly. She had deeply admired his skill, spent many an hour watching him as he trained and gentled—molding the ponies into equine stars on the pitch.

But watching him work Rosemary on the field today had been different. Noni hadn't been just casually appreciating Enzo's talent. No, she had sat there on her pony, silently going to delicious pieces as she watched him take control.

The way he leaned down to whisper calming words into Rosemary's ear, the way he showed no fear at all when the pony reared, just took her straight into a sharp and controlled little trot, the way he didn't seem to think of himself at all—just what the little red mare needed...It had driven Noni wild.

She shifted uncomfortably as she curried the pony, then ran a comb through Hex's glossy black mane, trying to calm her shaking hands. She was aflame. Agonizingly aware of Enzo in the stall next to hers. Unable to think of anything else but the aching need to be in his arms, under him, to feel every inch of his body against hers again...She leaned her forehead against the pony's neck and closed her eyes.

"Noni," he said, and she whipped her head up, startled to find Enzo standing alone in front of the stall.

They locked eyes. She felt the breath leave her body.

He reached over and unhooked Hex, calmly attaching the lead and then taking the pony out of the stall as Antonia stood there, suspended by her need.

She listened to the clip-clop of Hex's hooves hitting the clay floor as Enzo led her away. Then, after a moment, the much lighter sound of his boots returning to her alone.

"*Vamonos, chica*," he said. His voice was raspy and low.

She stood frozen, rooted to the spot.

"Come on, Noni." His face was still. "We have unfinished business."

She swallowed and nodded, following him out of the stall.

* * *

He led her into the office, locking the door behind them and pulling the shade over the glass door.

He would never be able to say whether she came to him or he to her, but in an instant, she was in his arms, her mouth on his, her hot little body writhing against him as she twined her arms around the back of his neck with a guttural moan.

He let himself get lost in her for a moment. Savoring her

soft, warm lips, her sweet little tongue as it darted against his, the way her hands moved relentlessly over him. He gripped her around the waist, fitting her body closer to his, breathing in her spicy scent, deliriously pleased to have her back in his arms.

"Enzo," she breathed, "we should talk."

He shook his head. "Later," he said, and pushed her up against the wall, crushing his mouth to hers, needing more.

She caught her hands in his hair and moaned, hooking one leg behind his knee and rubbing herself against him. He reached under her thighs and picked her up, allowing her to wrap both legs around him. He broke the kiss and trailed his mouth down her neck, over her almost bare shoulder, catching the strap of her tank top and pulling it down with his teeth, exposing the top of her breast.

She hissed in pleasure as he palmed the creamy mound, bringing it to his mouth as he hooked her shirt with the tip of his finger, tugging it farther down, freeing her sweet pink nipple.

"Ah, *mi corazón*," he moaned. "*Tan bella.*"

Someone rattled the doorknob and then a sharp knock sounded at the door.

They leaped apart with a gasp.

"*¡Momentito!*" exclaimed Enzo.

"Enzo? Why is this door locked?"

It was Pilar.

"Enzo?"

Noni groaned softly in dismay, desperately straightening her clothes. Enzo adjusted his jeans and smoothed his shirt. He shot Noni a questioning look and she widened her eyes unhappily but gave him a nod in response. He opened the door.

"*¿Qué está pasando?*" said Pilar as she bustled in. "Why—"

She stopped short, staring at Noni, a frown on her face.

There wasn't much use trying to hide anything, thought Enzo. Antonia's cheeks were bright red, her hair was a mess, and he could see the marks he had left on her throat and chest.

Still, she looked so mortified that he had to try.

"Ah, Pilar. *Buenos días*. Noni and I were just having a meeting about—er—"

Pilar rolled her eyes. "*Dios mio*, don't bother," she snapped. "You have always been the worst liar in the world. Actually"—she snapped her head in Noni's direction—"it's her I need to talk to." She looked wryly at Antonia. "There are people at my house. They say they know you."

* * *

Pilar stalked ahead, her big yellow dogs flanking her on either side as Enzo and Noni trailed behind her.

"Are you expecting anyone?" Enzo asked.

Antonia shook her head, looking mystified. "Maybe a delivery? I don't know why they'd come to the house and not the barn, though."

They rounded the corner of the house and saw a red Mazda Miata convertible parked in the driveway. Noni suddenly stopped and clutched Enzo's arm.

He turned to her. She had gone chalk white.

It was Noni's mother, dressed in a short sapphire blue tunic and high-heeled sandals; Jacob Van Dyke, wearing a fitted black dress shirt and dark jeans to match; and, between them, a little boy—maybe six or seven, judging from his size—with wild red curls and black-rimmed glasses.

The boy looked up at them with wide brown eyes. Noni's hand bit into Enzo's arm so hard that he flinched in pain.

Enzo watched Jacob Van Dyke give the little kid a nudge forward.

"Mama?" said the little boy, looking at Antonia. He tumbled forward and awkwardly wrapped his arms around Noni's waist, burying his face against her. "Mama!"

Chapter Nineteen

Antonia stood in Pilar's powder room, trying to catch her breath. Her hands were clutching the sink and she had her forehead pressed against the mirrored door of the medicine chest. She was hyperventilating.

There was a knock on the door. "Noni?" said Enzo. "Are you all right?"

She shook her head, trying to answer. Finally she sucked in enough air to choke out, "I'm okay. I'll...I'll be out in a moment."

"Noni"—Enzo's voice was low—"let me in."

"You know what?" she said. Even to her own ears, her voice sounded strange and high-pitched. "Why don't I meet you back at the barn in a little while? I think I should probably, um, talk to my mom and Jacob and..." Her breath felt short again as she trailed off.

There was a long silence, and then finally, "Okay. *Bien*."

She shut her eyes, swallowed hard, and leaned against the door for a moment. "Enzo?" she whispered. "I'm sorry. I know this must all seem crazy to you. I promise, I'll explain it all later."

She waited.

No answer.

She turned the knob and opened the door a crack. Then wider.

"Enzo?"

The hallway was empty. She heard the front door shut.

She pulled the bathroom door closed again and ran the water in the sink, splashing her face and then drying off with a hand towel. She looked at herself in the mirror. She pinched her cheeks, not wanting to scare Max with her ghostlike pallor.

Max.

She shook her head, hardly able to believe it. He was so beautiful. Those red curls. His hair had just been baby fuzz when she had last seen him. She and Jacob had always joked about what a little baldy he was, how slow his hair was to grow.

She smiled, remembering.

After he had hugged her outside, she had allowed herself to hold him for just one moment before she realized that she was either going to break down into sobs or hysterical laughter, and she honestly wasn't sure which it would be. Not wanting to alarm the child, she had gently extricated herself, stammered an excuse, and then bolted for the bathroom.

But she was calmer now. It was time to come out.

She took a deep breath, opened the bathroom door, and headed for the parlor.

* * *

They were all gathered in one end of the room. Benny and Jacob sitting, perfectly comfortable, on one of Pilar's tufted white couches. Pilar a bit off to the side, eyes narrowed as she looked at Benny. And Max, standing in front of a glass coffee table, examining a large dish of shells and sea glass.

They all looked up at Noni as she walked in.

She ignored the adults and went to straight to Max, squatting down on the other side of the coffee table.

He looked up at her warily. She smiled at him. "Do you like to collect shells, Max?" she said.

He blinked, his big brown eyes owl-like behind his glasses; then he nodded shyly. He held up a piece of green sea glass. "This kind is my favorite," he said, his voice barely above a whisper.

Noni nodded. "Mine too."

She allowed herself to just look at the little boy for a moment. Her chest felt tight as she hungrily took in his round, pudgy cheeks, the velvety soft golden hue of his skin, the spangle of freckles across his nose, his long thick dark red eyelashes, the gleam of his curls, the determined set of his little shoulders under his striped green and blue shirt, the dimples on the backs of his small square hands as he capably sorted through the shells...

She wanted nothing more than to gather him up in her arms, see if the heft of his little body felt the same when she held him, bury her nose in his copper curls and smell him—searching out that bright, sunny, sweet baby smell that she would never forget.

Her heart ached, and she wasn't sure if it was from loss or relief of having him near again.

"Why, that's not even a shell," put in Benny, plucking the sea glass away from Max's hand. "That's just garbage, really." She smiled broadly and chose a small spotted cowrie shell from the dish. "Now this is a pretty shell."

Max frowned.

Noni looked at her mother, exasperated. "Why would you say that?" She looked at Max. "Sea glass isn't garbage."

Benny rolled her eyes. "How is broken glass not garbage?"

"It's been transformed, Benny," Jacob interjected. "Garbage to art."

Noni glanced at him. He gave her a crooked little smile. She looked away, not wanting his help.

"Well," said Benny, "I suppose that's one way of looking at it."

Noni sighed, reminded that no matter how much she wanted to, she couldn't just sit here and look at Max's little hands all day. She had to find out what was going on.

"Pilar," she said nervously, inclining her head toward Max, "would you mind taking..."

Pilar looked at her inscrutably and then gave her the tiniest nod in response. "Max," she said, "do you like boats? Because I have a boat in a bottle in the other room that is really quite interesting. Would you like to see it?"

Max looked at her. "Okay," he said softly.

Pilar held out her hand. He hesitated, darting a quick glance at Jacob, and then took it.

Pilar led him out. "I have never been able to figure out how they got it in there. Perhaps you will know," she said as they left the room, sliding the pocket doors shut behind her.

Noni was suddenly uncomfortably aware that she was still squatting on the ground, looking up at her mother and Jacob.

She stood up.

Benny threw herself backward on the couch with a dramatic sigh. "I thought she'd never leave." She looked over at

Noni. "So, how many face-lifts has she had already?"

Jacob wandered around the room a bit, picking up various things and then putting them back down again. "This is a beautiful house," he said.

Benny snorted. "Carlos hated this place. Said it felt like a jail."

Jacob laughed, peering at a small Edward Hopper on the wall. "We should all be sentenced to such a jail."

"Why are you here?" said Noni, not wanting to hear any more about the house or Pilar's suspected plastic surgery.

They both turned their heads toward her, looking surprised by her bluntness. She felt her face flush but didn't waver in her gaze. "And why," she said, her voice shaking just the smallest amount, "did Max call me Mama?"

Jacob seemed to recover first. He gave her an easy smile. "Sorry about that. He was just so excited about seeing you again."

Noni shook her head in confusion. "How does he know who I am? Last time I saw him he wasn't even a year old yet."

Jacob shrugged. "Well, you know, of course we talk about you, Noni. And I show him pictures."

Antonia stared at him. Her heart was beating double time. "Why?"

Benny sat upright. "Why wouldn't he? You were a very important person in that little boy's life, you know, Antonia."

Noni turned to her mother, completely bewildered. "And why are you here with them?"

Benny smiled brightly. "Because Jacob invited me. He said he was coming up to see you and asked if I wanted to come along."

Noni looked at her mother and then at Jacob. She felt like

she was drowning. "Mother," she said at last, "would you please excuse us?"

Her mother arched her meticulously shaped eyebrows. "Can't wait to be alone again, eh?"

"Please," said Noni. She strained to keep her voice under control.

Benny sighed dramatically and stood up. "Fine. I guess I'll go make sure that old dragon Pilar isn't eating Max alive."

After she left the room, shutting the door behind her, Noni looked at Jacob. She felt like she was hurtled back in time, looking into his dark blue eyes.

"Noni," he said. His voice was soft. "I know this must be difficult."

"Honestly?" said Noni. "It's excruciating."

"I just," said Jacob, "I just wanted him to know you, is all. Your mother was right. You were important to him."

"But why now?"

Jacob looked away. Under his beard, she could see his jaw clench. "I've never stopped thinking of you, Antonia," he said gruffly. "Not a day has passed since you left that I haven't thought of you."

"*You* left *me*," said Noni. Her voice shook. "You left me and you took Max."

Jacob looked pained. "I know. But I had to. You know that, right?"

Noni felt her stomach twist at his words. Tears sprang to her eyes. She looked away from him and nodded.

"But," he said, "I will never forgive myself for hurting you that way. I thought I was doing the right thing. I thought I was protecting him. But then when I saw you at Benny's opening...I knew it had all been a huge mistake."

Noni stared at him, completely bewildered. He strode across the room and took her hand between his. She froze. Too shocked to pull away.

"I want you back, Noni," he said, looking her in the eyes. "I want us to be a family again."

Chapter Twenty

Enzo picked the wildest horse in the stable, a big white stallion named El Rey that was kept more for breeding than riding, and rode him down the twisting narrow path at the edge of the property that led to the Del Campos' private beach.

He needed to ride, and he needed to ride hard. Seeing the look on Antonia's face when that little boy had called her Mama and wrapped his arms around her—the strange combination of joy and terror—and then her refusal to explain things immediately after, Enzo had felt mired in secrets, overwhelmed by all that she had not told him.

He reached the edge of the beach. As if echoing his mood, the gorgeous sunny day had turned dark and stormy. Billowing black clouds were racing across the sky, and the sea was a tarnished silver, restless and turbulent. Enzo could see the whitecaps in the water.

"Ya!" He tapped his heels into El Rey's sides and took him galloping toward the water, only turning him once the big horse's hooves hit the surf.

They flew down the empty beach, the frigid water splashing against Enzo's legs with every step of El Rey's stride.

The salty wind whipped at Enzo's face, and the sound of the surf roared in his ears. He pushed the stallion until he felt that he had, at least temporarily, managed to outdistance the demons that were chasing him.

He slowed the horse to a trot and then to a walk. El Rey snorted as Enzo twisted in his saddle to look over his shoulder, squinting down the beach and realizing he'd gone farther than he had intended. A fat drop of rain hit his face as he turned the horse to head back to the farm. Distant thunder rumbled, and Enzo could feel the stallion shudder slightly, so he gave him the lead. They kicked into a brisk trot, trying to outpace the weather.

Visibility was bad and Enzo cursed himself for taking the horse out to begin with. He'd let his own needs take precedence over the pony's, and he felt like an ass as the rain started really coming down and the stallion increased his speed.

Suddenly, as if out of nowhere, a black and white blur crossed their path and raced almost under El Rey's hooves. The stallion whinnied and shied as the blur separated into two blurs—one on each side of the horse—and Enzo realized it was Noni's dogs.

"¡Mierda!" Enzo swore, fighting to get the pony under control. The dogs kept going—racing down the beach past them, but then, from somewhere ahead, there came a long whistle, and the sisters circled round and came running back toward them again.

"Damn it, Antonia!" Enzo roared as the slight figure, still clad only in jeans and a tank top, came into view. She looked up at him as he brought the restless horse alongside her. Her face was pale and her long hair was plastered against her head and streaming down her back.

"Are you all right?" she said loudly.

El Rey kept dancing as Enzo fought for control. "I'm fine," he yelled back. "No thanks to your dogs!"

"I need to talk to you!" she shouted over the sound of the wind and the rain. She pointed to an old pier a little ways down the beach. "Meet me there!" And then, without waiting for his answer, she took off running for shelter.

* * *

It was dim and cool under the wharf but blessedly dry. The rain drummed on the wood above her as Antonia pushed her wet hair away from her face and rubbed at her arms, trying to get warm as she watched Enzo dismount and lead the horse under the shelter of the pier, tying him to a post in the corner.

He turned to face her, and Noni caught her breath. He was drenched through and his dark green T-shirt was clinging so tight that she could make out every line of muscle in his chest and abs. His black hair was damp and pushed away from his face, but drops of water still ran down his cheeks and neck and over his broad shoulders. His jeans were like a second skin, showing off his muscular thighs. Even his dark brown riding boots were soaked.

He licked the dampness off his full lips and she shivered.

"Cold?" he asked. His eyes were hooded and glittering with a dangerous intensity, but his voice was calm.

She shook her head and fought the urge to move forward, press herself against him.

"So, who's the boy?" he asked quietly.

She blinked. His words were like ice down her back.

"Not...not mine," she stammered. "I mean, not in the way you think."

He looked doubtful. "He called you Mama."

She took a deep breath. "I need to sit down," she said faintly. She sank into the sand, leaned back against a pillar, and closed her eyes for a moment, gathering her strength. Then opened them and looked up.

He stood with his muscular arms crossed over his chest, watching her, inscrutable.

"I met Jacob when I was twenty," she began, "and he was thirty-five. My mom and I were living in Berlin. We'd been all over the continent, traveling off and on for a couple of years, but then my mom read about this artists' collective in Berlin and decided it was something she needed to be a part of.

"She was making jewelry then, just beading stuff at first, but what she really wanted was to learn to work with metal. And the collective had a forge. Jacob was the teacher. As it turned out, my mom was really bad at metalwork—but I had the touch."

She absently traced the anvil tattoo on her inner wrist.

"Jacob was intense and handsome and ambitious. He worked with steel and iron—larger-than-life sculptures that were just starting to get some attention. Once he saw what I could do—how the forge felt so natural to me—he took me on as his apprentice. I was so happy. He was incredibly talented. For the first time, I felt like I was really good at something. And"—she hesitated briefly—"I'll admit, I had a pretty big crush on him."

The rain started coming down even harder, and a loud crack of thunder split the air. The white pony shook his head and whinnied in fear. Enzo hurried over to soothe him. He looked back at Noni. "Go on," he said, running his hands over the horse.

"Jacob had a wife. She was a dancer. Her name was Astrid. Jacob told me that she was an ex-junkie. That she used to do heroin before they got married but that Jacob had helped her get clean and that she was pregnant and they were going to have a baby."

Seeing Enzo's raised eyebrows, Noni shrugged. "He always said I was easy to talk to."

Enzo snorted.

"Anyway, Astrid had the baby, and that was Max."

"Max," said Enzo, like he was trying out the name.

Antonia nodded. "Max..." She wrapped her arms around herself, trying to get warmer. "At first, everything was good. Jacob had this new baby and this beautiful wife, and his art career was taking off. But then—I don't really know why—Astrid started using again."

Enzo slowly nodded. "Ah."

"Yeah. He tried to get her to go to rehab—you know, for Max. But she wouldn't. Or she couldn't, I guess. I don't know. So Jacob would bring Max to the studio because he couldn't trust Astrid to take care of him. He never knew if he was going to come home and just find her nodding out. But he had to work, of course, so he would bring Max in, and I started watching the baby for him. Just a little at first. Then more and more. Jacob and I...we got closer. Nothing happened between us, Jacob would never have done that to Astrid, but there was definitely a connection."

She pushed her wet hair back out of her face again.

"Mostly, though, it was about Max. He was such a sweet little baby." She smiled to herself, remembering. "He looked worried all the time back then." She looked at Enzo. "Isn't that funny? That a baby could look worried?"

"It sounds like he had a reason to be worried."

She gave a little bark of rueful laughter. "Well, yeah, no kidding because . . . Astrid OD'd. She died." She looked away from Enzo for a moment, fighting the lump in her throat. "It was awful," she finally whispered.

A look of pain passed over Enzo's face. "I can only imagine."

"Max was still really, really young. Not even six months old. Jacob didn't have anyone else to help, and he was such a mess, and he needed someone. Max needed someone. So I just, kind of stepped in, you know?"

Enzo shook his head. "Where was your mother, *niña*?"

Noni snorted. "My mom? Oh, she was around, I guess. But she never liked babies. She wasn't going to help. When I told her that I was moving in with Jacob and Max, I think she was relieved, honestly. She wouldn't have to support me anymore or stay in Berlin any longer. She wanted to go to Istanbul."

She was quiet for a moment. The rain continued to fall.

"So, at first we were, you know, like a little family. I stayed home at the flat with Max, and Jacob went to work, and we did stuff like have dinner together every night. Stuff I had never done before, really." She looked up at Enzo and smiled. "I loved it. I really did."

She smiled softly to herself.

"Jacob worked a lot. But he was an artist, you know? That's what an artist does. I was used to that because of my mother. But the difference between Jake and my mom was that when Jacob was there with me, he was really there. All of his attention just completely focused on me. It was . . . intoxicating, honestly."

She noticed Enzo's scowl and hurried on.

"Mostly, though, it was just the two of us—me and Max—

and for the first time, I felt like someone was really...mine. And that I was his. I would hold him and rock him and give him his bottle, and he would look up at me, just stare at me, with these huge eyes, so serious and worried, while he ate. Sometimes he would reach up and touch my face, pat my cheek or tug on a lock of my hair..."

Her throat hurt. She swallowed.

"But it was also hard. I mean, I loved Max. I loved him so much. But he was fussy and didn't sleep well, and just— he cried a lot. Sometimes it seemed like there was nothing I could do make him stop."

"And what about his father?" asked Enzo. "Could he make him stop?"

Noni felt her smile twist. "Like I said, he worked a lot and, you know, he needed his sleep because he had to get up early. I was the one staying home. It was up to me to get Max to sleep."

Enzo shook his head but said nothing.

"Anyway, one day, Max got really sick. Like a flu. Fever and a cough, he wouldn't take his bottle, and he couldn't sleep. It was terrible. I took him to the doctor, but they just said it was a virus, and he would get over it and just to make sure that he got lots of fluids and bring him back if his temperature went up again. He was like that for three days straight. He just kept crying, and he wasn't sleeping; he was so miserable. I didn't sleep at all. I was so exhausted. Jacob had an exhibit coming up—a huge deadline—so he was working night and day. He would have helped me if he could, but it was really something that could make or break his career. He basically had to stay at the studio twenty-four-seven."

Enzo shook his head but remained silent.

"So I was taking care of Max the best I could, but then I

got sick, too. Or, I don't know, maybe I was just tired. Because if Max wasn't sleeping, neither was I, right? In any case, Jacob was working late...and..." She trailed off. Not sure that she could talk about it. She had never talked about it with anyone.

"What happened, *querida*?" His eyes were softer now, concerned.

She looked down. "I fell asleep," she said. "I was just so, so tired, Enzo. And he was crying, but I couldn't keep my eyes open anymore. I felt like I was going to pass out. So I put him in his crib. I thought I would just let him cry a little bit. That I would lie down, just for a moment..."

She swallowed. The words were caught in her throat. "He was blue," she whispered. "When Jacob got home, I was asleep and Max was in his crib—he wasn't breathing. He was choking."

Enzo looked at her. "But he was okay in the end."

She looked up at him, felt the tears start down her cheeks. "He almost died, Enzo. He could have died. The doctors told Jacob that if he hadn't gotten there in time..."

"But he did get there in time. He didn't die."

She looked away. "It didn't matter. The point is, I didn't even notice. He was choking to death, right there next to me in the crib, and I didn't even wake up. I was just like my mom. I tuned out. I wasn't paying attention."

He shook his head. "Noni, that's ridiculous."

"I was in over my head. It was too much for me to handle."

"It was one mistake, *niña*. Everyone makes mistakes."

She shook her head fiercely, wiping her eyes. "Not like that, they don't. It was my fault. I put him down even though he was still crying. I knew he was sick but I put him down anyway."

135

She shivered.

"I was there every day at the hospital. I would stay by his bed while Jacob was at work, just watching Max every moment, making sure it didn't happen again, you know? I slept there every night on a little cot."

Enzo shook his head.

"After a few days, he got better, and it was time for him to be released. I was so happy, so relieved. I was packing his little bag, gathering up this little bear I had bought him from the gift shop, when Jacob came in and told me to stop packing and sit down."

She stared blindly out at the storm.

"He said that they weren't coming home with me. That they were leaving."

"Wait. He left you? Why?"

"He said that it was obviously too much for me. That he never should have dragged me into all of it to begin with. That he needed to know that Max was going to be safe. That I wasn't meant to be a mother. I didn't know what I was doing."

Enzo looked incredulous. "That's insane."

She shook her head. "No. He was right. I was in over my head. It was too much for me. I wasn't built to be a mom."

"I'd say you were doing pretty well, all things considered."

"No. No. Jacob did the right thing. He did it because he loved Max."

"But you loved him, too."

She shrugged. "That didn't matter." She rubbed her eyes and then wrapped her arms back around herself again. "I never saw Max again after that."

He was quiet for a moment; then he walked over and squatted down next to her. "You know that none of that was your fault, don't you?"

She stared down at her feet. "He was so sick."

"Not your fault."

"He was in the hospital for days."

"Not your fault."

"He almost died."

"But he didn't."

She buried her head in her hands. "He wasn't mine to begin with and I didn't deserve him."

He pulled her into his arms. "Ah, *querida*, it sounds like you deserved him more than anyone else in his life did."

She sobbed then. Collapsed against his chest and shook with tears.

"In all these years, I've never forgotten him. I've thought of him every day. Wondered how he was doing. Prayed that he was okay. So when I saw Jacob at the opening..."

He held her closer. "I know, *niña*. I know."

He kissed the top of her head. She looked up at him. "He looked good, though, right? He looked healthy, happy?"

Enzo nodded. "He is a beautiful little kid."

She smiled through her tears. "He really is." She sighed and laid her head back on Enzo's chest. Her voice dropped low. "Jacob said...he said that he wants to try again. To be a family again."

Enzo froze in her arms. "And what did you say?"

She shook her head. "I don't know. It seems crazy, right? After all these years?" She took a deep, shuddering breath. "At first I thought maybe...he heard about my inheritance. But Jake was never like that. He wanted fame. He wanted to be able to make his art. But money never meant anything to him. I honestly don't think it's the money."

"So what is it?"

She ducked her head, smiling shyly, still hardly able to believe what Jacob had said. "He...he said that Max needs a mother. That he'd made a huge mistake pushing me away. I mean, seeing Max again, hearing him call me Mama..." She swallowed, raising her eyes to Enzo's. "It's a second chance. A second chance to do it right this time. And I just don't think...Enzo, I can't turn that down."

Enzo hissed as if she had burned him and tried to pull away from her. She clung to his arm.

"I'm sorry! I'm sorry! I know I shouldn't be telling you any of this. It's not fair to be talking to you. I know that things are complicated between us. But...I miss my best friend, Enzo. I need him now."

She looked up at him. She reached to touch his face but he caught her hand in his grip halfway there.

"*Querida*." His voice sounded choked. "I can't be your friend."

They locked gazes. His eyes were wild.

And then he reached down and kissed her.

Chapter Twenty-One

He knew he shouldn't, but he couldn't help himself. The agony of having her so close, the realization that he was going to lose her for good...He crushed her body to his, searing himself on her lips, pushing her down into the sand.

She groaned and twisted under him, running her hands down his body and feverishly kissing him back. The storm picked up and the rain started to fall even harder. Thunder crashed, a bolt of lightning lit up the air, and he pulled back just in time to see her beautiful, tear-stained face, her onyx eyes glittering.

"Don't stop," she whispered. "I want this. Right now, I want this."

His breath caught in response. The thunder crashed again as he renewed his charge, yanking off her wet clothes as she pulled at his. Then they were naked, trembling together in the cold sand as he rained kisses down on her, licking and biting and touching every part of her body that he could reach, and she frantically did the same, raking her nails down his back, biting at the hollow of his throat, and then gasping as he pushed himself between her legs and slid into her.

He groaned and shuddered in pleasure as she moved beneath him, arching her hips to bring him in deeper. Being inside her was red-hot ecstasy. He felt engulfed by her. He could see nothing, smell nothing, hear, taste, feel nothing but Antonia.

He buried himself in her again and again, didn't even try to hold himself back. He wanted her. He wanted all of her. And she took him, again and again, but underneath the blissful feeling of her body connecting to his, he felt a throbbing, frenzied panic.

He was losing her.

Her hips whipped against him in a delirious tattoo, and he could feel her muscles pulsing around him as she reached her crest and tumbled over the edge, crying out her pleasure. Her peak brought on his own, and he pulled out just in time, aware of the fact that they hadn't used protection. Fire raced through him. He felt her shudder under him, feeling, as one last spasm shook him, a twist of agonizing sorrow.

They breathed in unison as she lay under him, her arms still clenched around his back, her legs twined in his, her bare skin pressed to his bare skin. For a moment, he fooled himself, thinking, surely she would not let go.

But then all his fears were confirmed when she bent her head to his shoulder and wept like a woman who had lost something that she knew she would never have again.

Chapter Twenty-Two

The morning after the storm was bright and beautiful. The world looked washed clean. The ocean breeze felt cool against her cheek as Noni climbed out of her truck and squinted, searching out the room numbers on the motel doors.

Her mother was crashing with an old friend in Sag Harbor and going back to the city later that afternoon, but Jacob and Max were staying at this motel in Southampton. He'd given her the address the day before.

She found the room number she was looking for but paused a moment, her heart in her throat. She still ached, body and soul, from her time with Enzo. They had stayed twined together in the sand until night fell, the dark all the more relentless because the storm refused to let up. They were shivering with cold, silent, with nothing left to say, but neither of them could seem to make the first move to disconnect.

It was El Rey who finally decided for them. The big horse got sick of waiting and suddenly broke his tether. They leaped up to catch him, and Enzo managed to grab hold of his bridle before the pony could bolt into the night.

He had turned back to Noni then. "I have to get him in."
His voice was filled with anguish.

She nodded, wordless, and then walked over to him and
gave him one last kiss before turning to go.

She didn't look back. She couldn't...

She took a deep breath and knocked on the motel door.

Jacob answered, his sandy hair mussed, wearing just a T-
shirt and boxers and rubbing the sleep out of his eyes.

He looked good, thought Noni. He was still lean, with incredibly muscular arms from all the metalwork he did. He
had a few new laugh lines around his eyes and she couldn't
decide if she liked the beard, but overall, the years had been
easy on him. There was no doubt that he was still a very at-
tractive man.

When he saw her standing there, he broke into a huge
grin. "Antonia," he breathed. "I knew you'd come." He took
her into his arms.

She bit her lip and briefly hugged him back but then
stepped away.

"We have a lot to talk about," she began, but then, from
inside the room, came Max's little voice.

"Daddy?"

"Hang on, little man," answered Jacob without turning
around.

"But, Daddy, I peed."

"Yes, sure, okay. Good job."

"No, I mean, I peed in the bed."

Jacob groaned, rubbing his hands over his face. "Okay,
hang on, buddy. We'll take care of it."

And just like that, Noni followed him in, picking up
pretty much where she had left off all those years before.

* * *

Enzo sat at the little table in his apartment, staring at his phone. Finally, he palmed it, flipped it over, and dialed London.

He'd already called Mark the night before and told him he would sign on as *piloto* of his new team if the job was still open. The young billionaire had been delighted and wanted to start making plans right away, chattering about the horses he'd bought and the new polo field he'd installed on his property, but Enzo had made a strained excuse, promising to come over the next day and ending the conversation as quickly as he could.

He listened to the phone ring, still not sure just how he would say what he needed to say.

"Enzo. *¿Que pasa, amigo?* Everything going okay?" Alejandro sounded relaxed and happy.

Enzo could hear the sound of a crowd in the background. "*Todos bien,* Jandro. Are you at a match?"

"*Sí.* It's hopeless, though. A bunch of fat Englishmen on expensive ponies. We should have gone to Argentina first. We'll never find our fourth at this rate."

Enzo frowned. *And now you'll have to find a piloto, too.*

"Listen, Jandro, I have something to tell you..." He took a deep breath and decided to just say it. "Mark Stone has offered me a job as *piloto* for his new team, and I feel it's an opportunity I just can't pass up."

"What? Mark Stone? I don't understand. What are you talking about?" Alejandro sounded shocked.

"I'm going to start right away. I'm sorry."

"Right away? But can't this wait until end of the summer at least?"

Enzo shook his head. "I know I'm leaving you short-handed. But please know that this simply can't wait."

"How much is Stone paying you? We'll match his salary."

"It's not about the money, Jandro."

Alejandro sounded bewildered. "If it's not the money, why would you do this, Enzo? I thought you were happy with us? Are we not *compañeros*?"

For a moment, Enzo had considered telling him the truth—after all, Alejandro was not just his boss; he was also his friend. But then he decided that Noni deserved her privacy. She could tell her family what had happened only if and when she wanted to.

"Believe me, *amigo*, it's complicated, but I would not be leaving if I did not absolutely have to. That's all I can say."

Alejandro was silent for a moment and then he said softly, "Okay. *Bien*. I am very sorry to hear this news."

They discussed hiring a temporary worker to replace him while the Del Campos were away, but Alejandro decided that Noni could handle things until he or Sebastian could make it back.

"I'll go to the barn this morning and let the grooms know what's going on. Make sure everything is in order before I leave," said Enzo.

Enzo heard Alejandro sigh. "I hope you will be happy in your new job, *amigo*. You know I wish you only the best."

"*Gracias*. And thank you for everything. I mean that, *mi hermano*."

Chapter Twenty-Three

Watching Max play on the beach, hearing him giggle and run from the shallow incoming waves, watching his sturdy little figure jump and splash in the water, seeing the sun glint in his red-gold curls absolutely mesmerized Noni. She felt greedy. Like she had been starving and someone had just laid out a feast in front of her. He was so beautiful. And happy. She hadn't even realized just how much she had missed him, just how sharp that ache still was, until she had him in her sights again.

Jacob sat beside her on a towel in the sand, almost close enough to touch her. She darted a glance over at him. He was watching Max with his brow slightly knit, looking almost worried, but then he seemed to sense her gaze and looked over at her and smiled.

She bit her lip. He'd always had the warmest smile. And when he truly turned his attention on her, he had a way of making her feel alternately thrilled and overwhelmed, as if she were staring straight into the sun.

"This is kind of amazing, right?" he said. "I mean, me, you, Max...Doesn't this feel right, somehow?"

She looked down, unable to maintain eye contact. "I don't

know quite what it feels like yet," she admitted, glancing back up at him. "But I'm happy to see Max so happy."

He nodded, looking back at his son. "He does seem happy, doesn't he?" He sighed. "It's been a while."

She cocked her head. "What do you mean?"

"Just—" His phone rang, interrupting him. He dug it out of his pocket, glanced at it, and then stood up. "Hey, I'm so sorry. I have to take this. Can you keep your eyes on Max?" Without waiting for her answer, he put the phone to his ear and walked briskly away from her.

Noni blinked, then looked back at Max, who suddenly seemed a little too far into the waves. The water was almost to his knees. Noni stood up.

"Max?" she called, hurrying toward him, thinking about riptides and jellyfish, mentally running through what she knew about mouth-to-mouth resuscitation. "Max, you want to come out of the water for a minute and look for some shells with me?"

The boy looked up at her, the sunlight flashing on the lenses of his glasses. "Okay," he said solemnly. Then he put his little hand into hers. It was damp and cold from the sea, but Noni was suddenly flooded with happiness. She had to stop herself from laughing out loud.

They walked along the water line together, stopping now and then to pick up little treasures they found in the sand.

"I like this beach," announced Max after they found an almost intact sand dollar. "It's better than the one in Spain. The one in Spain had sharp little rocks that hurt my feet. Sand is better."

Noni nodded. "I agree. When were you in Spain?"

Max shrugged. "Last summer. We go every summer. This is the first summer we won't go, Dad says."

Noni raised her eyebrows. "Why not this summer?"

Before he could answer, Jacob came jogging up to them, a big smile on his face. "You guys were way down here! I had to run to catch up!"

Max smiled at his dad and rushed over to show him the handful of shells and pebbles he had found. Jacob squatted down next to him and gravely poked through the treasures, admiring each one in turn.

"Hey, kiddo," said Jacob, "I've got an idea. Why don't we make a sand castle and we can use all these rocks to decorate it?"

Max nodded excitedly in agreement.

"Okay, you start digging the moat, and I'm just going to talk to Noni for a second over here, okay? We'll be right back to help." He looked over at Noni. "You mind?" he said quietly. "Something's come up."

She followed him a bit up the beach, out of earshot from Max.

"I need a favor," he said. "That was my agent on the phone."

"Oh?"

"Yes, and it was great news. The Berlinische Galerie just had a guy drop out of their emerging artist showcase, and they want to bring some of my pieces in instead."

She smiled, thrilled. The Berlinische Galerie was top tier. "Oh, wow, Jake, that's huge! Congratulations!"

He nodded. "I know. It's a once-in-a-lifetime thing, right? But the catch is, it's very last minute, and they want me there right away. Like, tomorrow basically."

She felt her smile dim. "So...you and Max are leaving?"

"Well, that's the favor. This is such a big deal, Noni. I know you understand what it means to be asked to participate in something like this. I know this might be a huge imposition, but I really can't take Max with me. I'm going to be working night and day. I don't have proper child care lined up, and I just thought...maybe he could stay here with you?"

Noni blinked. "Leave him here? With me?"

"It would only be a couple of weeks."

"Weeks?" she croaked.

"I mean, this would be a chance for you guys to really get to know each other again, right?"

She shook her head. She suddenly felt panicky. "I don't think...I mean, I can't take care of him, Jacob."

He touched her arm. "Hey, there is no one I would trust to take care of him like I trust you to, Noni."

"But—"

"You're great with him. He loves you. You guys will have a blast."

"He hardly—"

He stepped closer and his voice dropped. "Noni, I know it's a lot to ask. I know it is. But it's the Berlinische. This could make my career. I might not ever have this chance again."

She looked at him. His eyes were pleading. She looked back at Max, who was intently digging a trench with a stick he'd found. His little shoulders were hunched over and the seat of his swimsuit was covered in wet sand. She smiled in spite of herself.

"I guess maybe I—"

"Yes!" He grabbed her into a hug, lifting her off her feet. "Thank you!"

"Jake," she laughed. "Put me down!"

He gave her a big smacking kiss on her cheek and put her back onto the ground, but he didn't let go.

She stared up into his eyes for a moment, and she saw his face soften. "Noni," he said huskily, "I—"

"Daddy! Noni! The moat is done! Come help me!" Max's clear, sweet voice carried over to them.

Jake laughed and dropped his arms, stepping away from her and striding back toward his son. "Okay, buddy, here I come! We can do a quick sandcastle, but then we've got a change of plans..."

Noni stood where he left her, watching the two of them as they started piling sand in the middle of the moat. She felt excited, thinking about having Max all to herself for two whole weeks. It was more than she could have asked for, really. But at the same time, she felt a cold finger of fear slipping up her spine. Why should Jacob trust her? Who was she to take care of this child? What if something happened again?

"Come on, Noni!" called Jacob. "Come help!"

She blinked and shook her head, pushing her doubt away as she hurried over to join them.

Chapter Twenty-Four

Enzo watched the four players as they raced across the field. Mark Stone hadn't been kidding when he said that Raj Khan and Lachlan Walker were pros. The big, bearded Indian, Raj, rode with the grace and agility of a much smaller man, and the sandy-haired Australian, Lachlan, played with an impressive intensity; he had no mercy on the pitch. They would give the Del Campo brothers a run for their money.

Mark had taken his advice and hired David Jefferson, the young groom from the Wellington stables. Enzo watched the kid as he bent for the ball and sent it flying, his wide, white smile gleaming against his cocoa-colored skin as he followed the ball. What an arm. The kid was a little green, and he sometimes took dangerous risks, but he had incredible potential. It was amazing to Enzo that this kid had grown up in the projects and had only picked up a stick in the last few years. With some training and time on the pitch, Enzo thought that he'd be as good as anyone he'd seen play.

Mark had asked Raj Khan to play number three and captain for now, but Enzo felt sure that David would eventually take over that spot.

The only weak point was Mark Stone himself. The billionaire could barely keep his seat on the million-dollar pony he rode, and the only time he hit the ball seemed to be through sheer luck.

But, Enzo reminded himself, he had been spoiled by all those years watching Hendy play on La Victoria. Lord Henderson had been the kind of patron who actually knew what he was doing on the pitch. Some of the billionaires who funded high-goal polo teams were more like Mark—they paid to play. And by play, that mainly meant just being on the field while the pros ran circles around them.

Still, he thought as he watched Mark happily follow the other players down the field, he had to give the man credit for enthusiasm. The guy looked like he was having the time of his life.

Raj called a time-out, and the players left the field, handing off their mounts to the waiting grooms. Enzo walked over to Mark, who was chugging an enormous energy drink on the side of the pitch.

"So," said Mark, his lips faintly blue from the drink, "what did you think? Pretty great, right?"

Enzo smiled. "A lot of talent on that pitch. You picked some strong players."

"Thanks for tipping me off about David," said Mark. "I was a little worried when I met him. He's just so frigging young, but the kid plays like an absolute monster."

Enzo nodded. "He plays like he has no fear. Which is both good and bad, you know? I would like to see him be a bit more careful on the pitch. But we can work on that."

Mark grinned and slapped him on the back. "That's what I'm paying you the big bucks for, Rivas. I want to win."

Enzo raised his eyebrows. "Well, we have four strong players. That is a good beginning. But we will have to see how they come together as a team."

Chapter Twenty-Five

Max was seasick.

Noni couldn't believe it. The boat was so big, they were secured to the dock, the current barely moved under them, but the kid was literally green in the face.

Liz placed a bowl of hot soup in front of him. "Just take a few sips," she wheedled him. "I promise you that it will help."

Max shook his head and looked up at Noni miserably. His big brown eyes were shadowed underneath his little horn-rimmed glasses. He hadn't slept at all the night before—he said his stomach hurt too much.

"Just try a spoonful, Max," agreed Noni. "Don't you want to feel better?"

Max looked leery as he slowly dipped his spoon into the bowl and then brought it, trembling, to his lips.

He swallowed.

"There! Now, that wasn't so hard, was—"

Noni was interrupted by the little boy spectacularly throwing up all over the table in a panoramic splatter of vomit.

Liz looked up at her, an almost comic look of horror etched

on her face. "I think you better get him back on dry land," she whispered.

* * *

After giving him a bath and changing his clothes, Noni brought Max to the farm for the day, hoping that getting him off the boat would do the trick. But those hopes were dashed the minute they got out of her truck and he threw up on Pilar's hydrangeas.

"I'm sorry," he said miserably as Noni wiped his mouth with a tissue.

"It's okay, hon," said Noni, rubbing his little back. "It's not your fault you're sick. Come on, let's go see if Pilar will give you a drink of water so you can you rinse your mouth."

They knocked on the kitchen door and Pilar answered, her ridgebacks calmly wagging their tails on either side of her. She looked at Antonia imperiously, but her face softened when she saw Max, who looked just about as pathetic as a little kid with tummy trouble could look.

"I'm sorry to bother you, Pilar," said Noni, "but I'm afraid Max has got a touch of seasickness. In fact, he just threw up in your garden, so we were hoping for a glass of water."

"Sorry," offered Max shyly. "I tried to aim for the dirt, but I think I got your flowers."

Noni was surprised by the slightest twitch of a smile on Pilar's face.

"*Pobrecito*," said Pilar. "Of course. Come in."

They walked into her big old-fashioned kitchen. Not for the first time, Noni admired the antiqued brick floor, the big porcelain sink, and the warm wooden counters that had a rich, glowing patina from years of use.

She sighed happily. She loved Pilar's kitchen.

"Sit down, *hijo*," said Pilar, waving Max over to the long painted farm table. She squinted at Max as he swayed while crossing the floor. "Actually, you look like you need to lie down. How about the library? You can curl up on the couch and watch some of Tomás's cartoons while I make you some tea that will help your stomach."

"Oh, you don't have to do that," said Noni. "I was going to set him up in the office in the barn. There's a pretty comfortable couch in there."

Pilar was already leading Max out of the kitchen. "Nonsense," she said firmly. "The stable is no place for a sick child. He needs to rest quietly."

Noni bit back a protest, knowing that Pilar was right. She had been worried about taking Max to work today, but she couldn't leave him on the boat that made him sick, and with Enzo gone, her brothers were counting on her to make sure the barn was taken care of.

"Thank you," she said when Pilar returned. "I hope we're not putting you out."

"Of course not," said Pilar, briskly filling the little copper teapot and putting it on the stove. "I know how miserable seasickness can be. I do not care for boats myself."

Noni smiled, remembering Sebastian telling her how much Pilar loathed the yacht. "It's really nice of you. I'm hoping that he'll get used to it after a while."

Pilar frowned. "It won't get better through exposure. How long do you have him for?"

Noni bit her lip. "Two weeks. Jacob had to fly back to Berlin for some work. You really think he won't get better?"

Pilar shook her head. "Just worse. And it can be dangerous. He will become dehydrated if he's sick long enough."

Noni felt a small surge of worry blossom in her gut. "Oh no. That can't happen. I'll have to rent another place to stay."

Pilar scooped some loose-leaf tea into a tea ball and dropped it into a china cup. "This time of year? It's high season. You won't find anything."

The worry turned to panic. "Oh God. You're right. I know you're right. Maybe if I get a Realtor, they'll be able to help? I think I have a number somewhere..." She took her phone out of her pocket and desperately started scrolling through her contacts.

Pilar dripped some honey into the cup. "You could stay here," she said casually.

Noni's head shot up. "What?"

Pilar kept her eyes on the cup as she shrugged. "The house is practically empty. It's just me and the dogs. I have plenty of room."

Noni blinked. "No, no, we couldn't put you out like that."

Pilar finally looked at her. Her eyes flashed. "Don't be stubborn. The boy can't stay on the boat," she said flatly.

Antonia swallowed. "Thank you," she said. "That's incredibly kind."

The kettle whistled.

Pilar waved her off as she turned toward the stove. "But those mongrels of yours will have to stay in the barn."

Chapter Twenty-Six

Enzo asked David to meet him at Mark's barn early that morning. He wanted to work with him a little before the other players arrived. Over the past couple of days he'd noticed the young player making some reckless mistakes on the pitch. Enzo knew the kid was just trying to prove himself to his more experienced teammates, but he was jeopardizing not only his own safety, but also that of the ponies and the other players.

Enzo thought he would only make it worse if David was confronted in front of his teammates, so he quietly asked him to meet privately. He didn't want to embarrass him or put him on the defensive.

Mark's barns were brand-new. State of the art. Big enough for two hundred ponies, though Mark had only half that many at this point. He planned on filling the rest of the stalls by starting his own breeding program, based entirely on cloning.

Enzo couldn't help feeling a bit uneasy about being *piloto* to a team where no one really knew the ponies yet. He had no doubt the horses were all of excellent pedigree and in great health—Mark had gone on a multimillion-dollar buying spree that left the horse world buzzing in awe—but Enzo knew that each horse was an individual, and it was vital that the players knew their mounts.

It would take months, he thought, walking through the high-tech barns before he really knew these ponies like he had known the Del Campo horses.

He frowned, not wanting to think of the Del Campos. Not wanting to think of Noni...He knew it had been the right choice to move on, to cut off contact. But that didn't mean thoughts of her didn't crowd his mind almost every moment of every day.

And the nights were worse.

Enzo shook his head, trying to push his thoughts away as he opened one of the stalls. He needed to concentrate on this team now.

He had chosen a pony at random so that he could multitask by taking the measure of the new horse while he was working with David.

The pony was a piebald mare. The nameplate on her stall door said *Sadie*. She clamped down her tail and pricked her ears forward when he entered the stall. Enzo approached her slowly, knowing the signs of a nervous horse.

"There, there, *pequeña*." He kept his voice low and calm. She snorted unhappily as he advanced toward her. "No worries, little girl," he said as he slowly reached out his hand to touch her neck.

She shuddered a bit when he touched her, but he kept talking and started scratching along her neck and behind her ears. After a moment, he felt her relax enough under his hand that he was able to put on the lead and take her out of the stall to get groomed.

David had arrived by then, and Enzo told him to go pick a pony for today's lesson.

"Any one of them?" said David. He looked like a kid in a candy store who had just been told he could have whatever he wanted to eat.

"Your choice," answered Enzo, grinning. He liked to imagine how this must all feel to David, having gone from the streets of Philadelphia to being trained to be a top-tier, high-goal player.

David led out a little chestnut, and they groomed and tacked up side by side.

"Where are you staying?" asked Enzo as he tightened the girth around Sadie's belly.

"In a guest cottage on the estate," said David. "It's ridiculously dope. Mark had them built especially for the team. I'm surprised he didn't offer to put you up as well."

Enzo shrugged. "He did, but I have a place already. A little studio I'm renting."

David shook his head. "You're crazy, man. No way is it as nice as Stone's cottages. I have three bathrooms for just one person!"

Enzo laughed. "I'm good with one."

David suddenly looked serious. "Hey, Enzo, I don't think I ever thanked you for recommending me to Mark in the first place. He told me you were the one who sent him my way."

Enzo nodded. "I just told him you had talent. You did the rest."

David smiled shyly and glanced over at him. "Well, thanks for what you did. And thanks for working with me today. I know I've got some stuff to learn. This is a huge opportunity and I really don't want to blow it."

"You won't," Enzo assured him. He grinned at the kid. "Not as long as you listen to me anyway."

* * *

Noni walked back to the farmhouse in the dark, grateful for the cool evening breeze that wafted over her. She stretched, exhausted. Her days were longer than she liked now that she was doing both her farrier work and filling in for Enzo. She was usually dressed and on the pitch while it was still dark out, squeezing in some polo practice before Max woke up in the morning. After that, she went directly to the barn and started her work before the first feed. And this, she thought to herself unhappily, certainly wasn't the only time that she had arrived home well after Max's bedtime.

Noni felt that she was failing to connect with Max. There simply wasn't any time. She tried to make a point of coming back up for lunch every day, but even then, Max happily chattered away to Pilar and responded to any questions Antonia might have for him in shy, one-word answers. Pilar usually brought Max down in the late afternoon for a quick riding lesson or so he could watch Noni do smith work or supervise the horse training, but of course, Noni was always working when he was there. It was hardly quality time.

That said, Noni didn't know what she would have done without Pilar. She had thought it would be simple enough—that she would just bring Max along to the barn in the morning and keep him there with her as she worked. It had only taken her about an hour on that first day to realize what an idiotic idea that had been. Noni worked with fire and nails and hot metal—not exactly the safest environment for anyone, never mind a restless seven-year-old child. And if Max wasn't bored, he was hungry, and if he wasn't hungry, then he was underfoot or getting into things he shouldn't be. He was fascinated by the horses, but he had no experience with them, which meant that he didn't know the rules and hadn't yet developed a healthy respect for the big animals' more dangerous capabilities.

By the time Pilar had come down that first morning, bringing Max a light jacket since the day had been cooler than expected, Noni had already plucked him out of a stall, pulled him down from the hay loft, and pushed him away from the rear end of a pony just before he was backed over. He had been having a temper tantrum, literally kicking and screaming in Noni's arms as Pilar let herself into the barn.

Pilar shook her head and tsked when she saw them. "What's going on here?" She didn't look at Noni, just bent down to Max's level and addressed him instead. "*Ay,* what could be so terrible, *niño?*"

Max had stopped fussing at once. He looked warily at her, then up at Noni, and then back at Pilar.

"She won't let me ride the horses." His little lips still trembled. "She says that I need lessons, but I can do it myself."

Noni rolled her eyes. "Which was exactly what he was trying to do when I caught him trying to climb up Hex."

"Hmm," said Pilar, unsuccessfully hiding her smile. "Well, Noni is right, *señor.* You do need lessons. But"—she plucked him out of Noni's arms—"perhaps I can give you a first one right now." She looked over at Antonia. "*¿Bien?*" she said.

Noni nodded gratefully. "Yes. Thank you. I'm so behind."

Pilar snorted. "But of course you are."

Before Noni could respond, Pilar had turned and carried Max off to search out the oldest and most docile pony in the stable.

After that, Pilar had taken him home for lunch, and that night she had told Noni that he might as well stay with her during the days. She wasn't busy, and besides, Max was an easy child.

Noni knew that it was the smart thing to do, that it was the *only* thing to do, really. She couldn't have Max being endangered in the barn, and she couldn't miss work because her brothers were counting on her not to, but she felt a pang of loss when she agreed to it. She had imagined this time with Max in such a different way.

Still, Noni knew that she should be grateful to Pilar and she tried to remind herself of that gratitude every time Pilar was brusque or sarcastic or downright mean to her. Pilar obviously liked Max immensely, but she still treated Noni as an unwelcome stranger in her home.

It was starting to feel like two against one, thought Noni as she continued her walk up the road to the house. And then she was immediately ashamed of the thought. It was good that Max liked Pilar and Pilar doted on Max. Pilar was saving Noni's hide. No doubt about it. But still, deep down, she couldn't help feeling like this was just more proof of her inability to care for Max in the way he deserved.

Pilar was in the sunroom, wearing a trailing silver robe, her dogs at her feet. She was drinking a martini and reading a book. She barely looked up over her reading glasses when Noni came in.

"Is he asleep?" said Noni.

Pilar arched an eyebrow. "I would hope so. It's nearly ten thirty."

Noni sighed. "Things were crazy in the barn today. I thought I'd never get out of there."

Pilar nodded. "You miss Enzo," she said casually.

Noni blinked, not sure of what to say. Her heart suddenly felt like it was being squeezed.

Pilar looked up at her and her face softened a bit. "Oh," she said, "I did not mean it that way. I just meant that he kept things running smoothly. That you are doing his work, too."

Noni nodded, still unable to speak. She felt a knot rise in her throat.

Pilar sighed. "You had better sit down and let me make you a drink."

Pilar stood up as Noni sank down in the nearest chair. "I'm sorry," Noni said, shaking her head. "I don't know why I—"

Pilar waved her hand. "You do not have to explain," she said as she walked over to the sideboard. "In fact, I would prefer you did not." She freshened up her own drink and then grabbed a cut crystal glass and poured some Jameson in, neatly adding a little glug of water from a gleaming silver pitcher and then handing it to Noni.

Noni looked at her, surprised. "How did you know this was my drink?"

Pilar shrugged and sat back down in her chair. "I guess I have attended enough parties with you over the years to know what you drink." She raised her glass to Noni. "*Salud*."

Noni returned the salutation and took a large gulp. "Thank you," she said, savoring the warm liquor as it slid down her throat.

Pilar leaned back in her chair and closed her eyes for a moment. "Max had a good day," she said without opening her eyes. "He helped me in the garden this morning, and we went for a walk on the beach before dinner. He played in the water a bit."

Noni tried to smash down a pang of jealousy that unfurled

in her gut. She took another sip. "That sounds like a perfect day," she forced herself to say.

"I am thinking that he needs a different pony. And maybe a better teacher. He has a knack for riding, but he will not learn much riding old Tuffy. She can barely make it round the ring. If we really want him to learn, he should have someone teaching him who knows more than I do."

"Maybe I could teach him," said Noni, desperately trying to calculate when she could take that kind of time out of her day. Maybe if she didn't ever eat lunch...

Pilar shook her head. "No. That is impossible. You do not need another task in your day. I will find someone."

Noni nodded reluctantly. "I guess you're right," she said sulkily. And then, appalled at how ungrateful she sounded, she added, "I mean, thank you. Thank you for everything, Pilar. I couldn't do this without you."

Pilar sniffed. "No, I suppose you could not." She drained her martini and gestured for Noni's glass. "Let me freshen you up."

She crossed back over to the sideboard. "So, I am still confused as to how you know Max. He was your *hijastro*—your stepson?"

Noni looked away, avoiding Pilar's eyes. "Sort of. Jacob and I lived together while Max was still a baby."

"And where is Max's mother?"

"Dead," said Noni. "She died not long after he was born."

Pilar looked at her speculatively. "*Que tragedia*," she said, handing back her drink. "And so you took on another woman's child."

Antonia met her gaze. "I never thought of Max that way."

Pilar nodded and sipped her drink. "And then things ended, I presume?"

Antonia nodded. "Yes."

"Did you end it or did he?"

Antonia looked away again. "He did."

"And you were no longer in Max's life?"

Antonia shook her head quickly. "No."

"Was that your choice?"

She shook her head again.

Pilar was quiet for a moment.

"That must have been difficult," she said softly.

Noni shrugged, trying to keep herself calm.

"But now you and this Jacob...you are..."

"No. I mean, not yet. Maybe. I don't know."

"Hmph," said Pilar, sitting back down. "Bad timing. I always thought you would end up with Enzo."

Noni blinked. "Always?"

Pilar delicately lifted one shoulder in a shrug and reached to pet one of her dogs. "That poor *chico* has been in love with you for years."

"Love? No. Why would you think that?"

Pilar shot her an amused look. "Any woman with eyes could tell."

Noni laughed nervously and took a large gulp of her drink. "I think I should go to bed now," she said, standing up. "I'm exhausted. Thank you for the drink. Drinks, actually," she corrected herself.

Pilar gazed at her placidly. "*Buenas noches, hija*." She put her glasses back on and picked up her book.

"Good night," Noni said as she hurried from the room, still clutching her glass.

* * *

Antonia stood outside Max's room for a moment, feeling torn. She wanted to banish all her thoughts of Enzo before she looked in on the little boy.

She put down her drink on a hall table and closed her eyes for a moment.

Pilar had surely been teasing her with her talk of Enzo being in love. Sure, yes, they were good friends. Certainly they had discovered that sex between them was explosive, to say the least. But that didn't add up to love. Did it?

What did it matter, anyway? Whatever there had been between them was over now. She had Max to think about. Max and Jacob. She didn't think she could survive losing this boy for a second time.

She had made her choice.

She carefully turned the knob and pushed open the door. Max was staying in the spacious room that Alejandro and Sebastian had shared as boys. They could have had their own rooms, of course—there were plenty of bedrooms in this house—but Pilar had told her they had preferred to be together when they were little.

Pilar had laughed, recalling how indignant Sebastian had been when the teenage Alejandro had finally announced he wanted his own room.

The room had obviously not been changed since the boys were young. There were model airplanes hanging from fishing wire on the ceiling. Posters of various Argentine soccer players and polo stars. A bookshelf that ran from floor to ceiling crammed with picture books and comics.

Max was curled up in one of the two twin beds. It was warm in the room, and his cheeks were flushed a soft pink. He had kicked off his blankets. Noni opened the windows to let in the breeze and then pulled the covers back up over him. She stared longingly at him. Was there ever a more beautiful child? She reached to push a damp copper curl off his forehead but stilled her hand halfway there. She didn't want to wake him. She turned to go instead, stumbling over his shoes and almost falling.

"Damn it!" she hissed.

Max turned in the bed and briefly opened his eyes. "Noni?" he said sleepily. "Is it time to get up?"

Noni hurried back to the bed. "No, baby, it's still night-time."

He took her hand. "Will you stay with me until I go back asleep?"

She felt a thrill of joy to be asked. And then she laughed softly. Max had never liked to sleep alone. "Of course, buddy," she said.

She lay down on the bed next to him. He snuggled up against her, resting his head on her shoulder.

"Good night," he said, and closed his eyes.

She felt happy tears well up as she gently pushed back the soft curls from his brow and then dipped her face to his head, giving him a kiss and taking a deep breath of his warm, sweet scent, searching for that familiar baby smell.

She smiled. Not exactly the same, but pretty damned close.

Chapter Twenty-Seven

David was riding Sadie this morning, the little piebald mare that Enzo had taken out with him the other day. She was a spooky mount, not totally reliable, but fast and agile, and she loved the pitch. David had taken a shine to the horse while watching Enzo ride her and had taken her out several times in the few days since then, using her as a starting mount whenever he could.

Enzo considered the team as he watched them gallop together across the field. They were definitely getting better. Things were starting to gel. Raj had turned out to be a solid team captain. He had an easygoing nature that everyone liked, but his size and mastery on the pitch made it very clear who was in charge. Lachlan played great defense as number one, and David was only getting better and better as number two.

Even Mark had improved quite a bit. Though he was still light-years behind the other players as far as his skills went, his excitement about the game and his willingness to spoil his team with the latest gear, the best ponies, and practically anything else they wanted kept everyone in very good spirits, indeed.

Raj called a time-out and the team handed off their horses to the grooms. Mark took off his helmet and walked over to where Enzo was standing on the sidelines.

"How'd we look?" he said with a big grin. "Amazing, right? I mean, I can just feel it. We're gonna kick ass, don't you think?"

Enzo laughed. "Well, you are definitely making improvements," he said. "Lachlan might consider being a little less aggressive about—"

"When do you think we'll be ready to play?" Mark interrupted. "I want to play a game."

"Okay," said Enzo. "Against who, exactly?"

Mark shrugged. "I don't know. Anyone. How about La Victoria?"

"La Victoria?" said Enzo. "Well, first of all, they are down a player right now."

"All the better!" said Mark. "They'll have to get some chump they don't even know for Four."

Enzo smiled to himself, remembering when Mark was exactly that chump. "And second of all, the Del Campos are in England right now, scouting."

Mark shrugged. "We could fly the ponies out. Meet them in London."

Enzo laughed. "Mark, I hardly think there's reason to do that. I am certain that we could find some perfectly good players to scrimmage with around here."

Mark pouted. "I don't want perfectly good players. I want to try us out against the best. Do you think we could take them?"

"I think we would grind your little team into dust," came a cheerful voice from behind them. "And we would not even need a fourth player to do it."

Enzo and Mark turned around and saw Pilar Del Campo standing there, smiling wickedly. She wore gray linen slacks, a light blue sweater, and a pair of diamond studs in her ears so large that Enzo thought that even Mark must be impressed.

"Hello, Pilar," said Enzo, genuinely glad to see her.

"*¿Como estas?*" she said.

"*Bueno. ¿Y tu?*" returned Mark.

Pilar turned to him and laughed. "Who is teaching you *español*? Your accent is terrible."

"My wife," said Mark cheerfully. "And she agrees with you."

Pilar laughed again. "Go away, Mark," she said, waving him off. "I am still very angry with you for poaching our *piloto*. Poor Noni has had to work double time all summer because of you."

Enzo frowned.

"He came willingly," said Mark with a grin. "And Noni can take it. She's a big girl."

Pilar shooed him off. "*Andate.* I need to talk to this traitor."

"Okay, okay." Mark offered her a goodbye kiss on each cheek, which she calmly took as her royal due.

She tucked her arm into Enzo's. "Come, show me the new barns. I hear they're utterly vulgar."

Enzo smiled and nodded. "That is true."

He led her across the pitch toward the stable, slowing his walk so she could keep pace.

"Is Noni really working double time?" he said to her.

She nodded. "*Sí*, and it's all your fault. I still cannot believe you ran off like that." She shook her head. "Like a scared little boy afraid of a garter snake."

He shook his head. "It was just time for a change, Pilar."

She rolled her eyes. "Oh, do not bother to lie to me, *hombre*. I know exactly why you left. And I am right in saying that you were frightened. She scared the living daylights out of you."

"Who scared me?" he said, trying to sound casual. "I don't know what you are talking about."

"Who?" scoffed Pilar. "That little *bruja* with Carlos's eyes. That is who. I think you know the one—that girl you have been in love with since the day you met her?"

He looked sharply at her. "I don't know what—"

"*Ay, dios mio*, stop. You are really the most terrible liar." They reached the stable and Enzo pulled the door open for her. "Listen, I didn't come here just to talk to you about Noni. I actually need something else..."

* * *

Noni was examining the front hoof on Alejandro's favorite horse, Tango, when Pilar and Max came into the barn. Noni's dogs rushed to greet them.

"Noni!" shouted Max as he came running to the stall. "Pilar says I get a new teacher today!"

Noni carefully lowered Tango's foot back to the ground. "Oh?" she said, looking at Pilar. "You found someone? That was fast."

Pilar smiled. "Oh, *sí*, our little Max deserves the best, do you not think?"

"Yeah!" yelled Max, romping with the huskies. "The best!"

Noni grinned at him. "Of course." She looked back at Pilar. "Who is it?"

"Me, I'm afraid," said Enzo, stepping around the corner. He frowned at Pilar. "You forgot to mention that you did not actually run this by Noni first."

Noni's dogs left Max and rushed to Enzo, circling around him and whimpering in excitement as he petted them.

Pilar shrugged innocently. "I thought it would be a nice surprise."

Noni stared at Enzo, her heart in her throat.

"Pilar," said Enzo, "you know I would not have—"

Pilar cut him off. "Okay, *muy bien*. Max, this is Enzo. Enzo, this is Max. I will come back in an hour," and she started toward the exit.

"But—" said Noni.

"Max," called Pilar as she walked away, "when you come back up, you may bring Noni's dogs. They obviously like you and I imagine they are not too happy in the barn. If we keep them away from *mis perritos*, it should be okay."

Noni blinked in astonishment.

"Have fun with the lesson!" Pilar said over her shoulder as she slipped out the door.

Noni and Enzo stared at each other awkwardly.

Enzo shook his head. "She didn't—"

"I know," said Noni quickly.

"So . . . ," said Enzo.

"So . . . ," echoed Noni.

"So, where's my pony?" said Max.

They laughed. Noni was relieved to have something else to focus on. "Right, yes, fair enough. So, he's been riding Tuffy, but we think he's ready for someone a little more challenging. Actually"—she looked at Tango, who was standing patiently in the stall—"Tango might be a good choice."

Enzo reached past her to scratch the pony's nose. "Tango loves to teach," he said, smiling at the old horse.

He was standing so close to Noni now, they were almost touching. She took a step back, hyperaware of his presence.

"You want to ride Tango?" she said to Max.

"*¡Sí!*" he answered enthusiastically.

Enzo laughed. "Has Pilar been teaching you *español*, little man?"

"*Sí,*" said Max.

"Okay, then, *muy bien*. So, what's the first thing we need to do before we ride?"

Max instantly became serious. "Groom and tack up," he said.

Noni smiled as she clipped the lead onto Tango's halter and handed it to Enzo. "You see? He already knows what he's doing."

Enzo handed the lead to Max, who looked at him with huge eyes. "I get to lead?" he breathed.

Enzo gave him a nod. "Absolutely. Let's take this pony to the grooming station."

Noni watched them as they walked away together. Her dogs came into the stall with her and settled at her feet.

She had missed Enzo with a dull, steady ache every moment since he'd left, but suddenly, as he walked away from her, that dull ache twisted into something sharp and unbearable. Just seeing him again, the strong lines of his shoulders, his slow easy smile, the calm, competent way he acted with both Max and Tango, it simply took her breath away.

I love him, she thought to herself.

The words shot through her like a bullet. She dropped the small knife she had been holding to trim Tango's hooves and she felt her knees give way. She grabbed the wall for support.

"Oh no, no, no," she said out loud. "This is not good. This is not okay."

A passing groom gave her a questioning look. "*Está bien*, Noni?"

She tried to straighten up. "I'm...I'm fine, Luis. Thanks."

He nodded, but as soon as he had walked on, she slid down the wall and put her head on her knees. Her dogs shoved their noses at her, wagging their tails, worried. Noni felt like she might actually pass out.

The situation was impossible. Just when she felt like Max might really be back in her life, just when she thought she might see a future with Jacob...

She heard Max and Enzo laughing together down the hallway and closed her eyes, both savoring the sound and feeling like they were simply making things worse.

Why did Pilar have to meddle? Noni sat up, suddenly infused with righteous indignation. None of this would have happened if Pilar hadn't butted in!

She stuck her head out the stall door and watched as Max and Enzo headed out the back, toward the covered ring; then she scrambled up.

"Stay," she told the sisters as she headed the opposite direction out of the barn, toward the house.

Chapter Twenty-Eight

The boy had some natural talent, thought Enzo, as he watched Max bob up and down on Tango's back. They'd had to bring the stirrups all the way up, and his little legs barely straddled the pony's broad back, but he was keeping his balance and managing to hold on.

"Max," asked Enzo, "have you ridden a pony off its lead yet?"

"No," said Max, his big eyes shining under the visor of the black riding helmet he was wearing. "Can I?"

"I think maybe you are ready," said Enzo, unhooking the lead but keeping his hand on Tango's bridle. "Just put your hands like this." He placed the boy's hands on the reins. "Keep them soft. You do not want to pull hard or it will hurt Tango's mouth. Keep your back nice and straight, and when you want to go right or left, you can tug the reins just a tiny bit in the direction you want to go. Just a little tug—Tango will understand you. You do not need to pull hard."

Enzo could hear the boy's loud, excited breathing. "Okay, ready?"

Max nodded and Enzo let go of the bridle but kept close and walked alongside them just in case.

"I'm doing it!" said Max. He sounded amazed. "I'm steering the horse!"

"*¡Excellente!*" said Enzo. "Let's go once more around the ring and then we will quit for the day."

He watched the little boy with pleasure. His glasses were slipping down his nose, his cheeks were pink with excitement, his penny-bright curls stuck out from under the helmet, his skinny little arms were clenched and stiff and held uncomfortably high, but he had a huge smile plastered on his face.

Enzo's chest got tight. He could only imagine how hard it must have been for Noni to lose him, what a gift it must feel to have him back in her life.

He had refused Pilar at first when she had asked him to come give Max some lessons. He'd claimed he was too busy, suggested that one of the grooms start him out instead.

"Well, perhaps that would work if you had not abandoned us," said Pilar, carefully examining Mark's new stables, "but the grooms are all too busy picking up the slack you left behind."

Enzo exhaled in exasperation. "The barn has more than fifty workers, Pilar. I find it hard to believe that I have left such a huge hole."

"Well, you did," said Pilar shortly. "Besides, I want this boy to have a real teacher, not just a groom."

Enzo looked at her, puzzled. "But why do you care? Who is this boy to you?"

Pilar raised her eyebrows and shrugged. "I like him. He makes me laugh. Besides, this is not about who the boy is to me. This is about who the boy will be to you."

"What are you talking about?"

"When you and Noni reconcile. You will need to know Max."

Enzo made a noise of frustration. "We were never together, Pilar. How could there be a reconciliation?"

"Tsk tsk tsk, there you go, lying again."

Enzo turned to her. "Why are you getting involved? You don't even like Noni."

Pilar nodded, considering. "You know, that used to be true. I used to look at her and all I could see was Carlos. And I am not saying that it is very different now. Most of the time that is still the situation. I do not like her. But you know"—she paused and leaned over a stall door, calling a pony over to her with a little whistle—"when I was married and the boys were very young, Carlos was almost never around. He was always traveling, and even when he was home, he was usually out late or, you know, with one of his women."

Enzo blinked, surprised that Pilar would speak about this so casually.

She looked at him, amused. "What? You think I did not know he had women?" She blew out a little huff of air. "Believe me, I knew. Anyway, sometimes when I see Antonia with this boy, I see someone else. Not just Carlos. Maybe I see a little bit of myself, honestly. She works so hard and she worries so much, and she has no man to help her. And that reminds me of me. Which does not mean I like her. It just means maybe I understand her a little bit."

She looked at Enzo intently. "I had a long, unhappy marriage, Enzo. I think you know something about that, no? Unhappy marriages?"

Enzo smiled grimly in response.

"I stayed in that marriage because I loved my children and I thought I was doing what was best for them. And who knows?" She shrugged. "Maybe I was wrong to do that, or maybe I was right. But I was never happy, and I would not wish that on anyone. Not even someone I do not like."

She looked away from him, leaning over and scratching the pony's neck. *"Me comprendes?"*

"Yes," he said quietly. "I understand."

* * *

Antonia huffed up the drive, filled with self-righteous anger. Pilar had finally gone too far, and Noni was going to find her and tell her so. No holding back. No keeping her temper. The old woman had no right to meddle in Noni's life.

She crashed through the kitchen door, fully expecting to find Pilar in her usual place at the kitchen table, cup of tea in one hand, a book in the other.

But the kitchen was empty.

"Pilar?" Noni called. She checked the dining room and the sunroom. They were empty, too. She turned and walked up the stairs to the second floor.

Pilar's bedroom door was ajar, and Noni heard a rustle from inside. She thrust through it, not knocking. "Pilar, I have some things I need to—Oh my gosh, whoa!"

There were Pilar and Hendy, in bed, under the covers, looking up at her.

"Oh! Oh my God! Sorry! Sorry!" Noni threw herself out of the room and flattened herself against the hallway, covering her eyes with her hands. "I didn't see anything! I swear!" she called back, her voice cracking with embarrassment.

She heard Hendy's dry little chuckle, followed by Pilar's somewhat more exasperated voice. "Antonia," she said imperiously. "Come back in here."

Noni shook her head frantically. "That's okay! I'm good!"

Pilar sighed, annoyed. "Antonia. Come in. Now."

Noni squeezed her eyes shut, opened them again, grabbed the door frame, and then slowly inched her way back into the room. She kept her eyes on the floor. "Um. Hi," she said.

"*Ay, dios mio,*" muttered Pilar. "You can look at us. We are perfectly respectable."

Noni gradually slid her eyes back in their direction. They were both sitting up in bed, the blankets pulled up to their shoulders. Noni gave a sigh of relief. "I'm so sorry," she said again. "I had no idea that Hendy was here."

"He just got back," said Pilar, patting his arm affectionately. "It was a surprise."

"Straight off the plane," said Hendy happily.

"Does this mean that Jandro and Sebastian are home, too?" asked Noni.

"*Sí,*" said Pilar. "They're stopping in the city first, but they'll all be up later tonight."

"Are they home for good? Did they find a fourth player?"

Hendy shook his head. "We saw some excellent prospects but haven't made any offers just yet."

"So why did everyone come home, then?"

"Why, darling girl," said Hendy, "your thirtieth birthday is this weekend. Did you think we'd let you celebrate without us?"

Noni froze, a lump in her throat. "Oh, wow, you guys didn't have to do that. I mean—"

Pilar rolled her eyes. "Do you think I raised a couple of chimps? Of course your brothers will be here for your birthday. Do not make plans for Saturday. It's all been taken care of. Now, get out of my room."

"Okay," said Noni, "thanks." She knew she was grinning foolishly, but no one had ever planned a birthday party for her before. "I'll just, uh, keep Max around the barn for a bit longer."

Pilar shot a look at Hendy from under her lashes and gave him a sultry smile. "*Sí*, why don't you do that?"

Noni stepped out the door.

"Oh, Antonia!"

She stuck her head back in the room. "Yes?"

"What did you come storming into my bedroom for to begin with?"

"Ah," said Noni, still smiling, "nothing. It was nothing, Pilar."

Chapter Twenty-Nine

The house was full of family the next day: Alejandro and Georgia and little Tomás, Sebastian and Kat, and it looked like Hendy would be staying on as well.

Before breakfast, Noni, afraid the house might be too crowded, offered to take Max and find another place to stay.

Pilar just glared at her in response.

"You think my home cannot accommodate nine people? In 1932, this house once comfortably boarded all the members of the U.S. Senate and ten congressmen on top of that. My dining room table alone seats twenty-five and that is without the extra leaf. Now stop being ridiculous and go fetch Max before your *café con leche* gets cold."

Max was racing around his room with four-year-old Tomás. They were sharing the room.

"Just like *Tío* Sebastian and *Papí* used to," said Tomás, who was obviously quite enamored with the older boy. "It's like we are brothers, too!"

Antonia smiled nervously at that description. "Time to get dressed, Max," she said. "Pilar has breakfast on the table."

Max obediently went to the bureau and pulled out a T-shirt and shorts. He unself-consciously took off his pajamas and stood in his underwear for a moment. Noni felt a pang in her heart at the sight of his skinny little bare chest. He looked like a featherless baby bird.

"Noni," he said, "Tomás calls Pilar *Abuela*. Should I call her that, too?"

"What? Oh no, that means 'grandma.' Pilar isn't your grandma. Put your clothes on, honey."

Max slowly pulled on his shirt and shorts. "Well, she kind of is, isn't she? I mean, she is the mom of your brothers, and you are kind of my mom, right? Since my real mom is dead."

Noni took a deep breath. "Oh. Oh, buddy. It's a little more complicated than that."

"I mean, there's also Mama Cecelia. She's kind of my mom, too."

Noni froze. "Wait, who?"

Max struggled to zip up his shorts. "Mama Cecelia. Daddy and I lived with her for a long time." He got the zipper up. "But we don't anymore."

"Huh," said Noni, but before she could pursue the conversation further, Sebastian swept in and grabbed both boys up into his arms. "*¡Desayuno!* Come on, *muchachos*! *Abuela* says breakfast is getting cold!"

They both yelled in glee, happily pounding Sebastian on the head and shoulders as he carried them out of the room.

Noni hesitated in the doorway for a moment.

"You too, Noni," Seb called back to her. "*Mamá* baked *media lunas*. I can't remember the last time she made such a fuss."

Noni smiled and went downstairs.

* * *

Enzo ate breakfast on the patio of a café in the village, content to sit with his book and coffee and bask in the perfect Hamptons weather. Mark had gone back to California for a business trip, and much to Enzo's chagrin, he had given the entire team the long weekend off while he was gone.

"What?" he'd said when Enzo had tried to suggest they could practice without him. "Practice without the patron? Come on, that's crazy talk!" He'd winked at Enzo. "Besides, they're all already so much better than me. Last thing I need is them improving even more while I'm gone."

The waiter brought Enzo his goat cheese and spinach omelet and he put down his book. He watched the street as he ate. He thought he'd never get used to the sight of all the Ferraris and Porsches and Maseratis that inched by in the slow Hamptons traffic. The summer people were tanned, toned, and casually (if impeccably) dressed and all seemed to drive cars more suited to Kuwaiti princes (of which there were actually more than a few) than the laid-back villagers they liked to pretend to be.

Still, Enzo was comfortable here. Aside from the cars, it was actually less flashy than Wellington. He liked the little villages and their immaculate beaches. He liked the pretty shingled cottages and neat little dooryard gardens. He liked that he never had a bad meal, and he liked the sunset over the sound and the lively nightlife. And people knew horses here, of course. Which was always a good thing.

He finished his breakfast and looked at his watch. Only nine in the morning. He considered what he wanted to do with the rest of his day. He wasn't used to having this kind of free time on his hands.

Pilar had invited him to Noni's birthday party on Saturday and he was still deciding whether he'd go. Antonia had been strangely distant with him after Max's lesson the day before. He'd told her how well Max had done, and she had just smiled and nodded politely, then asked Max if he wanted to go into the village with her to get some ice cream, thanked Enzo, and left. It didn't even seem to occur to her to invite him along.

He wondered if this was how it would have to be with them from now on—always at arm's length.

Enzo paid his bill and decided that whether he was going to the party or not, he should buy Noni a gift. It was her thirtieth birthday, after all, and she was, if nothing else, still his friend.

At least, he thought with a little shiver, he hoped that to be true.

Chapter Thirty

Breakfast was loud and chaotic and messy and completely wonderful. Pilar, along with Liz, the chef from the yacht, had cooked up an elaborate meal of Argentine pastries and fresh fruit, eggs prepared to order, and succulent sausages from the farm down the road. The *maté* was poured and platter after platter of food passed around the table as Sebastian and Alejandro entertained everyone with stories of all the terrible players they had seen in London.

"Oh!" laughed Sebastian. "Jandro, tell him about that fat Scot who fell off his pony at the Ascot Park game. I thought he must have been a patron—no offense, Hendy—but no, he was a three goal player!"

"I think his *papá* bought him the team," said Alejandro with a grin. He was dandling Tomás on one knee and trying to get him to eat a forkful of eggs.

"No," said Georgia, who was seven months pregnant and still in her pajamas, "I asked around. It turns out he's very closely related to the queen. Did you know that he offered to fund the team in full if we would let him on?"

Sebastian looked at his brother, one eyebrow raised. "You failed to mention this to me, *hermano*."

Alejandro shrugged. "If you truly want to hand the team over to a fat Scot who falls off his horse, I am more than willing to discuss it."

Both of Noni's dogs were lying under the table. One growled at Pilar's dogs, which were sitting patiently by the kitchen door.

"¡*Basta!*" said Pilar firmly.

To Noni's astonishment, the dog stopped growling. Pilar reached down and scratched her ear. "They just need a firm hand," she said casually.

"So, Kat," said Hendy, "did you finish your script?"

Kat, Sebastian's wife, laughed. "Don't you know it's impolite to ask a writer if she's finished yet? You might as well ask me what I weigh."

"Sixty-eight kilos," said Sebastian, deadpan.

Kat shot him a deadly look and hit him with her napkin.

Noni sighed happily. It was everything she had always dreamed it would be. She'd had meals with her brothers and their families before, of course, but never in their home like this, and never with Pilar.

Noni realized that Pilar was the heart of everything. She joined in occasionally, but always with an eye to making sure that the food was kept warm and that there was a seemingly endless supply of it, that the table was set beautifully, that there were fresh flowers and linen napkins, that the coffee was served hot.

Max spilled his juice and Pilar had it wiped up so quickly that half the table didn't even notice it had happened.

Pilar was happy, thought Noni. She was happy in a way that Noni had never seen from her before. She beamed at her sons and their wives, she cooed over Tomás and Max, and every so often she would sneak her hand over to Hendy and gently squeeze his arm or rest her hand on his. When Noni told a little story about one of the ponies in the barn that seemed to have become emotionally attached to a billy goat, she was shocked to look across the table and see that Pilar was smiling rather fondly at her.

Granted, Pilar immediately followed up that smile by sharply saying that Noni should know better than to let prized ponies mix with an animal that had horns. But she had, at least for a moment, definitely smiled at Noni.

The only thing missing was Enzo. Noni could just imagine him at the table, fitting in so easily with everyone else. He would play with the children and tease her brothers and gallantly compliment Pilar's cooking. He would ask Alejandro about Valentina's budding dance career in California. He would ask after Hendy's knee, question Georgia about the health of the ponies, and make Kat tell all the latest Hollywood gossip. Noni imagined him turning to her and giving her that slow, devastating smile—the one that melted her from the inside out, the one that held so much promise for later, once he got her alone.

Antonia sighed to herself, longing for him.

Then her eyes rested on Max as he munched on a *media luna* pastry and happily gazed around the table, a smear of chocolate on his cheek.

Jacob needed to have a place at this table, she reminded herself. Not Enzo.

She sat for a moment, trying and momentarily failing to imagine how Jacob would fit in.

She shook her head. He would be fine, she reassured herself. Everyone always liked Jacob. He was a great father, a good man, and a brilliant artist. What was not to like?

After breakfast, Jandro and Georgia wanted to go see the

ponies, and Sebastian, Kat, and Pilar offered to take the boys down to the beach. Noni decided she would go to the barn first and then join up with everyone at the beach.

"Oh, and tomorrow, Noni," said Georgia before they all left, "Pilar has instructed Kat and me to get you out of the house. So we've booked a spa day."

"Women only," said Kat firmly as Sebastian opened his mouth and then shut it, a disappointed look on his face.

"Spa in the morning, and then we'll shop for something to wear for the party. Our treat," said Georgia.

Noni shook her head. "Aw, come on. You guys don't have to do all that."

"Yes, they do," said Pilar. "I need you out of the house for preparations."

"What about Max?" said Noni.

"He's going to help me," said Pilar.

"Oh?" said Noni, lightly poking Max in the shoulder. "Did you know about this all along?"

Max giggled. "I'm very good at keeping secrets," he said.

The group was just heading out the kitchen door when the front doorbell rang.

Pilar wrinkled her forehead. "Who could that be?"

The housekeeper slipped out to see who it was and the little boys followed.

In a moment they heard Max's joyful shout. "Dad!" he yelped. "Dad, you're back!"

* * *

Enzo had looked all over town, in and out of every little boutique and shop, trying to find the right gift for Noni, but nothing had seemed quite right.

It wasn't that there weren't beautiful things. This was the Hamptons—there were *nothing* but beautiful things all around him. Carefully cultivated, one-of-a-kind, immaculately arranged, beautiful things. With equally beautiful people offering them for sale.

It didn't help that he knew, as of tomorrow, Noni would be heir to hundreds of millions of dollars and could surely buy any little thing that caught her eye here or anywhere else.

Chocolates or flowers wouldn't be enough, a bottle of good Scotch was too impersonal, lingerie too painfully intimate...He supposed jewelry was the answer—a necklace or a bracelet, but he didn't see anything he could imagine her truly loving.

He wished he could take her for a vacation somewhere to celebrate. He imagined flying her to Paris, staying in a little flat with a view of the Seine. Or Venice, where they could get lost among the canals. Or even better, home to Argentina, where he could show her the country that he loved so well...

The common thing among all these daydreams was that he had her to himself. That it was just him and her—alone again. Nothing to distract them. Nothing to keep them apart. He felt that he would give all that he had for that possibility.

Hell, he thought, he would give all that he had for just five more minutes under the rainy boardwalk, for a moment or two in her arms again, anywhere.

He wandered into an antique shop, surprised to see how dusty and overstuffed the place was. Unlike the minimalist boutiques he'd been shopping in, this place felt as though, if he picked up even one thing, he might create a domino effect and knock over an entire store's worth of teetering goods.

The elderly salesclerk didn't even look up from the magazine she was thumbing through when he passed by.

He examined some ancient books, sneezing from the dust and wiping his now grimy hands off on his jeans when he was done handling them. He flipped through some old records, giving up when he realized that Noni wouldn't have a record player. He peered through a smeared display case of jewelry, hoping to find a literal diamond in the rough.

He almost gave up after being startled by a large orange cat that sprang out at him, hissing, when he lifted an old quilt off a sprung horsehair couch. He carefully sidestepped the angry feline and had just turned to go when he saw it, stacked in a corner among some old umbrellas and carved wooden canes...

The perfect present.

Chapter Thirty-One

When Jacob came into the kitchen with Max in his arms, Noni noticed a little twinge in her stomach that felt uncomfortably like disappointment.

He was wearing a black T-shirt under a somewhat wrinkled blue dress shirt. He looked tired and a bit wary, glancing nervously at her brothers, who flanked her on either side.

She took a deep breath and smiled, trying to push down her uneasy feelings. "Jacob!" she said. "You're back so early!"

He smiled at her, putting Max down with a little pat on his head. "I finished up early so I could be back for your birthday."

Noni looked at Pilar, who shook her head. "I certainly did not tell him."

"No, Benny mentioned it to me"—he winked at Noni—"but I'm sure I would have remembered the date, anyway." He took a step closer, lowering his voice. "Actually, I was hoping to whisk you away for the weekend. I thought maybe—"

"No, no," said Pilar loudly. "That will not do at all. Noni

is having a party here." She waited a very long beat before she reluctantly added, "Which I suppose you can come to if you wish."

"Oh," said Jacob, smiling, "well, of course. That's very kind of you to offer."

Pilar shrugged. "I'm going to the beach. Who is coming?"

"Me!" yelled Tomás.

Max looked at his father. "Can we, Daddy?"

"I was hoping to talk to Noni a bit, Max, but maybe later we—"

"I will take him," said Pilar. She looked at everyone else. "Don't you all have somewhere to be?"

"Um, thank you!" called out Jacob as Pilar herded everyone out the back door. Pilar, followed by all four dogs, slammed the door behind her without answering.

He looked at Noni. "Wow, Benny wasn't kidding about Pilar. She's a formidable old thing."

Noni frowned. "My mom doesn't know Pilar at all. I don't know why she insists on acting like she does."

"Anyway"—he caught her in a hug—"I can't believe we're finally alone."

She stepped back gently. "Actually, we're not." She looked over at the Liz, who gave her a smile and a wink as she was carrying in the breakfast dishes to the kitchen. "Why don't we go out to the gardens?"

* * *

It was a hot and muggy day. The air felt saturated, and the roses and lilies were looking sulky and wilted. Their scent hung heavy on the air.

As she led Jacob down the path, Noni chattered mindlessly, trying to cover up her uneasy feelings. "Max has been learning to ride," she said, "and Enzo says he's actually really good."

Jacob frowned. "Horseback riding? That seems awfully dangerous."

"Oh no, we kept him on the safest ponies, and either Pilar or Enzo was always with him, plus he always wore a helmet."

His frown deepened. "Pilar and Enzo? Where were you?"

"Well, I had to work. But don't worry, they both really liked Max and—"

He cut her off. "Listen." He took her hand. "We can talk about Max later. Right now I just want to talk about us."

She met his eyes and he smiled at her, lightly touching her face with his fingertips. "I missed you so much, Noni. Even just these few days away . . . it feels like a miracle that you're back in my life again."

She nodded, thinking of Max.

"You don't really need to go to this party, do you?"

His hand was warm against her skin. "Pilar's party?"

"I have a much better idea. In fact, it's all planned out." He took a large envelope out of his jacket and handed it to her. "Happy birthday."

She stared at the envelope for a moment.

"Open it," he encouraged her.

She did. In it was three airplane tickets.

He grinned. "We're going to Mexico. Just you, me, and Max. For a birthday celebration. It's all planned. We leave tonight."

She gaped at him. "What?"

"There's a little seaside town called San Blas. You'll love it. Super romantic. I figured we can stay at least a week or two, maybe longer if we really like it—"

She thrust the tickets back at him. "No. I mean, I'm sorry, but I can't. I have a job, Jacob. I can't just up and leave with no notice. Besides, Pilar has already been planning, and my brothers and their families flew all the way back from London to be here for me. I'm not just going to take off at the last minute."

He shook his head. "I don't want to ruin anyone's plans, but I just thought this would be good for us. Give us a chance to have some time together. A chance to get to know each other again. Let Max see what it's like to have a real family."

She blinked, conflicted. "That sounds lovely. It really does. And I definitely want that. But can't we go after the party? Maybe a few weeks from now? I need to make sure that Jandro and Sebastian have someone to cover the stables. You see, Enzo quit and I've been picking up the slack while everyone was in London. I can't just leave them without warning."

Jacob shook his head. "Listen to you. You sound like their slave. Why are you at the beck and call of your half brothers?"

She stepped back, stung. "I'm not. I work for them. They pay me. And like any other job, I can't just decide to go on vacation on a whim without checking in first. Plus, I'm not about to run out on a party that has already been planned for me. That would be awfully rude."

She didn't want to tell him that it was the first time anyone had ever planned a birthday party for her. In fact, she remembered the year she had spent with him; he had missed her birthday altogether.

He looked away and seemed to collect himself and then turned back to her and gave her a dazzling smile. "Okay. I get it. I'm sorry. I was being selfish. I just...just wanted you to myself, you know? But hey, at the very least, have dinner with me tonight. I'm staying at a friend's place on Shelter Island while they're out of town."

"Yes, okay," she agreed, relieved that he'd stopped pressing. She took his hand. "I'm sorry that I sound so ungrateful. It's an amazing gift. Thank you. I'm sure we can change the tickets for later, right?"

He nodded. "Absolutely."

She took a deep breath and then stood on her tiptoes and kissed his cheek.

He caught her face in his hand before she pulled away and bent eagerly to her mouth.

She kissed him back. She felt she had to. She thought of Max. She thought of the family they could have. The family they used to be.

She smelled the cloying scent of overwarmed flowers. She felt Jacob's tongue, rough in her mouth, his hand slowly sliding down her back...

He broke the kiss and looked into her eyes, smiled at her and stroked her cheek. "I missed you so much," he whispered.

She closed her eyes.

She would not let herself think of Enzo.

* * *

Enzo had ended up at the stables anyway, exercising a couple of the horses he didn't know well enough yet. He was just putting the last one into its stall for the night when his phone rang. It was David.

"Enzo? Where are you?"

There was music and laughter in the background.

"I'm at the stables. Where are *you?*" said Enzo, amused.

"I knew it! I knew it! Raj, you owe me twenty bucks! He's at the barn! Man, Enzo, we're supposed to be on vacation! Come on, we're at this great bar on Shelter Island—it's right on the beach. Come join us."

Enzo shook his head. "Are you even legal to drink, David?"

David laughed. "Come on, man, I'm twenty-four!"

Enzo smiled. "I thought you were younger."

"Come oooon! Wait...here. Raj wants to talk to you."

Enzo listened as the phone got shuffled around. Raj's deep, accented voice came on.

"Enzo, you must come. I need you. I think I am the oldest person in the place by a decade at least."

Enzo laughed. "That's what you get for bar hopping with a bunch of kids."

"Indeed. However, as captain of the team, I must remind you that a team is not made entirely on the field. There are other ways of bonding."

"Like flaming tequila shooters!" yelled Lachlan in his thick Australian accent.

"That sounds like a nightmare," said Enzo.

Raj laughed. "I promise you will not have to drink any tequila shooters. Come and join us. For the team."

"For the team!" shouted Mark and Lachlan together in the background.

Enzo groaned. "Fine. Text me the address."

He hung up the phone and did one last tuck check before he left for the night. Mark had more than enough staff who lived on site, so Enzo didn't have to close down the barn, but he liked to be sure that everything was under control.

It was still light out when he got into his truck. As he drove to the Shelter Island Ferry, he turned off his air-conditioning and rolled down his windows. The best thing about being near the beach was that even when the days turned hot and humid, the air always cooled down in the evening.

The line for the ferry was surprisingly short for a Friday night, but Shelter Island wasn't exactly the most popular spot for nightlife. The island was one of the quieter, less developed parts of the Hamptons. The gentle hills and forested swaths of land made it feel a step or two apart from some of the more crowded villages and towns. He wondered how his rambunctious teammates had ended up out there.

He parked his truck on the little ferry and then got out to stand at the front of the boat and enjoy the view. The sun was lower now, and the light danced across the water in glittering sparks. The sea air was cool against his face, and, not for the first time, Enzo reminded himself that he was a very lucky man.

He had a job he loved and he got to work with the kind of horseflesh that he'd only dreamed about growing up in Argentina. The ponies he trained were world class, and it was a pleasure to just be near them. He lived in beautiful places all over the world. He made more than enough money—a ridiculous amount, actually, now that Mark was paying his salary. And it was easy to live well, to make sure his mother was taken care of, and still put a good chunk aside every month.

He watched the dark forested shore loom ahead as the ferry skipped through the water, and frowned. What more could a man ask for? he challenged himself. What more could a man want?

Her onyx eyes swam up into his head like a vision. Her silky hair. Her creamy shoulders. Her soft lips...

He shook it off.

All at once, he was glad that he had agreed to come out and drink.

Chapter Thirty-Two

The house Jacob was staying in was exquisite. A gray and white three-story Greek revival perched high up on a hill over the sound. They parked on the circular driveway and stood side by side for a moment, taking in the incredible view of the sunset reflecting off the water.

"The guy who owns this place is a Wall Street broker," said Jacob to Noni as he unlocked the front door, "but he has an amazing art collection. He actually has two pieces from my Fire series in the garden. You remember those?"

Noni nodded, recalling the huge, intricate steel and iron orbs that had a hollow in the center for bonfires. She had helped Jacob forge them.

"Those were some of my favorites," she said. "I'd like to see them again."

"I'll show them to you later. We can come back after dinner and light a bonfire or two."

They were alone in the house. Max had begged to stay the night at Pilar's again, wanting to continue the fun he was having with Tomás. Pilar had said she didn't mind, that she wanted Max to be there in the morning to help her get started on the party, anyway.

The house was as beautiful inside as it was out. Hushed and opulent, with gleaming dark wood floors and warm halos and pinpricks of light designed to show off the breathtaking collection of art on the walls.

An appreciation and knowledge of art were among the few things that Noni was grateful that Benny had given her. The only times she could really remember her mother paying her any real attention was when she took Noni through the countless museums and galleries, big and small, in all the towns that they had lived in through the years.

Some of Noni's best memories were the mornings when she would wake up and find her mother at the kitchen table, dressed and waiting, a cigarette in one hand and a cup of coffee in the other. She would hand Noni a glass of juice and announce that she was skipping school, that there was something she wanted her to see.

And Noni saw amazing things. It was surprising what exhibits passed through even the most out-of-the-way places. They saw Picasso sketches and a lesser Caravaggio; she stood inside a Louise Bourgeois spider and found an entire collection of Chagalls in a tiny town the artist briefly lived in.

If you knew where to look, Benny had told her, you could always find something worth seeing. And Benny always knew where to look.

For the longest time, Noni had assumed she would be an artist because Benny assumed she would be an artist. And, she had to admit, she did have some talent. Perhaps even more than Benny did.

However, no matter what medium Antonia tried—watercolor, oils, sculpting, ceramics—it always felt like work. She always felt like she was struggling against something, pushing at a stone that she could never quite budge.

Working with Jacob at the forge was the closest she had come to really liking the work she was doing, but even then it didn't feel like a calling or a passion. More like an interesting hobby.

It hadn't been until she had combined the forge with the ponies that something had clicked for her. That she knew she had finally found what was she was meant to do.

The only other time she'd felt that sensation was the first time she'd played a game of polo, smashing that ball across the pitch as her pony ran at full tilt under her.

Another calling—another passion—she had realized at once.

"Take a look around," said Jacob. "I'm just going to change real quick."

He turned up a wide staircase, and Noni watched as he climbed, objectively admiring his broad back and slim waist and the way his wheat-colored hair curled a little at the ends.

There was no doubt that he was a very handsome man, she reminded herself as he reached the top of the stairs and disappeared down the hallway.

She went into the kitchen to get a glass of water and wrinkled her nose when she saw all the high-tech gleaming stainless steel surfaces. The stove alone must have cost tens of thousands of dollars, she thought, running her hand over it. She much preferred Pilar's kitchen, with its warm wood counters, herringbone brick floors, and deep porcelain farmhouse sink.

Noni couldn't imagine anyone cooking in this kitchen, never mind actually sitting down to enjoy a meal.

She smiled as she recalled breakfast that morning, with everyone crowded around Pilar's big farm table.

Noni drank her water and then wandered back out into

the great room, peering closely at a painting above the fireplace. "Oh my God. It's a Modigliani," she breathed. "And a good one."

Jacob came back downstairs and stood next to her. "Holy shit," he said. He sounded awed. "Can you imagine? Actually owning one? You probably could, you know, after tomorrow."

She turned to him, surprised. "You know about that?"

His shrugged. "Your mom mentioned it to me." He grinned at her and raised his eyebrows. "Antonia Black, heiress. Very fancy." He nudged her with his shoulder. "What do you say? Will you buy me a Modigliani or two?"

She snorted and rolled her eyes. "Absolutely not," she said, laughing in spite of herself.

They stood in front of the painting a moment longer, just taking it in, and Noni relaxed a little. This felt nice, she thought, admiring this beautiful thing together. She slipped her hand into Jacob's and squeezed.

He turned to her and smiled. "I want to show you everything he has. There's a crazy Vermeer in his bedroom and I swear to God, he keeps four Kandinskys in his home gym. But we're going to be late for our reservation if we don't leave now. I thought we could walk. It's just down the hill."

* * *

The restaurant was packed when Enzo arrived and he was grateful that his teammates had come earlier and commandeered a table. The place was directly across the street from the beach, and most of the seating was outside, with small café tables lining the road and an open-air central courtyard inside, where there were several fire pits surrounded by low tables and lushly upholstered wicker couches and chairs.

As Raj had promised, the crowd was young. Young, beautiful, and scantily dressed, thought Enzo as he wound his way to the fireside space where David was waving him over.

"Hey, man!" yelled David over the throbbing music. "You made it!"

Enzo clasped hands with each of his teammates in turn.

David looked the most at home in the bar. He was a good-looking kid, and all his time working as a groom had given him a strong physique. He wore a white linen shirt, open halfway down his sculpted cocoa-colored chest, and loose white jeans. A style, Enzo smiled to think, copied from all of David's time working for the Del Campos. This was the uniform that Sebastian and Alejandro both tended to wear at their more casual functions.

Lachlan was a little more dressed down—in a red V-neck tee and faded jeans, his sandy hair carefully mussed, his sleeve of tattoos proudly displayed. And Raj was a little more dressed up, in a blue and white striped button-down, cut close enough to show off his formidable muscles. He also wore small gold hoops in his ears.

More than one young lady was looking their way. They were a fine-looking team.

"Here, mate!" said Lachlan, pushing a shot glass toward Enzo as he took his seat. "I saved you a shooter!" He frowned at it. "It's not on fire anymore, but I bet I could get it going again if you want."

Enzo almost refused it, but then thought, *Why not? What the hell.*

"No fire necessary," he said, and gulped it down.

The alcohol burned a trail down his throat and warmed his stomach as the rest of his teammates cheered him on.

* * *

The waitress showed Noni and Jacob to an ocean-side table. The restaurant was packed with the rich, privileged, and beautiful. Even the busboys were model-level gorgeous.

Antonia looked around at all the young partiers throwing back drinks and preening for each other. For a moment, she was almost glad that she had grown up poor. Certainly, going without had been hard in its own way, but getting to know her brothers had disabused her of the notion that the rich were necessarily happier than anyone else, and living a life like this, hyperaware of how you looked, what you wore, who you were with, where you were seen…it just seemed exhausting. She silently swore to herself that no matter how much money she had, she would never get sucked into this trap.

"It's nice, right?" said Jacob, unfolding his napkin and putting it into his lap. "Fun?"

Noni looked at him and felt rebuked. What was her problem? She was such a snob. All these people were just trying to have a good time on a Friday night. She didn't have to break it down into class warfare.

Still, when she looked at the drink menu and realized that they were charging twenty dollars for a glass of what she knew to be not-so-great white wine, she couldn't help but inwardly roll her eyes.

"It's a million-dollar view," she finally said. And it was. The sun was hanging low over the sound, with lazily drifting sailboats silhouetted against a dozen different shades of gold, pink, and lavender in the sky. The beach was a vast expanse of sand as fine and white as powdered sugar, punctuated by bright yellow sun umbrellas and tan, beautiful people strolling along in various states of undress.

She had to admit, once their overpriced cocktails and plates of *moules-frites* had arrived, it *was* fun in its own way. The food, the drinks, the beach, the view, the crowd, even the good-looking man smiling fondly at her across the table...who was she to complain?

She relaxed and happily bit into a French fry.

"Max said he had a really good time with you while I was gone," said Jacob.

Noni smiled. "More like a good time with Pilar. I was working so much I hardly saw him, but she seemed more than happy to hang out with him. They really hit it off."

Jacob raised his eyebrows. "Well, we're lucky that she could help out. I didn't realize you'd be working so much."

"Neither did I," said Noni, sipping her drink, "but when Enzo left, there was a lot to do."

Jacob nodded and dragged a fry through the sauce on his plate. "I feel bad that I saddled you with a kid when you had so much going on."

Noni shook her head. "No, no. I wanted to have him. I'm so glad I got the chance to see him again!"

He nodded again. "Why did Enzo quit, by the way? That seemed pretty sudden."

Noni bit her lip, not sure whether she was ready to go there just yet. But, she thought, if she wanted a healthy relationship with Jacob, she had to be honest.

"Well, you know that Enzo and I were...involved, right? I mean, just for a little while."

Jacob's blue eyes snapped a little. "It seemed that way to me, yes."

"When things ended, it was...difficult. I think he just felt like it might be awkward for him to stay on as *piloto* for my family."

Jacob cocked his head. "Do you really think of the Del Campos as your family, Noni? I mean, I don't remember you ever mentioning your brothers when I knew you."

Antonia felt herself color. She reached for her drink. "I didn't...like to talk about them back then. We didn't have a relationship yet. But we do now."

"And Pilar? Benny said that she's been nothing but awful to you."

"Well, I mean"—she smiled to herself—"Pilar's not an easy person, but lately it's been...different." She ran her finger along the edge of her plate. "It's funny, but I actually think having Max around has helped."

He laid his hand over hers. "I'm glad for you if that's true, but I guess I just hoped that you and Max would have the chance to spend some real time together."

She looked at his hand on hers and sighed. "Jacob, I want that, too. I can't tell you what it means to me to see him again. It's been...wonderful. He's an amazing kid, and I've missed him so, so much. There hasn't been a day since you left that I haven't thought of him. But...I have to be honest, I don't know if I can be the person you want me to be for him."

He opened his mouth to speak, but she interrupted.

"It's not that I don't want to. I do. I want it more than anything. It's just..." She felt her voice catch. "I don't know if I'm even capable of it. I don't know that I can be a mother. I mean, you told me yourself—I'm not built that way."

He tightened his hand on hers and closed his eyes for a moment. "Antonia." His voice was low. "There's something I have to tell you."

He opened his eyes and looked at her.

"When Max and I left, I know I told you that it was your

fault and that I didn't feel like he was safe with you. I know I blamed you for him getting sick. I know I did all that. But the truth is"—he looked away—"I was going to leave you anyway."

She looked at him, confused. "What?"

"I'd met someone. Long before that night. I'd been seeing her for a while. So when he got sick, I mean, I really was scared and angry, of course. That wasn't an act. He almost died. But what happened that night—it could have happened to anyone, and I knew that. I knew you were just so exhausted. I was so scared to tell you I wanted to leave. You'd been so incredible, helping me through Astrid's death, taking care of Max. I felt like such an asshole. I didn't know how to be honest. So when all that went down, it just seemed like an opportunity, the easiest way, I guess, to avoid having to tell you about Cecelia. I thought maybe it would hurt you less if you didn't know about her."

She tugged her hand out from under his. She felt like she couldn't breathe. "So you let me think that it was my fault...that I didn't deserve to be a mother to Max?"

"I know. It was the wrong thing to do. I realize that now. I was stupid and I was scared and I was fucked up. I mean, it had been such a terrible year with Astrid using again, and then when I lost her...I wasn't myself. And you were really young, Noni. You were great with Max, you were, but you were practically a kid. That scared me."

Antonia felt dizzy.

"And I'm not proud of his, but honestly, Cecelia was wealthy. Like, really wealthy. I knew that if I was with her, it would just be...easier. I knew that I'd be able to stop teaching, to concentrate fully on my art. And Max could go to good schools and be taken care of."

She pushed away from the table, started to get up, but he grabbed at her arm.

"I was wrong, Noni. I was so, so wrong. Nothing was easier with Cecelia. She was cold. She was disconnected. She believed in my talent—she helped me make it in the art world, but I don't think she ever really loved Max. She just thought he was in the way, you know? She hired all these nannies and she started talking about sending him away to boarding school...I just couldn't do that. I could never do that to him. He's my son. So we left her. And then I was back in the States, and I ran into your mom, and when I saw you again...it just seemed like kismet, you know? I realized what a huge mistake I had made. That you had really loved him. That you loved me...and I just threw that away."

He looked up at her, imploring. "I never meant to hurt you, Noni. I swear. I made a mistake. A horrible mistake. And I just...I just want to make it right."

She stood for a moment, her breath caught in her throat. "I...I need a moment." She stumbled backward.

He stood up. "Noni—"

She put her hand out. "No, don't. I just...I'm going to the bathroom for a second, okay? I promise, I'll come back. But I need a second alone."

He looked unsure but nodded as she backed away.

Chapter Thirty-Three

Enzo had to admit, he was enjoying himself. After that first shot, he'd ordered a couple of vodka and sodas, trying not to notice the inflated price of the drinks. His teammates were fun. Raj had a million and one amazing stories about playing polo in India—including an entire year when he'd actually played on elephants—and David and Lachlan kept up a running commentary, teasing and laughing as Raj spun his tales.

It was the best Enzo had felt in a while.

He got up to use the bathroom, surprised to find that he was a little unsteady on his feet. The drinks may have been overpriced, but they definitely weren't watered down.

The corridor to the bathrooms was long and dimly lit, and just before he turned into the men's room, the women's bathroom door flung open, and Noni walked out.

Enzo blinked, not quite trusting his eyes. Noni just stared at him for a moment, saying nothing. Her face was blotchy, and her dark eyes were red-rimmed.

"Noni?" he said at last. "What are you doing here? Are you okay?"

She shook her head mutely, rapidly blinking her eyes as if to hold back tears.

"*Querida*," he said. He took her hand and led her to the end of the hall where there was a small bench. He pulled her down next to him. "What's going on?" He didn't let go of her hand.

She closed her eyes, the tears silently slipping beneath her long, dark lashes. "There's too much to explain," she said. Her voice sounded rusty. "Can you...would you mind just holding me for a moment?"

Without question, he put his arms around her and held her close. She wrapped herself around him, laid her head against his chest, and sighed.

"I've missed you," he said. It hurt to say it.

She was silent. And that hurt even more.

He smoothed his hand over her hair. "Are you okay?"

She shook her head. "No." She looked up at him, her dark eyes huge and wet, her soft trembling lips a mere few inches from his. "But I'm sure I will be," she whispered.

He stared at her. He couldn't resist. He leaned over and kissed her, and after the tiniest moment, he felt her melt under him and kiss him back. A kiss not so much of passion as it was of exquisite, heartbreaking tenderness.

He closed his eyes and floated on that kiss, savoring the feeling of having her in his arms again. The warm, spicy scent of her, the silky brush of her hair against his cheek, the way her hands skimmed over his shoulders and rested lightly at the small of his back.

She broke the kiss and sighed, leaning her forehead against his. "I should go," she said.

He pulled her closer. "No," he said.

She shook her head. "Yes," she said, but moved closer to him instead. "You're coming to my party, right?"

He nodded.

She smiled. "Good." She kissed him on the cheek. "Then I'll see you tomorrow."

Without another word, she got up and walked away, slipping into the night.

He sat there for a moment, the taste of her lingering on his lips, still not totally sure that he hadn't imagined the entire thing.

Then he got up and walked back to his table.

"Boys," he said, "I need your help with something."

Chapter Thirty-Four

She and Jacob walked back to the house in silence. It was a beautiful night; the tall, full pine trees along the road whispered softly in the summer breeze. The first few fireflies of the season, little green orbs of dancing light, were darting among the shrubs and trees of cottage yards. Noni could feel the warmth of the residual heat collected from the day's sun in the blacktop beneath her feet.

She was walking with Jacob but thinking of Enzo. How he had just appeared in the moment when she needed him most. As he always seemed to do. How, seconds before she had seen him, she had felt like the world was ending. She hadn't been able to catch her breath, the ground had seemed to be shifting beneath her; she had just wanted to sink to the floor and weep and had contemplated doing just that.

But then, moments later, in the safety of Enzo's arms, she somehow knew she would be okay.

She drew strength from him. She always had.

She sighed.

Jacob looked at her. "I feel horrible," he said. "Like I've gone about this all wrong."

She laughed ruefully. "Was there a right way?"

He shrugged. "Maybe I shouldn't have told you at all."

She shook her head. "No. I'm glad you did. I mean, it's good to have some proof that I'm not actually the monster I thought I was, right?"

His face twisted in pain. "Is that really what you thought, Noni? For all these years?"

She kicked at a stone on the ground. "Yup. Pretty much."

"I'm sorry," he said softly. "God, I'm so sorry. Obviously I was the monster."

She blew out a little puff of air and shook her head. "It was a terrible year, Jake. You were going through some impossible things."

"I appreciate you saying that."

"Your wife died. You had a newborn baby."

"I know. But you were so good to me, good to us both, and I...I think I broke your heart."

She was quiet for a moment.

"Losing Max did," she admitted.

He nodded. "He's a great kid, isn't he? He turned out really well considering that he has such a screwup for a father."

She laughed. "He did."

"You were the only real mother he ever had, Noni. I mean that."

She bit her lip, thinking of the way she'd held him as a baby. The way she'd rocked him in her arms, the heavy droop of his head as he fell asleep against her shoulder. Holding him had felt better than anything she'd ever known.

She wasn't sure how she felt about Jacob. But she knew how she felt about Max.

They had arrived at the house, both a little winded from

the steep climb up the driveway. They turned and looked at the night sky reflected on the ocean. He reached for her hand, and she let him take it.

"That year wasn't always terrible, though, was it?" he said. "I mean, we had some good times, too."

She looked at him. "We did," she agreed.

He met her eyes. "And we could again," he said, smiling. "It's possible."

He leaned down to kiss her. After a moment's hesitation, she lifted her face to his and let him.

It was nothing like the kiss she had just shared with Enzo. That kiss had said everything; this kiss was mute. She fiercely wanted this to be easier, to have Jacob's lips on hers make her feel...anything, honestly.

But they didn't.

Maybe that didn't matter, she thought. There had been something between them once; maybe things would grow between them again over time. What was important now was Max.

She kissed Jacob harder, desperately hoping for something more. He shifted against her with a little groan. "Ah, Noni," he said, "I've missed this so much."

She broke away suddenly, hearing the echo of Enzo's voice in Jacob's words. She panted softly from the exertion.

He looked at her and smiled gently. "It's okay," he said. "We can take this slow. We have a lifetime ahead of us."

* * *

Enzo lay in his bed, watching the moon through the French doors to his balcony. It was late, but he couldn't sleep.

Seeing her had shaken him up badly. He wished he kept

a bottle of booze in his flat; the effects of the night's drinks had worn off long ago, and he was stone-cold sober now. But he didn't want to be.

He was fairly certain he had lost her for good. That last kiss had communicated so much. It had been filled with so much regret and longing...

He wondered if he would ever get over her.

What a fool he'd been all those years, making up reasons to hold back, refusing to act, wasting all the time they could have had. His excuses seemed so flimsy now that there was a real, immovable reason they couldn't be together. Who cared if she had money or not? Who cared who her family was? He knew, deep down, that she had never wanted him to be anyone but exactly who he was. She had literally told him that. Why had he ever doubted her? What exactly had kept him so stubbornly, stupidly frozen?

He shifted in his bed.

Fear. He'd been afraid he would hurt her like he hurt Agustina. He had thought that he would just be bringing about another disaster, that he would break her heart just like he had broken his wife's. But now he realized that he had never loved Agustina at all, really. That what had been between them had been insignificant—child's play—compared to what he felt for Noni.

Pilar had been right. He had loved Noni from the first moment he had seen her.

And he would never, ever stop loving her.

He turned over onto his other side, facing away from the moon, and then onto his back. He closed his eyes and thought of that first night at her house, out on the balcony. What had she said, exactly?

That it was not always like this. That it was almost never like this. That people can go their whole lives looking for something like what they had just felt between them—and die never finding it.

He had taken her back to her bed then. Literally carried her, kissing her the entire way there. He had laid her down on the bed and opened her robe and just stood back for a moment and looked at how beautiful she was. Her lashes, her lips, her breasts, her hair, her long legs, her creamy skin. And she'd lain there, calm and open, the look in her eyes filled with nothing but stars and heat.

He had trailed the tips of his fingers down her cheek, down her arched white neck. She shivered in pleasure and closed her eyes when he circled her breast, taking the time to graze her pale pink nipple, which hardened under his fingertips and made him throb with desire.

He had gone to his knees at that point and buried his face between her legs. God, he would never forget the taste of her—like sea and spice. The feel of her velvety thighs against his cheeks as she arched up against his mouth, laying herself open to him, crying out for more.

He grasped himself in the dark, thinking of her, and slowly began to stroke.

He remembered the way her breath quickened, the way she reached down and grabbed his hair in her fists, corkscrewing her hips against him as he licked and kissed, the way he felt her peak under his mouth, her whole body arcing in ecstasy, lifting off the bed as she cried out his name. The way he kept going, bringing her to higher and higher heights until she was trembling all over, thrashing under him, begging him to never stop.

He climaxed to the memory of how he had slid into her afterward, and she had instantly come again. He had never seen a woman so beautiful, so uninhibited, so wild and completely lost to her own pleasure. It was something he knew he would think of for the rest of his life. It was something he knew would come to him on his deathbed.

He was certain that he would leave this earth thinking of how beautiful Antonia had been.

* * *

Noni and Jacob reclined in deck chairs, side by side, drinking wine and watching the flames in Jacob's Fire sculptures. The statues were two balls of metal, one about eight feet in diameter and one about five. A mix of iron and steel, polished to a high shine. Noni still remembered treating the metal with various chemicals until they managed to get the exact look that Jacob envisioned. The metal was stretched into long circular bars, wrapped round and round, with small, lace-like holes throughout. Inside the balls were spaces for fire, which, when lit, reflected over and over on the lustrous metal and illuminated the pieces in their entirety.

It was truly great art, thought Noni, and when they were both lit, side by side, it was especially dramatic and beautiful.

She stretched in her chair and reached down lazily for her glass, sipping the dark, delicious wine, enjoying the heat and flickering light pouring off the sculptures.

"Noni," said Jacob, "I think we should leave for Mexico sooner rather than later. Like, maybe right after the party tomorrow."

She shook her head. "Jacob, I told you, I can't just leave my job like that."

He turned to her. "What is more important? Your job or the three of us? You, me, and Max? I feel like there's something coming between us here, that I can't reach you the way I used to. Your family, your job, something is in the way. I don't want to wait to have a clear path. I don't want to hold back."

She sat up. "Jake, come on. Just an hour ago you were saying we could take things slow. You said we had plenty of time. And I told you how important—"

"Antonia," he interrupted her. "I'm in trouble." His voice was different. Low and ragged. He sounded desperate.

A chill ran down her spine. She turned to look at him. "What do you mean?"

"I wasn't in Germany. I didn't get a call from my agent. There is no exhibition."

"What are you talking about?"

"I was in the city. I was talking to my lawyer. I . . . I have a trial coming up."

She sat up in the chair. "What happened?"

He wouldn't look at her. He stared into the fire. "After I left Cecelia, money got really tight. I haven't been selling much lately, and I haven't had time to make anything new, you know? So I just figured if I could make enough money to live on for a little while, I could get back to work."

He slowly picked up his glass, took a drink of his wine, and swallowed.

"I knew some guys. They told me it would be an easy sale. I was supposed to bring the stuff from Germany, sell it in New York, and that was it. A one-time thing."

"What stuff? What were you selling?"

"Heroin."

She groaned softly. "Oh God, Jacob. How could you? After Astrid?"

"I know. I was desperate. But it made this cosmic sense

to me somehow. Drugs had ruined my life. I thought that maybe now they could fix it, you know? It seemed like poetic justice.

"It was just going to be that one time, and then everything would be fine. Max and I would have been fine. But . . . there was an undercover cop."

She closed her eyes. "God, Jake."

"I tried to run, but she caught me, and now . . . my lawyer said we could make a plea deal. That I could name the guys I got it from to begin with, that I'd probably get five or ten years instead of twenty or thirty—but, Noni, that's too long. That's a huge chunk of Max's life—most of his childhood. And I'll never get my career back if I'm away that long."

He stood up and poked at the fire, causing a shower of sparks to fly through the metal and rise up into the night sky. "So, I thought . . . I thought that if the three of us . . . could just leave. Go to Mexico, like I said. They're not going to come after me. They won't bother. They know I'm small time. And with your money we could—"

"Jesus, Jacob!" Noni stood up and wrapped her arms around herself. She was suddenly freezing. "Is this why you came to find me? For my money?"

He turned to her and caught her by the shoulders. "No! No, I swear. When I told you I wanted to be a family again, my lawyer was still saying that he thought I could get through this with no jail time at all. I never thought I'd be locked up. I thought that all of this was like, a sign—leaving Cecelia and then getting caught, and then seeing you. I thought it was a second chance. That I could start our lives over, me and Max and you. But when I found out that I couldn't get a better plea deal, I just thought, why not go? Get out. Who needs to live in the States, anyway? Plenty of people leave and never come back. You've lived all over the world. This isn't your home."

He let go of her and ran his hands through his hair. He had tears in his eyes. "Please, Noni." His voice was ragged. "This is our chance. Our chance to get it right this time. For Max. He needs me. He lost Astrid. He lost you. I've been his only constant."

He broke away as a sob ripped through him.

She stared at him, numb. "I need you to take me home now, Jake."

"Noni—" He stepped toward her.

She raised her hand, stopping him. "I'm not saying no, okay? I just...need to think. Please, take me back to Pilar's. We'll get through tomorrow first. There's so much going on. We'll talk again after the party."

Chapter Thirty-Five

Noni opened her eyes to see Max standing by the bed, a tray in his hands with coffee and fruit, a croissant with a lit candle in it, a single yellow rose in a vase, and a hand-drawn picture of what looked like her two dogs. "Happy birthday!" he trilled. "Happy birthday, Noni!" He turned back to the door. "I did it, Pilar! She's awake!"

Her dogs looked up from their place on her bed, tails thumping in unison.

Pilar stood in the doorway, beaming at him. "*Que bueno, hijo.*"

Antonia had to smile. Max looked so pleased with himself, his little cheeks pink with pleasure as he handed her the tray. "Pilar made the coffee, but I cut up the fruit. Blow out your candle!"

"Don't forget to make a wish," added Pilar.

Noni closed her eyes and paused, holding her breath. She truly did not know what to wish for.

* * *

Her mother showed up in her red Miata just as Noni was leaving the house with Georgia and Kat.

"Happy birthday, darling!" Benny swept Antonia into her arms and rained kisses on her face. "I can't believe you're thirty! I mean, how is that even possible seeing that I'm still twenty-nine?"

She looked around, laughing at her own joke.

"Mom," said Noni, detaching herself from her mother's grip. "I didn't know you were coming."

"Well, of course I'm coming." She swept back her long blond hair and straightened the red cotton romper she was wearing. "I'm your mother. It's your birthday. But"—she looked from one woman to the next—"where are you going right now?"

"Haven. It's a spa in Sag Harbor," said Kat. "Birthday treat. Do you want to join us, Benny?"

Antonia's heart sank.

"Oooh, wonderful!" cooed Benny. "Just let me get my purse."

* * *

Noni sat next to her mother in the back of Kat's Mercedes, lost in thought.

Georgia turned around. "I feel bad hogging the front seat, Noni. It is your birthday, after all." She looked at Benny. "Or maybe you'd like to sit in front, Mrs. Black?"

"For God's sake, call me Benny," said her mother.

"You're like thirty months pregnant, Georgia," said Kat. "Now stop trying to be a martyr. You have to sit in front because you're so dang big, we'd never be able to pry you out of the backseat."

"Do you know what you're having?" asked Benny.

Georgia sighed. "Twin girls. And I'm terrified."

Benny made a face. "I would be, too. Can you imagine what twins will do to your"—she gestured south—"down there? God, one kid was bad enough. I don't think mine was ever the same after Antonia was born." She dropped her voice. "She weighed almost nine pounds, you know."

Kat laughed.

"Mom!" said Noni, pulled out of her thoughts. "What is wrong with you?"

Georgia shook her head. "Believe me, she's not saying anything I haven't already thought about pretty much obsessively. I mean, I pee every time I sneeze and that's only after one fairly little kid."

"Here's the spa!" sang Kat in her Southern accent. "Massages, mani-pedis, facials, steam room, mud baths!" She reached back and patted Noni on the head. "I'm so glad it's your birthday. This is going to be awesome."

* * *

Noni tried to enjoy herself. She had a hot stone massage, but her masseuse said she'd never worked on someone so tense before. She had a full-body scrub, followed by a seaweed wrap, but she'd felt panicky and claustrophobic, lying there waiting for her toxins to be drawn out.

Now she sat neck-deep in the whirlpool, her face covered in yogurt and crushed caviar, her hair pinned up in a towel. Her mom and Kat sat next to her, each with a different colored mask on. Georgia sat on the edge, just dangling her feet, since she couldn't do high temperatures because of her pregnancy.

Noni was trying very hard to look like she was having a good time, but she knew, from the worried looks that kept passing between her sisters-in-law, that she wasn't fooling anyone.

Except for Benny, of course, she thought wryly. Her mother was chattering happily about everything from her latest bikini wax to her next art opening. As usual, she was completely oblivious to anything that might be going askew with her daughter.

The spa attendant came in to tell them it was time to remove their masks. They all got out of the water, toweled off, and wrapped themselves back up in thick, soft terry-cloth robes.

Benny latched on to Kat's arm as they headed back to the salon, telling her she thought her own life story would make an amazing movie. Georgia hung back with Noni for a moment.

"Hey," Georgia said. Her wide hazel eyes looked even bigger under the creamy green mask she wore on her face, "is everything okay?"

Noni smiled. She had liked Georgia from the moment her sister-in-law had first signed on as veterinarian for the Del Campo team years before. She was warm and smart, and Antonia desperately wished she could confide in her.

"Can I ask you a question?" Noni said.

Georgia cocked her head. "Of course."

"You'd do anything for Tomás, right? I mean, anything to protect him?"

Georgia wrinkled her brow. A glob of the mask chipped off and hit the floor with a little splat. "Of course. Wouldn't any mother?"

Noni looked over at Benny wryly. "Well, most moms, maybe."

Georgia laughed.

"So, even if the thing you had to do to protect him was unethical or dangerous? Or even if it was something that meant you'd be giving up a lot—giving up everything, really. You'd do it?"

Georgia nodded. "Look, Noni, I would die or kill for Tomás if I actually thought he needed me to. But I'm dearly hoping it won't ever come to that. What is this all about?"

"Nothing." Noni shook her head. "I just wondered." She hugged her sister-in-law. "Thank you for taking me out today. It's been great." She looked at Georgia and laughed. "Oops, smeared some caviar on your robe."

* * *

She locked herself in the bathroom and called Jacob.

"Noni?" he said. He sounded relieved. "I didn't think I'd hear from you until later."

"Can you meet me?" she said. "I'm in Sag Harbor."

* * *

She'd told them she was running out for chocolate. That she wasn't going to survive on green juice and salad all day. It was her birthday, for goodness' sake. She was going to sneak in some of the good stuff.

They all agreed that it was a great idea. "Maybe we should get a pizza, too?" offered Kat. "And wine? I didn't realize the menu here was limited to nonfat everything."

"That sounds perfect," said Noni. "I'll get it all. We can sneak a picnic in the rock garden after we get our toenails done."

"But I'll go," said Kat. "You shouldn't have to do that."

"No, no," said Noni, hurriedly heading out the door. "I'm already dressed."

* * *

Jacob was sitting in the coffee shop waiting for her. He looked exhausted and rumpled, though Noni was pretty sure she didn't look any better herself.

He stood up when he saw her and kissed her on the cheek, his prickly beard scraping her skin. "I'm so glad you called," he said. "I mean, I was willing to try, but I don't know if I could have made it all the way through the party."

She smiled nervously. "Let's sit down," she said.

They sat down and she bit her lip. "Jake," she said, "you know I really care about you, and I would do anything for Max."

He looked hopeful. "So—"

She raised her hand. "I haven't stopped thinking about this since last night. I've been round and round."

He nodded and grasped her hand.

She looked at him and then took a deep breath. "First of all, I will get you the best lawyer there is."

He pulled his hand away. His eyes went flat with dread. "You're not going to do it."

She shook her head. "I'm sorry, but it doesn't make any sense. Think about it. I mean, how would we even be able to leave the country? Do you and Max have fake passports? Even if you did, think of what this will do to Max. We'd always be on the run. What kind of life would that be?"

He shook his head frantically.

"Listen, listen. I have a plan," she said pleadingly. "Like I said, I will get you a new lawyer. I can afford the best there is. If they can't fix this right away—and I bet they can—then we will just keep trying, and I will take care of Max while we do. And even if worse comes to worst, five years or ten years isn't forever. I will make sure he calls you every day, and I'll bring him to visit every chance we're given, and I promise that he will understand that, even though you did a not-so-great thing, you did it for good reasons. I will keep you guys close. I swear I won't let that change."

"Noni—" he said again.

"And once you're back out," she rushed on, "I'll help you then, too. I can finance whatever you need to get your art career back on track. I can make this easier."

His eyes darted around the room; he looked like he might bolt.

She took his hand again. Her voice was urgent. "Jake, listen to me—you can't do this to Max. You can't make him pay for your mistake. It's not fair to him. Try to imagine what his life would be like with you guys always moving around, always on the run." She tightened her hand on his. "I actually know exactly what that's like, and it's miserable. It's no way for a kid to grow up. Please don't do this to him."

He stared at her, stricken. "But what about us?"

She glanced away. "Jake, I—"

"You and me. What about us?"

She looked back at him, tears in her eyes. "I've been over and over it and I just don't think I can make myself feel that way any—"

He held up his hand, cutting her off. "Don't," he said. "You don't have to say anything else. I get it." He smiled sadly. "It was always a long shot anyway, right? Even before you knew I was a crook."

She squeezed his hand. "But you'll let me help you, right? You'll let me do whatever needs to be done for Max?"

He took a deep breath and blew it out again. "Yes. Okay. I know you're right. I was panicking. I wasn't thinking clearly."

She smiled, relieved. "Don't worry, okay? We're going to take this one step at a time. We're going to figure this all out, I promise."

He smiled back at her, brought her hand to his mouth, and kissed it. "Thank you, Antonia," he said. "I'm never going to forget this."

"Okay," she said, glancing at her watch. "Shit. I have to get back at the spa. They're waiting for me. You're still coming to the party, right?"

He nodded. "Wouldn't miss it for the world."

Chapter Thirty-Six

Enzo stood nervously in front of Del Campo stables. He was decked out in a Team Stone jersey, white jeans, and riding boots. Lined up next to him were Raj, Lachlan, and David, all in their riding gear as well.

Alejandro, Sebastian, and Rory, their third player, were also in their La Victoria uniforms and standing next to the other team, waiting.

"She should be here any moment," said Enzo. "I told Pilar to bring her down as soon as they got back."

Alejandro glanced at Enzo and shook his head. "I am still not totally understanding what we are doing here. She wants to watch us play a game for her birthday? She has seen a million games."

"I still don't understand how we're playing without a fourth guy," said Sebastian.

David shook his head. "Mark's going to kill us when he finds out we played a game without him."

Enzo rolled his eyes. "Mark will be fine." He looked at Sebastian. "You will understand soon, okay?" Then to Alejandro, "This is a special game. Just—Oh, here they come!"

Pilar, escorted by Lord Henderson, Benny, Georgia, Kat, and Noni, came walking down the driveway. The women made a pretty picture, all wearing their breezy summer clothes, laughing and chatting, not yet noticing the men standing in front of the stables.

Enzo knew the moment that Noni saw them. Her eyes met his and she froze. She seemed to understand his intentions immediately. Her cheeks flushed and the look in her eyes shifted between excited and alarmed.

As they walked up, Pilar looked at Enzo and winked. He smiled.

"What is all this?" said Benny, wrinkling her nose. "Polo? I didn't know there'd be a game today."

Enzo stepped toward Noni, keeping his hand hidden behind his back. "Happy birthday, Antonia," he said, and offered her the vintage polo mallet he'd found in the antique store, all bound up with a red bow.

She reached for it, her eyes wide. Their hands met with a little shock of electricity.

He bent toward her. "You've got this," he whispered.

He turned to the Del Campo team. "Gentlemen," he said, "would you care to play a little stick and ball?"

* * *

After changing into her riding gear, Noni laughed nervously to herself as she mounted Sunny. She still couldn't believe this was happening. It felt like a dream.

She wasn't sure she was ready. She had been practicing as much as she could, but her time on the pitch had been short, and she hadn't played with a team of any sort since she left Wellington.

Her brothers and Rory rode up on their mounts, flanking her.

"Apparently, I'm to be surrounded by Del Campos on all sides," said Rory, grinning at her.

"I'm a Black," she said automatically.

He raised an eyebrow. "You're looking awfully like a Del Campo to me right now, darling," he said before he rode out to the pitch.

She looked at her brothers.

Seb shook his head. "None of us knew you played, *niña*," he said. "Why didn't you say something sooner? We could have been having so much fun."

Noni bit her lip. "I...I didn't think I was good enough."

"I'm sure you will be fine. Don't worry." Seb wheeled his pony around and headed out to the pitch. "Jandro and I will protect you!" he yelled back over his shoulder. "We'll take it very slow. We'll play an easy game!"

Alejandro glanced at her, a thoughtful expression on his face. "I wonder if we'll need to," he murmured before he followed Sebastian out to the field.

Enzo came riding up then. She stared at him, suddenly shy. She had seen him ride a million times, but she'd never seen him in uniform. He looked beyond handsome.

He smiled at her beneath his riding helmet. That slow, dazzling smile that made her heart ache. "*¿Estás bien*, Noni?"

She looked at him. "I'm scared witless," she admitted.

He laughed and shook his head. "Your brothers have no idea what you can do. They are going to be blown away."

She bit her lip nervously. "I sincerely doubt that."

He rode in a little closer. She fought the urge to reach out and touch him.

He leaned in and almost touched his cheek to hers. "You

deserve to be out there," he whispered. "This is in your blood, *niña*."

* * *

Pilar acted as the referee at the throw-in. The players lined up parallel to one another.

Pilar stood stick straight, her skirt ruffling in the breeze. "Since we have a party to get to later," she announced loudly, "this game will be abridged to four chukkas. All other usual rules apply."

As soon as Pilar rolled in the ball, Raj burst through and sent it hurtling toward his goal. The players followed, thundering down the pitch.

Noni paused—just a split second—before she raced to follow, cursing herself as she fell behind.

David picked up Raj's pass and changed the line of the ball, heading toward the goal. Sebastian charged forward, coming at David from an angle. He slammed his horse into David's, bumping him out of the line.

"*¡Lo siento, hombre!*" he shouted with a grin as he passed the younger player by and took control of the ball.

But just as he turned and raised his arm to send the ball flying, Enzo came from behind and hooked Seb's mallet with his own.

"*¡Lo siento, hombre!*" echoed Enzo to Seb, giving his old employer a friendly mocking salute.

Raj cut in and picked the ball back up, and with one powerful stroke, sent it through the goal just as Pilar blew the whistle to signal the end of the first chukka.

Noni raised her mallet and gave a short cheer for the other team, but she felt humiliated. She'd hardly even made it into the fray. She hadn't even touched the ball. She was trailing her team like a child. She was a disgrace.

* * *

It played out that way for two more chukkas. The teams were almost evenly matched, with the ball possession being equally shared on both sides.

Alejandro handed La Victoria two goals in the second chukka, thundering down the pitch so fast on his bay stallion that no one could keep up with him, and the Del Campos took the lead.

Then, in the third chukka, David paid Sebastian back in kind and bumped him, taking possession and making a point of his own, and Lachlan's horse managed a pony goal when Rory accidentally drove the ball right under the horse's feet and the pony kicked it right through.

Enzo watched Noni, worried. She wasn't playing as badly as she had in the first chukka; she did manage to block a shot or two and to grab the ball once or twice, but she certainly wasn't showing anyone what she was truly capable of, either.

Pilar blew the whistle for the end of the third chukka, and the teams went off the fields for fresh mounts.

Enzo knew that it was nerves, not a lack of skill, that hindered Noni. She was standing to the side, fiddling with her boot while she waited for a fresh mount, very obviously avoiding her brothers.

For a moment, Enzo wanted to go to her, comfort her, offer her words of advice.

But then the groom brought her Hex, and at the sight of the little black mare, Noni's face lit up. She rubbed the horse's nose and pressed her forehead against the pony's neck.

The determined look in Antonia's eyes as she swung up on the pony told Enzo to stay where he was.

He thought this chukka might be different.

* * *

Every polo player, even the very best, would say that their pony was at least 80 percent of their game. Bad pony, bad game. Great pony, and you were basically unstoppable.

Pretty much all of the Del Campo ponies were great ponies. They all had impeccable bloodlines; they had all been trained and groomed from the time they were tiny foals to be the top athletes they were today.

But for Noni, some were greater than others. And no pony was better than Hex.

Noni had fallen for Hex from the very first day she walked into the Del Campo stables. She remembered it like it was yesterday. The long, terrible flight from Berlin to Florida, sitting next to Alejandro, feigning sleep, afraid to talk to her big brother lest he find out just how much of a mess she truly was.

She had hoped to outrun the fresh pain of losing Max and Jacob. She had hoped for a place to hide and lick her wounds. She thought she would take the money that her father had left her and go somewhere far, far away. Maybe even back to New Mexico. She'd wondered if the little adobe house with the red clay roof and blue tiled floors was somehow still there and miraculously available.

When she followed Jandro into the barn, it became obvious to her almost immediately that everyone in that barn knew, if not all of her secrets, at least enough to judge her.

Every eye in the place had turned to her when she walked

through those doors; the hush over the barn was palpable. For a moment, she wanted nothing more than to leave. Flee. Get on that plane and go all the way back to her cold bed in Berlin. She didn't think she could stand it. She turned away, blindly petting a horse through its stall door, trying to ignore all the attention on her.

A movement caught her eye and she shifted just in time to see a tall, dark man staring at her from across the barn, and the shiny black pony next to him as it snaked its head out and nipped him right on the neck.

He cussed, surprised, and Noni heard herself laugh before she could stop it. Her eyes met the man's, and then she looked at his pony, and she somehow felt drawn to them both.

Antonia remembered her conversation with Enzo that day and knew that it was the beginning of both their friendship and their attraction. But something else she remembered from those first few moments in the barn—the way that little black pony's eyes had seemed to mysteriously echo her own feelings.

That pony wanted out of the barn, just like Antonia. That pony wanted to escape. And maybe it was as simple as a high-spirited beast tired of being locked up and longing to run free in the fields, but for Noni, it seemed much more profound. For her, it as if Hex were the only living thing in the barn that truly understood her. As she had stood there and scratched the little horse's ears and received an affectionate nibble in return, Noni fell just a little bit in love.

After Jandro had finished giving her a tour of the barn, Noni walked out back and spied Enzo and Hex galloping across the field in the distance. They were spectacularly beautiful. They moved so gracefully together that Noni imagined that they might sprout wings at any moment and take to the sky.

She stood, frozen in place, watching them canter from one end of the field to the other, the tall, dark, handsome man and the radiantly shining black horse. For the first time since Jacob had left, Noni felt something flutter through her that she had been certain she would never feel again. She felt something that she would almost call joy.

* * *

With Hex under her, nothing could stop her. She was flying down the pitch, her stick in hand, slamming into Raj, sending the big man and his horse off the line of the ball. Then she was hooking David's mallet as he tried for an offside shot, allowing Sebastian to pick up the ball and send it hurtling toward the goal. Then she was sailing through the air again, feeling the little pony's joy and ferocity and feverish enthusiasm for the game. She caught that ball as Enzo deflected it from the goal and sent it right back past him, scoring the winning point just as Pilar blew her whistle.

Her team cheered wildly as she and Hex spun around, triumphant.

Alejandro galloped up to her, beaming. "Well, I would say we found our fourth," he said, laughing.

Noni gasped, disbelieving, almost dizzy with joy.

"Oh boy," said Rory, shaking his head with a grin, "a whole team of Del Campos."

"¡Hermana!" shouted Sebastian. "What a play! Who the hell knew you could do that?"

"I did," said Enzo softly as he rode up next to her. His face was alight with pride.

She couldn't help herself. She didn't even think. She just leaned off her horse and threw her arms around the man she loved and kissed him with all the wild happiness in her soul.

They broke the kiss with a gasp, still touching forehead to forehead. "Thank you," Noni breathed.

"It was all you, *niña*," he said.

"And Hex." She grinned, patting the little pony underneath her.

"And Hex," he agreed.

"All right, all right, *basta*," said Pilar as she walked onto the pitch. "All very impressive, but you all need to go home and change for the party. Get going."

Chapter Thirty-Seven

Kat and Georgia had picked out something special for Noni to wear that night. They knew her dislike of skirts and dresses, so they found a simple pair of flowing black slacks and paired it with a scoop-neck black tank top, sparkling with silver threaded embroidery, and a pair of open-toed silver heels to match.

Noni looked in the mirror and sighed happily. Her hair was as lank and unmanageable as ever, and she couldn't decide what color lipstick she should wear, but the glow of the game was still on her face, and for once she actually kind of liked what she saw reflected back at her.

She went to the window and peeked out at the garden in the backyard. It looked enchanted, all lit up with candles, gold and silver paper lanterns strung through the air, and sparkling fairy lights entwined in every tree and shrub. It had been a warm day, and the summer fireflies were out, flitting from place to place, pulsing gold and green as they hovered in all the nooks and crevices of the yard.

There was a knock on her door and Pilar slipped in. The older woman was wearing a long white gown, spangled with curls of gold sequins that twisted in an undulating pattern down her dress. She wore enormous yellow diamonds in her ears and sparkling at her wrist. She sat down on Noni's bed and looked her over from head to toe, nodding in approval.

"*Que bonita*," she said. "And somehow not a dog hair to be seen."

The dogs in question rushed over to her, wagging their tails. Pilar smiled begrudgingly and gave them each a pat. "I guess you are not so bad when you are not harassing *mis perritos*," she said.

Noni laughed. "The garden looks spectacular, Pilar. Thank you so much."

Pilar waved her off. "Pfft," she said, "all smoke and mirrors. A few tea lights here, a few roses there. Anyone could do it."

"No," said Noni, and she approached the older woman and gave her a kiss on the cheek. "Only you."

Pilar's cheeks flushed pink with pleasure and she gently shoved Noni away. "*Ay, dios mio*, what a fuss."

Noni laughed and went back to her dressing table, holding up one lipstick and then the other. "You know," she said, trying to sound casual but wanting Pilar to know just how much this all meant to her, "this is the first time anyone has ever actually thrown me a party."

At those words, Pilar went very still, and an odd expression came over her face. "Well," she said finally, "then I suppose it is about time that somebody did."

Noni smiled and dug through her mess of a jewelry box, trying to find proper earrings for her outfit.

"So, Enzo after all, eh?" said Pilar, watching Noni in the mirror.

Noni blushed. "I don't know. I…I hope so. There is still a lot that needs to be worked out."

"And Max?"

"I think...I think he might stay with me. At least for a while."

Pilar smiled. "*Bien*. That is very good news, indeed." She shifted position on the bed. "You know," she said thoughtfully, "I used to think that the more a man could hurt me, the more it must mean that I loved him. If someone could make me feel so miserable, it was only because I felt for him so deeply, *comprendes*? Only now, when I've finally been lucky enough to experience something different, do I realize just how wrong that really was."

Antonia turned to look at her. "My father was not a very good man, was he?" she said softly.

Pilar shrugged. "Your father was a complicated man."

Noni blinked, trying to keep the tears back. "I'm ashamed to say this, but when I was a little girl, I used to imagine that he would come and...save me. I guess that's the best way to put it. My mother talked about him all the time." She rolled her eyes and smiled. "Mainly about how he didn't want to see me, of course. How he had abandoned us both. And even though I didn't know you, I...I thought that I hated you. You and Jandro and Seb. I thought that if you all didn't exist, Carlos would be mine, that he would come and scoop me up and carry me off, and I would have a whole different life. Something safe and beautiful."

Pilar smiled bitterly. "At least you had the excuse that you were just a little girl. I had similar feelings about you, and I was a fully grown woman."

Noni caught her eye. "But not anymore, right?"

Pilar chuckled. "No, *hija*, not anymore."

Noni looked down, smiling to herself, and started looking through her jewelry again.

Pilar stood up. "*Basta*. I cannot stand watching you rooting through that mess. Here, I have an early gift for you."

She handed Noni a small silver box. Noni took it gingerly.

"Pilar, you already created this beautiful party. You didn't have to get me a present as well."

Pilar shook her head impatiently. "It's not really a gift from me anyway. It's something that is rightfully yours. Open it."

Noni slid off the top of the box and gasped. Inside were a pair of glimmering black opal earrings, set in an intricate platinum filigree, and next to them was a ring to match. The stones were easily as big as walnuts and flickered with an eerie fire.

Antonia looked at Pilar, speechless.

"Go ahead. Put them on." Pilar nodded. "They will go very well with your outfit."

Pilar watched expectantly as Noni fastened on the earrings and slid the ring onto her middle finger. It fit perfectly.

Pilar nodded firmly. "*Bien*. They never looked right on me, but they were made for you."

She approached Noni and touched her chin, delicately turning her head this way and that. "For the longest time," she said, "all I could see when I looked at you was Carlos's eyes. It was like a bad joke. He finally dies, I am finally free of all his treachery, and you turn up, like a mirror of his gaze." She shook her head. "I hated looking you in the face. You were like a terrible reminder of all the parts of him that hurt me the most."

Noni looked down. "I'm sorry," she said softly.

Pilar tugged her chin back up and looked her in the face. "It was not your fault, *hija*. And the stupid thing that I was too blind to see was that your eyes were really not Carlos's at all. Actually, they were his mother's, Victoria's."

Noni blinked slowly. "My grandmother?"

Pilar nodded. "*Sí, tu abuela*. Who, by the way, was the most remarkable woman I have ever known. Hell," she laughed, "she was the most remarkable *person* I have ever known, man or woman."

She smoothed a lock of Noni's hair back from her face.

"If Carlos had any good in him at all, it was because of her. You not only look just like her, *niña*, but you also remind me of her. You have her warmth and her strength and her humor. Having you here these past weeks has almost been like having *mi madrasta* back."

She smiled softly, touching the jewels at Noni's ears.

"These were hers. She would have wanted you to have them. They were meant for a woman with eyes like yours."

"Oh," said Noni, throwing her arms around Pilar's neck, "now I'm crying! And it's all your fault!"

Pilar smiled and gently patted Noni's back. "*Ay*, such a fuss."

* * *

Enzo, back in his good suit, sat in the corner of the garden, nursing a vodka and soda and watching the crowd while he waited for Noni.

There were his teammates, David and Lachlan, who were talking to Valentina Del Campo, Alejandro's daughter. She had flown out from San Francisco this afternoon and arrived just after the game.

Valentina was all grown up now, with her curly black hair pulled back in a tasteful bun and the ramrod posture of a dedicated ballerina. She was the principal dancer with the San Francisco Ballet, last Enzo had heard.

Lachlan was obviously doing his best to get her attention, but it was David whom Valentina had locked eyes with, reaching down to brush an invisible something off his shirt.

Enzo smiled at Lachlan's frustration and the stunned look of luck on David's face.

Raj was at the buffet table with Benny, who was wearing a spectacularly short skirt. Even Enzo, with his mixed feelings about Noni's mother, had to admit she still had the legs to pull it off just fine. Liz, looking very professional in a white chef's coat, was on the other side of the table, which was absolutely groaning with delicacies. Liz smiled over at Raj and reached up to feed him a bite of something out of her hand. The big man rolled his eyes in appreciation and grinned down at the pretty little chef while Benny frowned petulantly off to the side.

Camelia, who used to be a groom for the Del Campos and was now Mark Stone's wife, was standing with Kat and Sebastian, waving her hands animatedly as she told them a story that made them all roar with laughter.

Alejandro and Georgia stood together at the edge of the garden. Jandro was slowly rubbing his hand over his wife's lower back. Georgia, wearing a red dress that was stretched to the max, looked beautiful, content, and particularly pregnant tonight.

Enzo turned his head just in time to see Jacob arrive. Max came rushing over to him and flung himself into his father's arms, enthusiastically pointing at this and that in the garden and chattering about how he had helped Pilar put the whole party together.

Enzo wished that Noni would hurry up and get there. He felt that he was going to pieces without her. He did not yet know what the kiss on the pitch had meant. While it was happening, it had felt like a declaration, a glorious promise, an expression of all that was unsaid between the two of them. But now that time had passed and his emotions had cooled, he wondered whether it had just been an impulsive moment of celebration on Noni's part and nothing more.

Because, he thought, looking over at Max as he pulled his father by the hand, excitedly leading him to the three-piece jazz band, here was this child.

This child whom Noni loved so much.

This child who had a father. And that father was here tonight as well.

Jacob turned at that moment and caught Enzo's eye. Enzo gave him a little half smile and a lift of his drink.

Jacob bent to his son's level for a moment and whispered in his ear. Then he left Max and walked over to Enzo.

"Pretty impressive spread," he said to Enzo. "I guess the Del Campos know how to do it up right."

Enzo nodded and took a sip of his drink. "Pilar lives for this sort of thing," he said.

Jacob nodded at the empty place at the table. "Do you mind?"

"Be my guest," said Enzo as Jacob sat down next to him.

"So," said Jacob, "has Noni talked to you about me at all?"

Enzo looked at him carefully. "I guess she has told me enough."

Jacob nodded slowly. "I need a drink," he muttered, looking around.

"Bar's over there," said Enzo, gesturing to the other end of the garden.

"Look," said Jacob turning back to him. "I'm sure you think I'm an asshole. I won't deny that I've done some stupid things. But I need you to know, I'm not just using Noni. I really do care about her. And Max, well, he adores her."

Enzo went still. A cold trickle of fear ran down his back. "Okay," he said, trying to keep his face impassive.

"So whatever happens—"

They were interrupted by Noni's dogs, which were suddenly at the table and doing their best to climb into Enzo's lap.

"Hello, boys." Noni appeared next to them, a vision in black and silver with glimmering gems dangling at her ears that set off the stars in her dark gaze.

"*Niña*," murmured Enzo, "you look *increíble*."

Jacob stood up suddenly. "I'm going to get that drink," he said, and hurried away.

Noni watched him go, a frown on her face. "What were you guys talking about?"

Enzo shrugged. "I am not sure, honestly. He didn't finish what he started to say."

Noni raised her eyebrows and sat down next to him. She took the drink from his hand and stole a sip, and then adjusted the lapel of his suit jacket and smiled. "Well, hello, Javier Bardem."

He smiled back crookedly in return.

"Isn't this beautiful?" she said, indicating the garden.

Enzo nodded. "Very."

"You know, I just had the most amazing conversation with Pilar," she began.

Suddenly he couldn't stand it anymore. Enzo still didn't know if he was going to lose her or not, but he did know that he couldn't just sit there and make small talk with her like they had all the time in the world.

All he knew for sure was that he had her with him now and that he was going to make the most of it.

"Dance with me," said Enzo, interrupting her.

The strains of "You Belong to Me" were playing softly.

"Oh," she said, blinking, "but no one else is dancing yet."

He took her hand and pulled her up with him. "I don't care. We can be the first."

She smiled and let him lead her out to the dance floor. "Okay, then. Let's be the first."

Chapter Thirty-Eight

Everything was nearly perfect. The party. Her new place on the polo team. Max happily playing with Tomás at the edges of the garden as the boys leaped about, trying to catch fireflies. The soft music...

And most especially, the man in whose arms she swayed, her head against his chest, breathing in his sweet and earthy scent.

Noni felt like she was home at last.

She shifted even closer to him, and their bodies seemed to melt together. She felt him throb against her and pressed even tighter in response.

"*Mi corazon*," he murmured hoarsely.

She looked up at him. He was so beautiful. "I love you, Enzo," she breathed.

He froze, stopped dancing, and his arms clutched her just a bit tighter.

"Why are you telling me this?" he finally said.

She laughed. "Wow. Just what every girl wants to hear after getting up the nerve to say that for the first time."

He took a step back from her. "I mean, are you telling me this because you want something more? Or are you telling me this because you are... saying goodbye?"

"Oh," she exhaled, "I thought you understood."

His eyes were wild. "I do not understand, Antonia. I need it explained."

She laughed. "I said I love you because I...love you. Because I need you. Because when I'm with you I feel strong, and warm, and happy. Because I know you would never hurt me. Because I know for a fact that what is between us is true, and real, and rare. Because I want something more from you, Enzo. So much more." She stood on her tiptoes and kissed him. A soft, slow kiss. Then she opened her eyes and looked at him. "Now you say it back."

He stared at her for a moment, wonder in his eyes. "*Te amo, niña*," he finally murmured. He pulled her back in for another kiss, all but crushing her in his arms.

Then he pulled away again. "What about Max?"

She nodded. "It's complicated. I have a whole crazy story to tell you, but I think he'll be staying with me for a while." She looked up at him, suddenly worried. "With us, actually, if you're willing."

He embraced her again. "Of course, of course," he said. There were tears in his eyes. "I would be so lucky to have you both."

Noni felt she was overflowing with happiness. It was a perfect moment on a perfect night.

And then her mother tapped her on the shoulder.

"Darling," she rasped. "Oh, daughter of mine."

Noni cringed. She could tell, from the soft slur in her voice, that Benny had already been overserved.

She turned and forced herself to smile. "Hi, Mom."

"Hello, Benny," said Enzo.

Benny ignored him and smiled brightly at Noni instead, tugging her away. Noni made an apologetic face at Enzo as she was being pulled across the floor, and he laughed and waved them off.

Benny stopped over by the bar. "I'm sorry to break up your little tête-à-tête, Antonia, but I haven't seen you at all tonight, and I just wanted the chance to say happy birthday to my girl."

Noni smiled. "Thanks, Mom."

"You know it's my birthday, too." She grinned. "I mean, quite literally, right?"

Noni laughed agreeably. "Absolutely. And thanks for that, too."

"Now, listen, darling." She started to rummage through the enormous purse she was carrying. "I have your birthday present in here somewhere . . . "

Noni watched her mother searching and smiled. Benny looked amazing. No one over thirty should have been able to pull off the tiny leather micro-mini Benny was wearing, but her mother was absolutely rocking the thing. Over that, she wore a body-skimming black CBGB T-shirt and a dark green kimono jacket. Her hair was loose and long. Six-inch stacked heel booties completed the outfit. The only way someone would have guessed her age would be if they noticed her hands, which were gnarled and scarred from years of working with kilns and forges and doing the detail work of her art.

Noni smiled to herself, wondering what her mother would think if she told her that she found her hands to be the most beautiful part of her . . .

"Ah," Benny said as she finally pulled out a wrapped parcel about as big as a slice of bread, "here it is. It's not much, but I thought you might like it."

Noni took the gift from her mother. "Should I open it now?"

She waved her hand. "Yes, yes, go ahead."

Noni carefully unwrapped the plain brown paper to reveal a small oil portrait that her mother had painted of the two of them. Noni as a little girl and Benny as a young mother.

Noni hugged her mother, truly touched.

"Mom, I love it. It's beautiful."

Benny leaned in, eager to show her daughter all the details of the work.

"You see here? I had to use the finest little brush to get that line. And see the color of your shirt? You remember that shirt? I had to mix paints a whole afternoon to get that color right."

It was one of the best things her mother had ever done, and yet Noni felt a twinge of sadness looking at it. There was something about the expression on both of their faces that seemed a little . . . lost.

Suddenly Benny went still. She reached over and touched Noni's ring.

"What's this?"

Alarm bells went off in Noni's head when she heard the brittle edge in her mother's voice.

"Oh my goodness!" Benny's voice rang with false excitement. "Those, too," she said, touching one of Noni's earrings. She squinted at them. "Those can't be real opals, can they?"

Noni's hand went to her ear protectively. "Pilar gave them—"

"Pilar?" said Benny. Her voice went up a pitch. "Pilar gave you this jewelry?"

"Well, not really," said Noni. She knew she'd said the wrong thing as soon as Pilar's name had come out of her mouth. "I mean, they were Victoria's, Carlos's mother? So really—"

"I know who Victoria is," her mother snapped. She yanked the painting out of Noni's hand. "I feel like an idiot. Why would you want this when you've already been given something like that?"

"No, Mom, don't be ridiculous. I love your painting."

Her mother snorted. "That ring alone must be worth tens of thousands." She looked at Noni, her eyes glittering. "I suppose even that doesn't mean much now that you're worth hundreds of Carlos's millions."

"Mom," said Noni, "that's not fair. Please, give me back the painting."

Benny shook her head. "No," she said as she shoved it back in her purse. "I'll get you something better later on."

She grabbed a glass and a spoon from the bar and clinked them together.

Ting ting ting.

"Hello?" said Benny.

Noni felt herself suddenly go stiff in dread.

"Helllooo," said Benny, hitting the glass again, this time a bit louder.

The band quit playing and the crowd quieted.

Benny laughed silkily, waiting for all eyes to be on her.

"So," said Benny, smiling a big smile, "for those of you who don't know me, I am Benny Black, Antonia's mother." She laughed and toyed with a lock of her hair. "Obviously, I had her very young."

There was polite laughter. Noni stood next to her, frozen. From across the room, she saw Pilar. The older woman was standing half in darkness, watching Benny with an unguarded look of pain on her face.

"Anyway, I just wanted to thank the Del Campos—and most especially Pilar—for putting on this lovely little party for my Antonia's thirtieth birthday." She turned and smiled sweetly at Noni, a glimmer of danger in her eyes. "I'm sure it's better than any soiree I've ever thrown for you, wouldn't you say, darling?"

Noni started to open her mouth to speak and then shut it again, knowing there was no right answer.

Suddenly, from her left, she felt Enzo's presence. He placed a comforting hand on her waist.

Benny picked up her glass and took a large gulp. "I mean, just look at this place," she said, sloshing her drink as she indicated the garden. "Carlos always used to tell me that he was absolutely dying to leave Pilar. That he couldn't wait to get out from under her controlling thumb. But who could give up such beauty? Such gracious living?"

Suddenly the crowd was even quieter than before. Everyone was frozen in place.

"Mom," gasped Noni. "Mom, stop."

"I mean, why not live in a sham of a marriage when there was all *this* to hold you here, right? Twinkle lights and delicious champagne and roses and lanterns. Life is beautiful here. Why would you ever leave?"

Alejandro and Sebastian quickly moved through the crowd, joining Noni and Enzo.

"*Señora*," began Alejandro, "that is quite enough."

Noni put her hand on her mother's shoulder. "Mom, please."

Benny shook her off and gave Noni and her brothers a wolfish grin. "Aw, look, Pilar's boys have come to defend her. That's so sweet. What good kids. And look, my daughter is defending her, too. Because," she said loudly, appealing to the crowd, "because Pilar has managed to buy my daughter just like she bought her husband." She turned back toward Noni. "Show them your birthday jewels, Antonia." Her smile twisted and an angry sob tore through her. "Show them how Pilar is going to steal you away from me, too!"

Noni stepped in close and took Benny by the arm. "Come on, we're going inside."

Benny pulled away, but before she could say more, Pilar had crossed the garden and stood defiantly in their way.

"Why did you never cash the checks, Benny?" she said quietly, ice dripping from her voice.

Benny looked at her and then looked away. "I don't know what you're talking about."

She started to walk away, but Pilar grabbed her by the arm. "The checks that Carlos wrote you every month. Every one of them came back uncashed. My lawyer explained this to me after Carlos died. From the sound of it, you and Noni could have used the help. So why didn't you cash them?"

"What checks?" said Noni.

Benny shook her head. "Why would I do that?" she said. "Why would I give Carlos any reason to take away my daughter?"

Noni felt dizzy. "Mom?"

Pilar raised her chin. "Whatever he felt about me, or you, I know Carlos would have never abandoned his child. She was his daughter, too. She needed help and you refused to take it."

Sebastian and Alejandro drew in closer to Noni, exchanging questioning looks.

"We were fine!" said Benny. "We didn't need his help. If I'd taken his dirty money, I'd have been playing right into his hands. It was hard enough, keeping ahead of him, moving every few months to make sure he didn't catch up. That money would have led him straight to us."

"Wait, he was looking for me?" Noni felt like the floor was tilting. "You told me he wanted nothing to do with us, that he didn't care."

Benny looked at her pleadingly. "He would have taken you away. Don't you understand? And now," she said, sobbing, "he has. He left you all this money and he delivered you right into the hands of his family. I mean, just look at you!" She flailed her hands at Noni standing with her brothers. "And now," she sobbed harder, "I'm going to lose you just like I always knew I would!"

She was starting to get hysterical, but Noni wasn't sure she really cared. She could only stand and stare.

"*Niña*," said Enzo softly, "I am going to take your mother out now, okay?" He looked at Pilar and the Del Campo brothers. "You've got Noni?"

They nodded as Enzo gently put his arm around the wailing Benny and led her through the crowd into the house.

Noni looked at her brothers. "Did you all know?"

Sebastian and Alejandro shook their heads.

Antonia looked at Pilar. "Why didn't you tell me?"

Pilar shrugged. "She is your *madre*. I did not want to come between you. It was not my secret to share."

Noni nodded, understanding. She took a deep breath and laughed rustily. "Oh God, I'm so sorry, you guys. That was horrible."

Pilar took her hand. "It is nothing. Come, let us get something for you to eat."

Noni nodded and then looked around. "Where's Max? Tell me he didn't see all that?"

Sebastian shook his head. "No, I'm sure he missed it. I saw Jacob take him inside the house before it all began."

* * *

Enzo gently took the drink from Benny's clutched hand, passed her a tissue, and waited patiently while she blew her nose.

They were in the sunroom. Enzo, hoping to calm her down, had led her in and shut the door behind them.

The sunroom was a long room that ran down the south side of the house. Instead of walls, it was made up of floor-to-ceiling leaded glass windows and had a magnificent view of the barn and the polo field beyond. On one end of the room was an enormous stone fireplace, almost big enough for a man to stand in. On the other end was a fully stocked bar. Pilar had furnished the room with comfortable antique green-painted wicker. A tastefully worn pink and green oriental silk carpet covered the brick floor. There was a large iron and glass coffee table with a top that folded back like a jewelry box, and inside Pilar displayed a revolving collection of bird nests, feathers, pretty seed pods, and other natural ephemera she had picked up around the farm. There were also several antique wrought-iron *étagères* that held Pilar's extensive selection of orchids and ferns.

Benny flopped down on a chaise lounge and glared at Enzo. "I suppose you think I ruined the party?"

Enzo raised his eyebrows and chuckled. "Well, there's still the cake. Perhaps that will help."

Benny's mouth quirked briefly at one side, but then she frowned again. She sat back in her chair and closed her eyes and sighed heavily.

"Fuck," she said, "I'm a horrible mother."

Enzo looked at her. "I don't know. You made Antonia into who she is today, and since I am awfully fond of how she turned out, I don't think you could have been entirely terrible."

This time Benny laughed. "So, you and my daughter, huh?"

Enzo nodded. "*Sí*. Me and your daughter."

Benny shook her head. "You don't know what you're getting into. This family will eat you both alive."

Enzo shrugged. "Perhaps, but I'm willing to take the risk. There is no life for me without Antonia."

Benny looked at him thoughtfully for a moment, and then looked down and slowly rubbed her fingers over the back of her other hand. "I'm getting arthritis," she admitted shyly. She sighed again. "I really did love Carlos, you know. And he loved me."

"I believe that."

"I was very young. Much younger than him. But we were like"—she made an exploding gesture with her hands— "fireworks, you know? I met him at a bar in the city. I was working as a cocktail waitress, putting myself through art school. He took me back to the hotel with him that night and we spent a week in bed."

She smiled to herself, remembering.

"But you know, it wasn't just sex. It was like we never ran out of things to talk about, either. We fascinated each other. There was chemistry between us, of course, but it was more than that. I thought, for a while, that we were actual soul mates."

Enzo nodded.

"When I got pregnant, he told me he was going to leave Pilar, that he wanted to start a new life with me. I thought I had done it, you know? I had found this amazing man, and we were going to have this beautiful child together, and I had my art and he had his horses, and we were going to have the most wonderful life..."

She reached over to claim her drink back from Enzo and took a sip. "But he didn't leave her," she said blankly. "All through the pregnancy, he said he would. But he never did."

"I'm sorry," said Enzo simply.

She nodded. "He only saw Antonia once, just after she was born." She smiled. "Noni was the most beautiful baby. You can't imagine."

He smiled in return. "I think I can imagine."

"I had already given up on Carlos. I knew he would never leave Pilar. That his family here was the family he had chosen. But when he held Noni, something happened. I watched him fall instantly in love. He looked at her in a way that I had never seen him look at anyone before." She laughed bitterly. "Certainly not me, at least. He looked...greedy, almost. That was when I knew that he would take her from me if he could. He didn't want me, but he wanted her. And that's when I knew we had to run."

She shook her head and rubbed between her eyes. "I know that Noni's childhood was hard in lots of ways. I was probably not always as on top of it as I maybe should have been. But at least we were together, right? A child needs her mother. I mean, what would she have been here? Can you imagine Carlos just coming home and plunking this kid in the kitchen and saying, 'Hey, boys, here's your new sister! Hey, Pilar, here's my bastard daughter!' You think Pilar would have just smiled and opened up her arms and embraced her?" She snorted. "Except that she did, I guess, as it turns out. But the old man had to die first before she was willing."

She looked at Enzo, seeming to take his measure with her

eyes. "You're not one of them, are you? You're not part of this whole crazy family dynasty thing?"

Enzo shook his head.

"So, what do you think? Do you think Noni is strong enough to deal with all this? All this money, this insane lifestyle...I just feel like it will ruin her. I'm afraid she'll get sucked into something she's not equipped to handle. She could lose a piece of her soul, you know?"

Enzo thought for a moment. "I was part of a family like that once," he said hesitantly. "I lost myself in the way that you worry will happen to Antonia. I understand what you're afraid of, because I think, if you had asked me that question even a year ago, I would have agreed with you. That you can't be part of something like this and not be changed for the worse. But Noni is strong. She already knows who she is. And this family—Pilar and Alejandro and Sebastian, Kat and Georgia—they are not what you think."

She looked doubtful and opened her mouth to speak, but he held up his hand.

"You were right about Carlos. Carlos was about the money and the image and the power. He was about winning and he cared very deeply about how people saw him. I think maybe you were right not to let him take Noni. From what I have heard, Jandro and Sebastian did not have the easiest of childhoods. Now that Carlos is gone...this family is somehow different. Did you ever meet Victoria?"

She shook her head. "No, but Carlos talked about her often."

He nodded. "I only knew her for a brief time, when I first started working for the Del Campos. But she was an extraordinary woman. While she was alive, Carlos, well, he was obviously not perfect, but she held him in check. After she died, he just seemed to lose his way. He ran wild. The family fell apart."

He looked out the windows at the dark summer night, considering. "Now, all these years later, it's like she's here again somehow. I mean, not her literal presence but her...spirit, her influence. When I see the Del Campo family together now..." He smiled. "Well, I think I would like to be a part of it."

He looked at Benny. She had tears in her eyes.

"As long as Noni and I are here, Benny, there will always be a place for you here, too. If you want it."

Noni reached out and grasped his hand. "Thank you," she whispered.

Chapter Thirty-Nine

Noni walked through the house, a plate of cake in her hand, trying to find Max and Jacob.

She wasn't quite ready to face her mother yet, though she knew it was inevitable. She thought that Enzo would be able to handle her, at least for a little while longer.

She smiled to herself. The man tamed wild horses, after all; even Benny Black should be easy compared to that.

Noni had already checked all over downstairs with no luck and was starting to worry a bit, but then she rounded a corner and saw her dogs, tails wagging, sniffing at the closed door to Sebastian and Alejandro's childhood bedroom.

"Good girls," she murmured, giving them each a little lick of frosting off her finger. She knocked on the door as she entered. "Jake? Max? You guys in here?"

They were standing by a half-packed suitcase on Max's bed. Max looked as if he had been crying, and Jake was running his hands through his hair in an exasperated way. When he saw Noni, he quickly reached into the suitcase and picked something up. "Finish up, Max," he said to his son before he turned back to Noni.

Noni looked at him and a sliver of fear struck her heart. "What are you guys doing? Why are you packing?"

"Daddy says we have to leave now. Before the cake even!" Max blurted as he carried over some clothes from the bureau.

Noni handed him the cake. "Well, here, I can take care of that, at least." She smiled at Jacob, trying not to show her worry. "Leave? To go where? What's going on?"

Jacob bent to retrieve a pair of Max's shoes from under the bed. "I can't do it, Noni," he said quietly. "I can't go to jail."

Noni's eyes shot to Max, worried about what the boy was hearing. She was relieved to see that he seemed distracted by his cake and a handheld video game he had found on the floor. "What...what do you mean? I thought we agreed—"

"No," said Jacob as he angrily threw the shoes into the suitcase. "You came up with a plan where everything worked out the way you wanted. You get Max, and you get your money, and you get to stay with Enzo. And I...I get conveniently shipped off so I'm out of everyone's way."

"No, that's not fair. That's not what...I want to help you."

He slammed the suitcase shut and locked it. "Oh," he said, "you still can."

She didn't notice the gun at first. He kept it very close to his body, hidden in his sleeve. After a glance over at his son, Jacob shook his sleeve back long enough for her to see it was pointed straight at her. She gasped, jumping back in terror.

He shook his head and whispered, "Stay calm. I know you don't want to scare Max."

"Jake, what are you doing? This is insane."

"I didn't want it to happen this way, Noni. I really do care about you. If you had just gone with the plan—"

"The plan was never going to...to...work," she stuttered.

He shrugged. "Well, now we'll never know, will we?" He gestured at her with the gun. "Get out of the way. We've got a new plan now."

* * *

Enzo and Benny were still sitting together in the sunroom when Pilar burst in. *"Perdon a mé,"* she said. She was a bit breathless. "Did you talk to Noni? Or Jacob or Max? One of the servers said they just saw them all drive away in Noni's truck."

Enzo froze. He felt an icy flood of fear fill his limbs. What if Noni had suddenly changed her mind? What if he had lost her after all?

Then he heard Benny gasp.

He turned to her. She was chalk white.

"Oh no," she whispered. "You guys, Jacob...Jacob is in trouble with the law...some drug thing...and he was so upset that Noni wouldn't..." She took a deep breath. "I told him that maybe if he just tried to talk it through with her, they could find a way to fix things. I didn't think he'd actually ever...Oh God, I think that he might have done something terrible."

Chapter Forty

Noni was relieved when Max finally fell asleep. She could feel the gun pressed into her side through Jacob's pocket as she drove, and she had been too terrified to answer the little boy's chatter and questions. She'd felt like she was hearing him from underwater.

"I don't understand what we're doing," she said to Jacob. She tried to keep her voice calm and matter of fact. She didn't want him to know how scared she really was. "Can you at least explain it to me?"

They weren't heading out of the Hamptons like she assumed they would be. Instead, he had told her to drive to the Shelter Island Ferry, and now they were in line to get on the boat.

"You don't need to understand," he said. "It will all be fine in a little while."

"Listen." She pinched herself to keep her voice from shaking. "I know you're scared. I know that you are under an incredible amount of stress. But...it's me, Jake. You don't have to use a gun on me. We can talk this through."

He shook his head. "I tried to talk it through. You didn't listen."

She slowly pulled onto the ferry and turned off the car. The ticket taker started making his way down the line, collecting money. He walked up to the window.

"Don't say a thing," hissed Jacob. "Don't even look at him. Just roll down your window."

She rolled down her window, careful to keep her eyes in front of her, even when the man said hello.

"Hey," grunted Jacob in return. "One way." He reached across her and handed the man some money and then took the ticket.

"Roll it back up," he whispered.

She looked at him. "Please," she said.

He gestured at the window. She rolled it back up.

He met her eyes quickly and then looked away. "I know this seems bad," he said. His voice took on a wheedling tone. "But I'm really doing this for Max. He needs you. I need you. We can't do this without you."

"Don't you dare use Max as an excuse," Noni spit out, suddenly enraged. "That's bullshit. You're delusional if you think you're doing Max any favors by dragging him into this. There are a million other ways we could fix this."

He shook his head violently. "Not without me going to jail. Not without Max losing his father. You of all people should know what it's like not to have your father."

She flinched as if he had struck her. "This is nothing like what happened to me. Nothing. He doesn't have to lose you. I told you I would—"

His face flamed red. "What kind of father would I be from behind bars? What would that do to Max? Seeing his dad in prison?" He poked the gun into her ribs. "Just drive," he said tonelessly.

* * *

Enzo sat in line for the ferry, feeling like he might shatter into a thousand pieces. He was sure he was going to go crazy with the wait.

Benny hadn't known where Jacob kept the boat, but she knew that he had managed to get one. The Del Campo brothers and their wives started searching in Southampton. They had driven to the nearest dock, where they kept their yacht, and Hendy, Pilar, and Benny had stayed behind to talk to the police once they arrived. But Enzo, remembering the other night when he had seen Noni on Shelter Island, had a hunch about where he needed to go.

The ferry slowly docked, bumping up against the pilings. The ticket taker stood in the front and started waving the cars off in what seemed like an excruciatingly sluggish way.

"*¡Vamos!* Come on! *¡Vamos!*" Enzo exploded, hitting the steering wheel with his hands.

Finally, the gate was lifted and he was waved on. It took all his willpower not to put the pedal to the floor.

"Hey," he said when the ticket taker came to his window. "Do you happen to remember an old blue Chevy truck getting on recently? There would have been a blond woman, a man with a beard, and a little boy with red curls in it."

The ticket taker nodded. "Actually, yeah. They were on the last trip round. Cute kid with glasses, right? And a real pretty woman."

Enzo felt his heart speed up. "Did they...did they seem okay?"

The ticket taker wrinkled his forehead. "Well, I guess so. The woman didn't really say anything. The guy just paid and took the ticket and then they all stayed in the truck on the way over. Is everything all right?"

Enzo swallowed. "I hope so," he said hoarsely.

* * *

Jacob ordered Noni to carry Max onto the boat. It was a small sailboat. Big enough for no more than two or three people.

Noni turned to glare at Jacob as she walked ahead of him. "I can't believe you would point a gun at your own child."

"I'm not," said Jacob. "It's pointed at you, not him."

"Whose boat is this?" she asked as she stepped gingerly on board, trying not to trip with Max in her arms.

"It doesn't matter," said Jacob. "He can afford to replace it."

She blinked. "So now you're stealing a boat, too. Jesus, Jake, can't you see how you're just making this worse and worse?"

"Stop it," said Jacob. "I don't need that. You're freaking me out. I need to stay calm."

She looked at him and felt a lump in her throat. "Please," she said raggedly, "please, don't do this."

He looked back at her; for a moment he seemed to hesitate. "You're scared," he said regretfully. He sighed. "I don't want to scare you, Noni. I just...I just need you to see reason, okay? I have to do this—for Max. I can't do it alone. I need your help. You're the only one I can trust." He looked at her sadly. "We were happy once. It will take a little time, but I know we can be happy again. And I'm not crazy. I understand this is a terrible way to start things off, but I don't have any other options."

"But you do have other options!"

He shook his head. "I don't." He seemed to find his resolve again. "Now, take Max downstairs. And don't try anything stupid, because I'll be up here, ready."

She closed her eyes in defeat and carried Max down into the cabin.

She laid him down on a little berth, took off his glasses, and looked around. She shivered. Ever since she had seen the gun, she'd felt like she was going numb, like she couldn't get warm enough.

She couldn't believe she didn't have her phone. She'd left it upstairs in her room at the house when she came down with Pilar, not wanting to be rude by carrying it to the party. Though she supposed it didn't make a difference. Jacob had already asked her to turn out her pockets and show him she wasn't carrying it.

The cabin was small, just two berths, one on top of the other; a tiny galley kitchen with a mess area; and a bathroom with a shower, sink, and toilet. Everything was very neat and well appointed, but she felt a tendril of panic as she imagined being trapped here with Jacob for weeks, maybe even months, on end.

Because she knew that's how it would be. She saw his plan now. He never needed a passport. He never planned on flying. A boat out was easy, and once they were in international waters, he'd be safe. They never needed to come back to the U.S. if he didn't want to.

She wondered dully if he actually knew how to sail. She wondered about their lack of supplies. The galley didn't look well stocked. She imagined he was counting on her money, but she wondered how he expected her to access any of it since her purse was back at the house.

She ached when she thought of Enzo. She hadn't had the chance to tell him what was going on with Jacob. In fact, she had confided in exactly no one. No one else knew. What if Enzo simply thought that she had chosen to go with Jacob? What if he thought she had left him again? What if everyone just assumed she had disappeared of her own free will?

Max stirred in his sleep, murmuring restlessly. She placed a comforting hand on his shoulder. "Shhh, shhh," she whispered. "Everything will be okay, buddy. Go back to sleep."

Then she sat down next to him on the berth, winded and freezing. *How, exactly was everything going to be okay?*

* * *

Shelter Island was small, but there were a lot of docks and marinas on it. It was, after all, *an island*. Enzo sped through the streets, heading for the first dock he could find.

He saw nothing suspicious at the first marina. A few old fishing boats, obviously empty, and a sailboat too small for a lower deck where anyone could hide. He asked a couple of guys who were hanging on the dock and drinking beer if they had seen a blue Chevy truck, and they both shook their heads no.

He tried to think it through before he went to the next dock. He couldn't just blindly search. He knew he was running out of time.

He had seen Noni at the restaurant across from Crescent Beach. She had been with Jacob that night. Perhaps Jacob had been staying close to that marina.

He did a U-turn and headed toward Shelter Island Bay.

* * *

Noni tiptoed to the top of the stairs and peered through the porthole on the door. She could see Jacob moving about, pulling ropes and setting the sails. Her heart sank. It seemed from the purposeful way he went about things that he actually knew what he was doing.

She crept back down the stairs and shot Max a worried glance. He was tossing and turning but still asleep. She went into the galley, looking for a knife.

She found several. She stood for a moment, holding a wickedly sharp, thin fish knife, wondering if she could bring herself to use it if necessary.

She looked at the blade and remembered the day, just after she had started helping Jacob with the forge, before Max was born, when Jacob had taught her how to make horseshoes.

It was an odd thing to start with, considering they were making art, not doing farrier work, but Jacob said that it was the first thing he had learned to make when he started smithing, so he thought it should be the first thing Noni learned as well.

Her enormous crush on Jacob had only grown that day. He had patiently guided her through the process, introducing to her to all the tools, getting her geared up with a leather apron and protective eyewear, showing her how to light the forge and use the bellows to get it hot enough, how to pick the right bar of steel, how to heat it to the proper temperature to make it malleable. She had been surprised that a bright orange-yellow signaled a more pliable metal than a darker red.

She remembered being burned for the first time. A spark had landed on her wrist and she had almost cried, it hurt so much. Jacob had laughed at her and softly rubbed the spot with a bit of lotion. He'd told her it was a rite of passage. He'd shown her all his own scars. And suddenly, in a rush, she'd imagined taking his hands in hers and kissing each burn, slowly and thoroughly and one by one.

They had hammered it together, taking turns. Noni had not yet built up the strength in her arms to hammer out metal for extended periods of time, but he had let her do the finish work. She had been ridiculously proud, when she had held up that first somewhat crooked but recognizable shoe. After it had cooled, he had presented it to her as a gift.

She still had it. She'd hung it above the door in her black-smith shop in Wellington, the U facing up so as not to let all the good luck run out.

She looked at the knife again. She looked back at Max, his bright red curls shining softly in the dim light. She put the knife down. She knew that she wouldn't be able to use it.

* * *

Her truck was there.

Enzo's headlights rolled over that familiar turquoise color and his heart almost beat out of his chest. It was just sitting there, empty, in the parking lot of the marina.

He pulled his truck right up next to it and jumped out, giving it a cursory glance as he passed it on his way down to the docks. This was a large marina, with a long row of boats floating along the boardwalk.

He kept to the shadowy side of the boardwalk, glad for the poor lighting and dark night. He did not want to be seen before he found them.

There were several boats with lights on. A small party was happening on one. A couple of young guys barbecued on the dock, while three women in bikinis lounged in beach chairs on the deck, laughing and talking. He could hear music from their radio, Adele belting out "Set Fire to the Rain." He slipped by them, holding his breath, praying he had made it in time.

At the very end of the dock, he saw a small sailboat with a lone man busying himself on board.

Enzo's breath caught in his throat.

It was definitely Jacob.

* * *

Noni heard Enzo before she saw him. There was a sudden pounding of feet on the deck above and then a shout and a crash. Max startled in his sleep, but Noni laid a hand on his chest and he slept on.

She inched up the stairs, fearful of what she might find above. She could see nothing through the porthole, just an empty deck, so she slowly pushed the door open and stuck her head out.

"Noni!" shouted Enzo. His voice was harsh and guttural.

She rushed out then, only to find Jacob, his face bleeding from a cut above his eye, standing with his gun trained on Enzo, who was sprawled on the deck, looking up at Jacob with an expression of pure loathing.

"Damn it, Noni, I said stay downstairs!" said Jacob. His voice was shaking.

She shook her head. "No." She made her voice soft and calm and continued to walk slowly toward them. "Jacob, this has to end now. Before someone really gets hurt. I know you're scared. I know you're panicking. But this will never, ever happen the way you think it will. I love Max, and I care about you, but we will never be happy together again. That is not going to happen."

She had almost reached him. She was close enough to touch him.

He panted raggedly, his teeth bared. "Why?" he ripped out. "Why can't we be happy?"

She swallowed painfully. Her throat was dry. "Because," she said softly, "because I am not in love with you. I am in love with Enzo. I can't stay with you. I won't. You'd have to keep me at gunpoint every moment of every day. That would never change. I would never willingly stay. I know you, Jake. I know you're not capable of that. I know you wouldn't do that to me. Or Max. Please, please, just put the gun down and let me help you."

She reached out a hand to touch him. Jacob kept his gun pointed at Enzo but turned to her. "Stop!" he barked. "I said stop!"

In that moment, Enzo leaped forward and threw himself onto Jacob. The gun went flying out of his hand.

The men grappled as Noni ran to pick up the gun, pointing it in the air and shouting, "Stop! Stop! I have the gun! Stop!"

But the men kept fighting. At first, Noni couldn't tell who had the upper hand. Jacob had the strength of a metal worker, but Enzo had the fury of someone who had just seen the woman he loved mortally threatened. Enzo took a hard blow to the face but then turned and hurled himself against Jacob, sending the taller man crashing to the ground. He started punching him, over and over, venting all the rage and fear that had been building up inside him since he had realized that Noni was gone.

"No, Enzo, stop!" screamed Noni. "You're going to kill him! Stop!"

Enzo didn't seem to hear her. The dull, wet sound of flesh pounding against flesh filled the air.

Noni pointed the gun into the air and fired.

Enzo stopped then, turning to look at her and letting Jacob slump to the deck.

Noni aimed the gun at Jacob. "It's okay," she said to Enzo. "I have the gun. It's over. I'm okay."

Enzo came to her, leaving Jacob as he pulled himself to a sitting position, coughing and spitting up blood.

"*Querida*," Enzo panted, "I was so scared. I thought—"

"Daddy?"

A small voice echoed over the water, silencing them all. The door to the cabin creaked open. They all froze.

"Noni?" said Max.

Noni quickly put the gun behind her back, and Jacob struggled up, raising his hand to hide his battered face from his son.

"Buddy," he said, his voice raspy and clogged, "go on back down, sweetheart. I'll be there in a moment."

"But, Daddy," said Max as he walked out onto the deck, "I don't feel good."

Jacob groaned desperately. "Okay, honey, just go back to bed and I'll—"

"I feel like I might throw up."

"He's seasick," whispered Noni. "Oh God, that's right. Jacob, he gets seasick. That's why we couldn't stay on the yacht? Remember? I told you."

Jacob stared at her for a second, and then all the fight

seemed to go out of him at once. His face went even paler and he seemed to collapse in on himself. He leaned against the side of the boat and closed his eyes.

"Max," he said. His voice sounded agonized, "Max, come here, babe."

Max went to his father, and Jacob picked him up and clutched him into a hug before the little boy could catch a glimpse of his father's bleeding face.

"Listen, baby," he said, tears running down his cheeks. "I want you to remember that no matter what, you are my best boy, and I love you."

"I love you, too, Daddy," said Max, his face against his father's shoulder. "You're my best dad."

Jacob leaned his face into his son's hair. He took a deep breath. "I want you to go with Noni and Enzo now, okay? I'm going to go away for a while, but I'll come back as soon as I can."

Max struggled to pull back and look at his dad. "Where are you going? Can I come?"

Jacob shook his head. "No, baby. Not this time. You'll be good with Noni, okay?"

Max's bottom lip started to quiver.

Jacob leaned down and gave his son a fervent kiss on his forehead. "You'll be fine, okay? Noni will take great care of you."

Noni passed the gun to Enzo behind her back and then stepped forward to Jacob. He buried his face in Max's hair for a moment and then passed the little boy over to Noni's arms.

Max began to cry and pushed his face against Noni's chest.

Jacob met Noni's eyes. He looked absolutely ravaged. "Just . . . let me go, okay, Antonia?"

She looked back at Enzo, who nodded. She turned back to Jacob. "Okay," she whispered. "Go."

"Thank you," he said.

"Jake," she said, "listen. I'll take care of him. I promise. Everything we talked about before—about him knowing that you're a good man—I promise that will happen."

He nodded. "I know."

He put his hand out, as if to touch his son's quivering back, but stopped just short and turned away.

Chapter Forty-One

They arrived back at Pilar's well after midnight. The lights from the party were still turned on in the garden, and the family came running out the front door as soon they pulled up.

Max had fallen asleep again, crying himself out, and Noni slipped him out of her truck and into her arms. Enzo followed them up the stairs to the house.

Not wanting to wake Max, they whispered to everyone that they were fine, everything was fine, that there was a lot to tell, but they would talk in the morning. Right now they all just needed sleep.

Noni's dogs followed them up to the bedroom Max had been sleeping in. Careful not to disturb Tomás, who was sleeping across the way, Noni and Enzo worked together to pull Max's clothes off and then tucked him into bed.

They stood together, watching him for a moment. Enzo's heart ached as he looked at the soft, innocent curves of the boy's face, the way his long dark red lashes brushed against his cheek, the way his mouth still worked a little in his sleep, like a baby sucking at a bottle.

This child had lost his mother before he could remember, and now he had lost his father, too.

Enzo reached down to brush a copper curl off his face and smiled at the featherlight feel of his hair.

Noni reached over and took Enzo's hand. "Thank you," she whispered. "Thank you for coming to find us."

He pulled her closer and kissed the top of her head.

The dogs, one by one, leaped lightly onto Max's bed. Enzo started to order them off, afraid that they would wake the little boy, but Noni put her hand on his arm, signaling him to wait.

If they had been in Noni's bed, the sisters would have curled up in their regular space at the foot of the bed, but this time was different. Mojo stretched out along Max's back, laying her head on the pillow next to his, and Luna fit herself on the other side, the top of her head right under Max's chin, wedging herself into the little boy's arms.

He opened his eyes then, just a slit, and turned in his bed, throwing one arm out over the white dog's neck and the other over the black dog, patting them both gently as their tails thumped in response.

The little boy and the two dogs lay there together like that for a moment. And then, with a sigh and a smile, Max fell back asleep.

* * *

Noni ached all over. Now that the fear and adrenaline had drained out of her, now that they were all safe back home, she felt so exhausted that she could barely make it to her room.

She turned to Enzo before going through the door. "You're going to stay with me tonight, right?"

Enzo nodded. "I don't think I could make it back to my place even if I tried."

She nodded. "Good."

She turned on the lamps by her bed, bathing the room in a soft golden light. It was only then that she really looked at Enzo's face. There was a bruise beneath his right eye and a cut on his cheekbone.

She reached up to touch his face and he flinched, so she stood on her tiptoes and slowly and carefully kissed his injuries instead.

His breath hissed and his eyes went dark. "Noni," he rasped.

She gave him a long, slow kiss on the mouth, savoring the sweet taste of him. She broke the kiss and leaned her cheek against his broad chest, feeling the warmth rush back through her limbs in an aching tingle, replacing the icy, numb sensation she'd felt all night.

"Let's take a bath," she whispered.

Her bathroom had a deep porcelain claw-foot tub, and she turned it on in a gush and left it to fill with the nearly scalding water.

She started to take her shirt off and paused, realizing with a start that she was still in her party clothes. The birthday party seemed days past, even weeks.

Enzo caught her hands and helped her pull her shirt off and then slide down her pants, exposing the black satin bra and bikini briefs underneath. He stepped behind her to unhook her bra and rained gentle kisses down her neck as he helped her remove it. She turned to him, just in her panties now, and pressed herself against him, laughing to realize that he was still in his good suit and that it was completely ruined. Dirty, torn, and stained with blood.

"Oh no, my favorite suit," she said, and giggled at the absurdity of it all.

He shrugged philosophically, his amber eyes dancing. "It's probably time to buy another one."

She helped him out of his clothes next, going slow because she could see that he was sore. First the jacket, then slowly unbuttoning his shirt, then slipping her hands into the waistband of his pants to untuck the T-shirt underneath, pulling it over his head, and trailing her fingers down his bare chest.

He took a sharp intake of breath. "Ah, *querida*, what you do to me."

She wrapped her arms around the back of his neck and kissed him, not holding back this time, delighting in the feel of her breasts pressed to his warm, bare skin, of the way his strong arms twined themselves around her waist and pulled her ever closer.

She felt him pulse and she ground her hips against him with a groan, then stepped back to help him remove his pants and boxer shorts, savoring the way he sprang out, heavy, hard, and ready for her.

She knelt, lightly scratching her fingernails down his back and legs, taking him in her mouth, loving the way he tasted, feeling such joy as he groaned and twisted his hands into her hair, letting her lick and suck until he gently pushed her away.

"Come back up here," he said. "That feels much too good."

She laughed and slowly stood, rubbing her almost naked body up against his until they were face-to-face again.

He kissed her until she was dizzy, plying her mouth with his tongue, running his hands all over her body, hooking her underwear with the tips of his fingers and dragging them down her legs with excruciating patience.

Then he cupped his hands around her rear and lifted her

onto the vanity counter. She shivered as he placed her down on the cool surface.

"Cold?" he asked.

"Marble," she answered, laughing.

She shivered in an altogether different sort of way as he gently moved her legs apart, kneeling in front of her and kissing his way up her inner thighs, one at a time, teasing her as he lightly caressed her curls with his fingertips. He sat back up for a moment, watching her face as he brushed his fingers over her and then let them go deeper, searching out the burning center of her and circling it with an almost casual expertise, all the while locking his eyes on her face as she writhed and moaned beneath his touch.

He bent his head back down to her. Just giving her the lightest of kisses at first, making her arch and burn for more. Then he grasped her thighs in his hands and pushed her legs even farther apart before parting her with one quick slash from his tongue and making her cry out in surprised pleasure.

He lapped at her slowly, taking his time. Trembling sensations coursed through her body, making her feel as if she were floating on currents of silky pleasure. She wrapped her hands in his hair and watched him, marveling at how he made her feel both wholly in her body and yet somehow outside it. She swore she could see a faint golden light—a radiance—that seemed to illuminate them both.

He lifted his head for a moment, staring into her eyes. "I will never get enough of you, *querida*," he said fiercely before bowing his head back down and parting her once more.

She started to tremble all over as he went deeper, licking and sucking, reaching up to cup her breasts in his hands, lightly pinching and flicking her nipples between his fingers as he continued to pleasure her with his mouth. She could feel herself falling over the brink now, the trembling turning into a buzzing, electrical flow and the light between them bursting into a radiant flame. He kept licking and sucking as he reached down and slid first one and then a second finger inside her, stretching her until she could feel him all through her body, and she tumbled over the edge with a sharp and wild cry. She felt like she was shattering into pieces even as he pulled her ever closer. She felt as if her body was built of nothing but shooting stars and billowing waves of joy. She peaked again and again under his strong fingers and agile tongue, until she was sobbing her bliss and begging for him to fill her in a different way.

And so he stood and placed her, still pulsing, back on the floor, turning her away from him and cradling her body within his own, slipping on a condom before sliding into her with slow, excruciating control, filling her deeper and deeper, his breath going ragged and uneven. His body trembling around hers with the effort of curbing his need. She felt her breath run short as she begin to peak again, every small movement sending her closer and closer to the edge, until he reached around and cupped one breast in his hand, teasing her nipple between his fingers, and slid his other hand down through her curls and into the very pulsing center of her, circling and rubbing. And then, just as she thought she could take no more, he pulled back and then thrust himself into her, no longer holding back but sheathing his full length deep inside her, and then out again and then back, losing all control as he took her over and over, sending her falling, falling over the edge. Because she could feel nothing else but this man she loved, nothing but his body, his soul, and his heart, all of which she knew, in that exquisite moment, to be hers and hers alone.

* * *

They floated together in the warm bath afterward, her body resting against his, heedless of the overfilled tub and the way the water lapped over the sides and onto the floor in little waves and drips.

The room smelled of roses and lilies, the sweet scents drifting up on the breeze. There was a soft glow from the garden below, the tattered remnants of Noni's first birthday party, fairy lights and lanterns, the candles long since burned out, but the fireflies still blinking their electric message of desire, swirling in graceful clusters in the warm summer air.

One luminous insect broke from the pack and rode the current of the breeze up and through their window, drifting over them and pulsing gold and then green in the hushed darkness of the room. They silently watched it hover, and it seemed to them a flickering, floating talisman of their luck. A reminder that, indeed, some people might search a lifetime for what lay between them...for what they held in their hands.

Epilogue

The bride and groom rode to their wedding. The bride rode sidesaddle on her favorite black mare and the groom on his beloved white stallion.

The groom dressed in a black cutaway morning suit, complete with a gray ascot, silk kerchief, and dove-gray gloves. He chose to forgo the traditional top hat at his bride's request.

The bride wore thick cream silk, with long lace sleeves and a bateau neckline. There was a subtle hint of the palest pink swirled through her heavy, elegant floor-length gown. At her throat and slim wrists glimmered clusters of large pink diamonds mixed with the tiniest of rubies and seed pearls. Her satin heels were likewise adorned with small bejeweled clips.

She carried her favorite flowers, blowsy red garden roses, in such a state of full bloom that she dripped petals as she walked down the aisle, which was fine since the twin two-year-old flower girls, while very cute, did a haphazard job at best of spreading their bounty.

The bride decided against a veil or any attendants other than the comically distractible flower girls. She walked herself down the aisle, thank you very much. At her advanced age, she was more than capable of giving herself away.

It was autumn in the garden, and there was a bite in the air, but the guests were, for the most part, cozily wrapped in cashmere and velvets and quite comfortable. The bride loathed summer weddings and would, she had previously announced, not risk the slightest chance of perspiring at her own ceremony.

The vows were of the traditional sort and not overlong but spoken in both Spanish and English. The groom, it had to be admitted, had a terrible Spanish accent and could scarcely be understood, but his bride knew that he had tried his hardest and gave him points for effort, nonetheless.

Some of the guests cried. Mainly on the bride's side. Her children were especially prone, though her sons did their manly best to be discreet.

The kiss between the bride and groom was shockingly amorous, and several guests found themselves quite warm, despite the brisk autumn breeze.

The reception was held in the same garden as the ceremony. A large, open tent was provided in case of rain, but the weather stayed dry as was predicted.

The decorative flowers were roses straight from the bride's gardens. Pink, cream and red. Some of the guests later argued over who would get to take the dizzyingly fragrant centerpieces home.

The food was, of course, spectacular, with a sumptuous buffet provided instead of a sit-down dinner, because the bride felt that food too perfectly plated was, perhaps, a bit bourgeoisie.

The cake was a towering affair. A traditional English fruitcake, iced with an achingly sweet white frosting, exactly as the groom had requested. The cake had been made three months in advance in order for it to "mature," as it needed to be lovingly fed many a teaspoonful of rum every day before it was deemed fit to be consumed.

The children were given fairy cakes of an ordinary vanilla and vanilla sort, though more than one dared try a bite of the rum cake with rather unpleasant results.

The two horses were allowed to stay for the party, tied to a fence post and peacefully grazing on the lawn. There were also multiple dogs at the ceremony. And, at one point, an errant billy goat.

The toasts were given by the bride's sons and granddaughter. They were heartfelt, moving, and in the case of her younger son, perhaps just the tiniest bit ribald.

The band was a multipiece jazz orchestra, as requested by the groom. The first dance was a tango, which was performed with such lusty enthusiasm and grace by the newly married couple that most of the same guests got warm all over again.

The other guests joined in the dancing, and there was particular attention paid to the chemistry between the bride's grown granddaughter, who moved on the floor like the professional dancer that she was, and the young handsome African American polo player who, it was whispered, had come from very rough beginnings.

The alcohol was top shelf; the bar was, of course, wide open; and the champagne was Veuve Clicquot, 1998, La Grande Dame Rosé.

The autumn trees had done as was expected of them— providing an astonishingly colorful canopy that arched over the wedding party and beyond, peaking in their beauty and hue exactly on the day that they were supposed to.

"Well, *of course* the trees cooperated," Antonia Black-Rivas was heard murmuring to her adoring husband, Enzo, as they whirled blissfully around the dance floor. "Because not even a tree would be so foolish as to deny Pilar Del Campo-Henderson exactly what she asked for on her wedding day."

AT AN INTERNATIONAL POLO TOURNAMENT IN
FLORIDA, COUNTRY VET GEORGIA FELLOWES
ENCOUNTERS SOME OF THE MOST GORGEOUS
THOROUGHBREDS—AND MEN—SHE'S EVER
SEEN. ALEJANDRO DEL CAMPO DESPERATELY
WANTS TO WIN THE SEASON'S BIGGEST POLO
TOURNAMENT—AND ALSO THE HEART OF
GEORGIA. BUT FIRST HE'LL HAVE TO CONVINCE
HER TO LOOK BEYOND THE PLAYER...AND SEE
THE MAN.

PLEASE SEE THE NEXT PAGE FOR AN EXCERPT
FROM

Nacho Figueras Presents: High Season

Chapter One

No!" Georgia laughed. "I have exactly zero interest in polo."

"Only because you haven't seen it played," said Billy. "It's actually amazing. The way they fight it out on the field, all snarled together, slamming up against each other, a sweaty, dangerous tangle of heaving chests and pumping legs..."

Georgia shook her head at Billy's handsome, teasing face on the Skype screen. "I can't tell if you're describing the ponies or the players."

Billy quirked an eyebrow. "Well, both, actually. Anyway, Peaches, please. For me. One week in Wellington. It will be so much fun! We'll do it right. And, okay, full disclosure, I've met someone, and I desperately need your opinion."

"Of course you do," said Georgia. Ever since they met at Cornell, there had been a never-ending series of inappropriate men Billy desperately needed her opinion on. "What's his name?"

"Beau."

"No. Seriously?"

"I know. It's a Virginia thing. He rides to hounds. Don't you love how that sounds? I think he might be The One."

She laughed. "Because he rides to hounds?"

"No, because he's cute, and sweet, and a little bit rich, and he does this thing with his tongue that makes my—"

Georgia threw up her hands. "Okay, okay, spare me the details."

"Honest, Georgie, this is not just about me. You'd love this place. It's sunshine and high fashion, perfect beaches, gorgeous people, million-dollar ponies, oh, and the wildest and most decadent parties you can imagine!"

"Yes, well, I sunburn on sight," she said, "and as for fashion, I believe that you once told me that I dress like last season's bag lady. Even the idea of a Palm Beach party makes me break out in hives, and besides"—she glanced out the window at the snowy, moonlit, upstate New York farm—"I have horses that need me here."

Since graduating with her degree in veterinary medicine, Georgia had been helping her dad on the farm and assisting in the village animal hospital. It wasn't exactly a challenge— basically she was handing out tick medicine and checking for worms, with the occasional trip to a stable in the case of a colic false alarm—but she knew she was lucky to have found work that let her be where she was needed.

The farm consisted of a dilapidated stone cottage and a sagging barn set on ten acres of meadow at the edge of the Catskills. The place was so ancient that it was practically open to the elements, and cost a fortune to heat. Without her help, Georgia knew her dad would sell, and she couldn't stand the idea of losing their home.

There were definitely days when Georgia wondered if she'd parked all her ambition the moment she had arrived back home, but her father had gone into debt to finance her education, and helping him now was payback. If she sometimes found herself daydreaming about missed opportunities and other, perhaps bigger, lives, she quickly shook it off. She loved the farm and she loved her father, and they both needed her. That was enough.

Billy rolled his dark brown eyes in frustration, visibly filtering a retort about what he obviously considered to be Georgia's sad-ass life. "Georgia. All respect. But there are horses, and then there are *horses*. The team that Beau is down here with are, like, among the top ten polo players in the world."

"Are there even ten people who play?"

Billy sighed in exasperation. "There are tens of thousands, probably. And you are absolutely missing the point. It's a sexy, savage game, and I'm telling you, you will love it. Plus, it's totally trending."

"Right," Georgia said. "Among the one percent."

"Don't be snarky just because you're stuck in the snowy wasteland not getting any. Please, Peaches. I really like this guy. And I think he really likes me. But you know how bad I am at this. Every time I fall for someone, he ends up sleeping with my cousin, or emptying my bank account..."

"Or stealing your car," snorted Georgia.

"Oh God, I can't believe that actually happened twice," he groaned, "but you see! That's exactly what I'm talking about. I need your unbiased opinion. You're the only one I can trust."

"Billy, I'm sorry, I just can't."

"Georgia, who was there for you when you found out that skinny hipster you called a boyfriend was secretly banging that waitress with the uni-boob?"

Georgia rolled her eyes and sighed. "You were."

"And who sat up with you all night drinking cheap wine and watching *Downton Abbey* until you felt better?"

She shifted reluctantly in her seat. "You did."

"And so, who is going to get her narrow ass down to Florida and make sure her BFF isn't making another colossal romantic mistake?"

Georgia gave a groan of defeat. "All right," she said. "Four days. That's it."

"Yay!" Billy cheered. "You're going to love it! Cocktails. Scandal. Strappy dresses. Trust me. It will be everything you need. I'll text directions."

Georgia snapped her laptop shut and fed the woodstove. As she climbed the stairs to bed, her shadow was animated by the flare of the fire.

She undressed, shivering at the window, staring up at the milky indigo sky and full moon. Slipping under the covers, she wrapped her arms around herself as she waited for her bed to warm. She started thinking about all she'd need to do before she left, what she'd need to pack...It was one of the hard parts about traveling—the way it made her so restless. The minute a plan was in place, everywhere her mind fell, there was something that needed to be done.

She closed her eyes, trying not to think, willing herself to relax while wondering why this little trip felt like something so much bigger, a kind of seismic shift. The bed slowly warmed but she couldn't let go. She lay there in the dark, a thousand thoughts flickering through her mind like so many fireflies on an inky summer night, each one determined to keep her awake and unsettled.

WHEN HER FATHER'S HEALTH BRINGS KAT
HOME TO WELLINGTON, THE LAST THING ON
HER MIND IS ROMANCE. BUT NOW SHE'S
FORCED TO WORK WITH SEBASTIAN DEL
CAMPO, A DEVASTATINGLY HANDSOME TABLOID
GOD AS WELL-KNOWN FOR HIS POLO PLAYING
AS HE IS FOR BREAKING HEARTS.

PLEASE SEE THE NEXT PAGE FOR AN EXCERPT
FROM

Nacho Figueras Presents:
Wild One

Chapter One

Katherine Ann Parker looked in the bathroom mirror and carefully applied a layer of dark red lipstick.

And then, just as carefully, she wiped it back off.

Too much. The last thing she wanted was to look like she was desperate.

She dug some ChapStick out of her bag and slicked it on, trying to ignore the Silver Lake hipster breathing behind her, impatiently waiting to wash her hands.

Yes, that was better. And everything else seemed to be working—her black hair, pulled back into a sleek chignon; the crisp white fitted button-down showing just a hint of cleavage; the modest gold hoops in her ears; the dark wash jeans that were tailored just so, the six-inch-heeled ankle boots...

She frowned. She knew her manager, Honey Kimmelman, would nix the boots. As a general rule, the men in Hollywood were short and didn't like to be reminded of that fact. And Kat was already tall, even without the heels. The boots pushed her up over six feet.

"Well, too damned bad," she said out loud. "This is a job, not a date."

"Um, excuse me?" said the hipster.

Kat blinked, embarrassed. She had forgotten she was not alone. "Sorry. Personal pep talk," she mumbled, and she moved aside so the girl could use the sink.

The girl washed her hands and left, shooting one last quizzical look at Kat as the door swung shut behind her.

Kat lingered at the window, looking out over the panorama of West Hollywood. She sighed dreamily. Even the bathroom at Soho House had an amazing view.

She checked her watch—it was time. She smoothed her hair, almost went for the lipstick again, and then stilled her hand and forced a deep breath. It was just a meeting, she told herself. She'd been to a million meetings. She could do this.

* * *

As Kat eased her way to the back of the restaurant, she made a point of pretending not to notice the multitude of celebrities and A-listers scattered around the private club. Soho House was, above all, discreet. A place where even the biggest stars could have lunch, take meetings, gossip, and relax, and be sure to go unbothered. Kat had reluctantly let her membership lapse when she could no longer afford the annual fees, but she was always happy to come back as a guest.

The movie exec, Dee Yang, rose from her seat, smiling, as Kat approached the table. Dee was younger than Kat, dark haired and pretty, wearing a navy sheath that showed off her toned arms. Kat liked her at once, could see the intelligence written all over face, and recognized her warm smile as genuine.

"Kat, so great to finally meet you," said Dee as they shook hands. "I'm such a huge fan."

Kat waved the compliment off, smiling. "Thank you. It's so good to meet you, too."

"And this is Steve Meyers," said Dee as she and Kat sat down. "He's producing the project."

A fiftyish man with graying hair, in jeans and a baseball cap, nodded but did not look up from his phone. "Hang on. Just one second," he said, texting away.

Kat glanced at Dee, who raised her eyebrows apologetically and passed her a menu. "Have you had the burrata?" she said. "I can't resist it."

"And ooookay," said Steve, putting down his phone at last. "Sorry about that. Couldn't wait." He gave Kat an obvious head-to-toe once-over before he stuck out his hand. "Nice to meet you, Kay."

"Kat," Dee corrected.

"Right, sorry. Kat."

Kat's heart sank as she watched his eyes dart right back to his phone. It wasn't hard to read the room. He didn't want to be here. Dee had obviously talked him into this meeting. He probably already had someone else lined up for the job.

She forced herself to look at her menu, trying not to let the disappointment show on her face.

"So, Kat," said Dee, "I notice a little Southern accent. Where are you from?"

Kat smiled. "My folks are originally from Georgia, but I grew up in Wellington, Florida."

"Wellington?" Steve said, momentarily interested, "I think my first wife went down there once for some expensive thing she had to buy a crazy hat for. Tennis? Cricket?"

"Polo, probably," said Kat. "Or some other horse-related activity. It's pretty much all horses all the time in Wellington."

She could just imagine Steve's first wife, tan and toned, her face a mask of Botox, taking out her frustrations about her jerk of a husband as she violently stomped divots on the field in her Chanel suit and oversized hat.

"That's right," said Steve, "polo. You ride?"

Kat shook her head. "Nope. I am not what you would call a horsey person."

Steve nodded. His phone pinged. "Oh man, it's a text from Michael." His voice sank to a conspiratorial whisper. "You know, *Bay*. I have to answer this."

As he turned away from the table, Kat tried to push down a rising wave of annoyance.

"So anyway," said Dee hurriedly, "I absolutely love *Winter's Passing*. It's one of my all-time favorites. I cry every time I watch it. And you were practically still in school when you made it, right?"

"About a year out," said Kat.

"It was a crime that it lost the Oscar," said Dee.

Kat smiled ruefully. "Well, you know what they say, just an honor to be nominated."

Steve looked up from his phone again, smirking. "But then... *Red Hawk*."

Kat felt the smile freeze on her face. "Yes. *Red Hawk*."

Steve made a clucking sound with his tongue. "Man, how much money did that one lose? It was some kind of record, wasn't it?"

Kat met his beady eyes defiantly. "Came this close to making the Guinness book."

Dee laughed. Steve didn't even crack a smile.

"Hell of a thing to be remembered for," he said. "And didn't you have a fling with Jack Hayes while you were filming? He dumped you right after the box office numbers came in, right?"

Kat fought the urge to stab him with her fork. "Something like that."

"Well, they should have known better, really. Talk about

ruining the source material. I mean, what little boy was going to want to see a girly version of *Red Hawk* comics?"

Kat stiffened. "And what Hollywood producer is so out of touch that he still thinks a bunch of little boys are driving the box office?"

Steve sniffed. "Yeah, because stunt-casting a female director obviously brought the audience out in droves."

Kat slowly counted to ten in her head before speaking again. "You know, I made a lot of mistakes on that film, but I'm pretty sure that being born female wasn't one of them."

He shook his head. "Shoulda stuck with what you know."

She cocked her head. "Oh? And what, exactly, do I know?"

"Rom-coms. Princess movies. Fifty Shades of Crap."

She stared at him. "You're kidding, right?"

He shrugged and looked back at his phone. "Your movie tanked. That says it all."

Kat felt her face flush, and some very choice words rose to her lips, but Dee hurriedly interrupted. "But that was all years ago," she said in a placating tone. "I'm sure you've done a ton since then, right?"

Kat took a deep breath and forced herself to turn away from Steve so she could give Dee her usual spiel about having some work in development, about how she was working on a new spec—but before she could even really start, Steve's phone pinged again.

"Oh, yep, gotta take this one, too," he interrupted.

That was it. She'd had enough.

She put her hand on his wrist and gave him her sweetest smile. "You know, Steve, I feel like we kind of got off on the wrong foot. Can we start over?"

He looked back at her, suspicious at first, but she just kept smiling until she saw the exact moment when he relaxed and a new kind of interest kindled in his eyes. His gaze slid down to her chest.

Bingo. She licked her lips in anticipation.

"It's cool," he finally said. "But I seriously gotta answer this text."

"Oh, is that Michael Bay again? Are you really friends with him?" Her Southern accent was suddenly thicker.

He smirked. "Played tennis with him just last week."

She looked up at him from under her lashes. "That is so amazing. I heard he only works with the best. You must be really good at what you do."

He straightened his shoulders. "I think it's fair to say that I know what I'm doing."

"I can see that." She smiled again, squeezing his arm. "I bet there's a lot you could teach me."

He raised his eyebrows. "I bet you're right."

She giggled. "Oh, hey, is that the latest iPhone? So neat. Do you mind if I take a look at it for just one little second?"

Steve chuckled. "Haven't seen it yet, eh? I had my assistant stand in line for twelve hours to get this thing." He passed it over.

Kat stood up, dropped the phone on the floor, and ground it under her heel.

"What the hell?" yelled Steve, his face going beet red.

Kat looked him in the face. "Oops. I'm so sorry," she said, deadpan. She stomped down again. "It must have slipped."

She smiled blissfully as she leaned even harder, enjoying the satisfying crunch of metal against metal.

Appendix

The Game of Polo

Each TEAM is made up of four PLAYERS. The players are designated positions from one through four and wear the corresponding number on their team shirts. Player 1 is primarily offensive; player 4 primarily defensive. Normally, the most experienced and highest-handicap players play positions two and three, with position three being akin to the captain or quarterback of the team.

HANDICAPS: Each player is given a handicap from −2 (the worst) up to 10 goals (the best). Only a handful of the greatest professional players achieve the prestigious handicap of 10.

Polo is played on a large grass field—or PITCH—that is 300 yards long and 160 yards wide. There are GOALPOSTS at either end, placed 8 yards apart.

THE GAME begins with players lined up in the center of the field. One of the two UMPIRES bowls the ball between the teams. The players then use a combination of speed, skill, and teamwork to mark each other—and to score.

Players SCORE by hitting the ball between the goalposts. A pony can score a goal for its team if it knocks the ball across the line between posts. After each goal, and at the end of each chukka, the teams change playing directions. Play resumes with another throw-in.

CHUKKA: The number of periods in which a game of polo is divided. Players change out their ponies between chukkas. There are generally six chukkas in a game (in Argentina there are eight) and each chukka lasts approximately seven minutes.

HALFTIME: At halftime, which is typically five minutes, the custom is for spectators to walk onto the polo field to tread in the clumps of turf—or DIVOTS—kicked up by ponies.

The horses ridden in polo are known as POLO PONIES, regardless of their height. Originally, no horse taller than thirteen hands and two inches (54 inches) was allowed to play the game. Though the restriction was removed early in the twentieth century, the terminology has remained.

Polo ponies can be Thoroughbreds or of mixed breed. What matters is that they are fit (they might run a couple miles during each chukka), strong, disciplined, intelligent, and love to play. Some of the finest ponies are bred in Argentina. Most ponies begin their training at the age of five, and this can last from six months to two years. As with their riders, it takes many years to master the game and most ponies reach their peak around age nine or ten. Barring injuries, a pony can continue to play until age eighteen or twenty.

During a game, a player will use as many as eight ponies—known as a STRING OF PONIES. The higher the level of competition, the more ponies in a player's string.

ABOUT THE AUTHORS

Ignacio "Nacho" Figueras is one of the most recognized men in the world as the global face of Ralph Lauren's polo line. Hailed by CNN as the "David Beckham of Polo," Figueras is also captain and co-owner of Argentina's award-winning Black Watch team. He has been featured on *Oprah* and *60 Minutes,* and *Vanity Fair* readers have voted him one of the most handsome men in the world.

Nacho currently splits his time between the United States and Argentina with his wife, Delfina, and their four children.

Jessica Whitman lives and writes in the Hudson Valley, New York.

You can learn more at:
NachoFiguerasPresents.com
Twitter @NachoFigueras
Facebook.com/NachoFigueras